Best Wishes,

TRECADNO

C P DAVIES

CANDY JAR BOOKS · CARDIFF
2022

The right of C P Davies to be identified as the
Authors of the Work has been asserted
by them in accordance with the Copyright, Designs
and Patents Act 1988.

© C P Davies 2022

Published by
Candy Jar Books
Mackintosh House
136 Newport Road, Cardiff, CF24 1DJ
www.candyjarbooks.co.uk

ISBN: 978-1-915439-49-9

Printed and bound in the UK by
Severn, Bristol Road, Gloucester, GL2 5EU

CHAPTER ONE

Chapel View Guest House

Trecadno stood perfectly still, as if deep in siesta, as the bus rolled into town. Not a soul stirred on the road around the chapel, and a haze hovered undisturbed over the hot pavements. A group of ragged sparrows dust-bathed on a patch of dried mud near the church, and sleeping crows formed a malingering line along the ridge of the chapel roof.

The bus stopped alongside the high chapel wall and discharged one passenger weighed down by two enormous suitcases. Anyone at the windows of the terraced houses around him would have recognised a newcomer in their midst. This was a place where everyone knew everyone, and anyway, the suitcases were a dead giveaway. On a late summer's day like this, the visitor – a youngish man of medium build – must have had an uncomfortable time on his bus. His shirt was unbuttoned to an almost indecent extent, and his short fair hair was so damp that he looked as if he'd been swimming.

Surveying the view before him, the man saw that he was in a town square – or rather a figure of eight, for at the centre of the encircling terrace were the town's church and chapel, separated by a narrow road. In the still heat of the afternoon, the two sombre buildings faced each other across the lane like two ageing cowboys preparing to draw.

The bus twisted away into the distance, pursued by a cloud of dust and fumes. Its former passenger remained fixed in position, flanked by his suitcases, peering at his surroundings.

If there had been a passer-by, he would have asked the way to Chapel View Guest House. If there had been a town map on display, he would have consulted it. Had there been a shop or pub in his vicinity, he could have entered and asked for directions.

There was a sudden confusion of chirrups as the sparrows took flight, and a face materialised close to the visitor's right elbow. It was large and round and possessed a small snout-like nose and very bushy brown eyebrows. It was attached to a rotund body covered in what seemed to be a floral tent.

'Good afternoon,' it said, in a gargle of Welsh accent.

The visitor took a step back and stared down at his new companion, too stunned to remember his manners.

'My name is Lavinia,' continued this very round female.

'Oh?'

'*Mrs* Lavinia Hughes, for your information. Though my husband has been dead these ten years.'

'Nice to meet you, Mrs Hughes, I'm—'

'*You're* young Mr John Simmonds, the new schoolteacher. We've been looking out for you.'

'Oh?'

Mrs Lavinia Hughes glared up at him from her position near his belt. 'You don't know who I am, do you?'

'Mrs Lavinia—'

'No, no! You don't know who I *am*. I am the lady who runs Chapel View Guest House. You wrote to me, wanting to book a room. "Arriving Thursday the twenty-eighth of August, 2003," you said.'

'That's right. Sorry, I didn't realise—'

'That's obvious,' Mrs Hughes snapped. 'But I suppose you've had a long journey, so we'll say no more about it. Now, you follow me, I'll have you right in no time.'

2

'You will?'

'A nice cup of tea is what you need.'

John picked up his cases and followed in Mrs Hughes' waddling wake. He noted flickering at the periphery of his vision that might have been sparrows, or a flurry of curtain-twitching.

As its name implied, Chapel View Guest House was close to the chapel, just thirty yards from the bus-stop.

'Fine houses, these,' commented Mrs Hughes, as she waddled across the dusty road. 'Well-made. Withstand earthquakes, they would.'

Feeling the quivering of the ground every time Mrs Hughes took a step, John decided that this was just as well. She stopped in front of a small blue door.

'Here we are!' she announced. 'This is Chapel View Guest House. *My* guest house. I run it all by myself. It's a big responsibility.'

'I'm sure.'

'And you never know, see. I'm a woman all alone.'

'Oh?' John did not see.

Mrs Hughes took a large key from a pocket in her pavilion-like frock and opened her front door with ceremony.

'Here we are! This is my hall.'

'Right.'

'It's got a radiator and a mirror.'

'Right.'

'I got central heating, mind. There's plenty who haven't.'

'Right.'

The hall was dark, and so narrow that Mrs Hughes was compelled to turn sideways in order to proceed.

'You can put your bags down for a minute if you like.'

There was so little space in the hall that the only way John could take advantage of this generous offer was by placing his suitcases behind him.

'No, no,' protested Mrs Hughes. 'You'll block the front

door if you put them there.'

'But I can't see how—'

'Mr Matthias the milk will be calling any minute.'

'Shall I take them upstairs to my room instead?'

'I haven't shown it to you yet!'

'Would you mind showing me, then?'

Mrs Hughes' chubby face began to redden. 'What about your tea?' she hissed.

'I would really love a cup of tea, Mrs Hughes. It's very kind of you to ask me.'

'I know it is.'

'But these cases will be in the way if I leave them here.'

Mrs Hughes glowered at him and proceeded to stomp up the staircase. It was of a steep and incommodious construction, restricting the access of anyone much above the age of eight. After a slow and laboured ascent, she stood triumphant on the landing. With further exaggerated huffing she edged up to a door at the back of the house and proudly pointed within.

'This is your room. Isn't it nice?'

John stood blinking at Mrs Hughes. There was no way he could see past her to give his opinion.

'I've made sure everything's aired,' she declared, as John followed her in with his cases, 'and I've given you my warmest flannelette sheets.'

John smiled weakly, beads of sweat dripping off him and onto the bedding.

The little room contained a single bed, a dressing table, and an armchair, all liberally covered with pink roses. A tiny wardrobe was squeezed into one corner, next to a window that overlooked the dim backyard. There was barely enough floor space for the suitcases.

'Mrs Hughes, I really need a desk,' he said, stating the first and most obvious of the room's many inadequacies. 'Could you perhaps remove the dressing table, which I'm not going to need, and put a desk there instead? It wouldn't have to be a proper desk, of course. A table would do.'

'A table?'

'Yes, you know, for writing, marking and so forth. And I hoped there'd be a kettle or a teasmade as well.'

'A *teasmade?*' A crimson flush flared around Mrs Lavinia Hughes' stumpy neck and worked its way up her abundant chins.

'For a hot drink first thing in the morning,' John responded haltingly.

'I am the only *teasmade* around here, Mr Simmonds. We don't have all those fancy things you get in London, and if I may speak plainly, we don't need them. You will find that my tea is the best you will get anywhere. It is remarked upon. Often. No one can make tea like mine, and that's a fact.'

'Oh. Well. I mean, I'm sure—'

'And if you don't mind drinking tea made by a mere mortal, I will be brewing some in five minutes.' With that, she marched along the landing and heaved herself slowly down the stairs.

John perched on the end tiny bed. Whether it was the heat of the day or his host's hair-trigger temper, he felt suddenly drained. He decided that a shower would help, but a brief exploration of the first floor of Chapel View Guest House revealed that the only bathroom, which happened to be next to Mrs Hughes' room, lacked a shower. He had a quick swill, changed his clothes, and promised himself a bath later.

He was soon back downstairs, hesitating in the doorway of Mrs Hughes' front parlour. The room was sun-baked and still, with empty white walls surrounding a sad-looking ceramic fireplace, a China cabinet, and three brown armchairs draped with antimacassars. John wondered whether life of any sort could be sustained in such a desert place. He soon got his answer.

'That room is for best!' yelled his hostess from the kitchen door. 'The *middle* room is for tea.'

John re-located himself to the adjacent room, a very tiny place, as dim as the parlour was bright. Two bulky armchairs had somehow been squashed inside it, along with a television and a coffee table that bore a tray of tea-things. Beyond this was a large window, but as it faced north, it let in little light. Outside, John could see a yard and a coalhouse, and beyond that, rows of earth ridges bearing the yellowing remains of potato plants. At the bottom of the garden there was a small blue bench in a patch of sunlight. Basking on the bench, a pudding-shaped tortoiseshell cat flicked a lazy paw at some red admirals hovering over a nearby bush.

Mrs Lavinia Hughes entered carrying a large brown teapot.

'Now then!' she announced with gusto. 'This will sort you out!'

The first sip of tea scalded his tongue, but John did not complain. Nor did he comment on the tea's extreme sweetness, even though he never took sugar. Indeed, he was so keen not to enrage his host, he forced himself to eat two garibaldi biscuits, despite his increasingly incapacitated tongue and dislike of currants.

'Pretty cat,' John said, to make conversation. 'Is it yours?'

'Cat!' exclaimed the landlady in disgust. 'Not mine, an' that's a fact. Agents of Satan, they are.'

'That's a bit strong, Mrs Hughes.'

'No, it isn't. They destroy wildlife, they do. Look at that thing trying to kill butterflies on the lavender.'

'It's buddleia, I think.'

'No, Tiddles, that is. Belongs to Avril Jones two doors down.'

'Ah.' John took a long, slow sip of his tea, Mrs Hughes

watching him contentedly.

'So,' she said, when she was satisfied that he'd consumed enough, 'you'll be starting next Monday I suppose.'

'That's right,' he replied. 'Monday, September 2nd.'

'They're far too long, school holidays.'

'Do you think so?'

'Definite. The children are running wild. You can't keep them occupied for eight weeks.'

'Six and a half.'

'Eight weeks is ridiculous,' Mrs Hughes continued. 'Ri-dic-u-lous! They'll have forgotten everything they learnt in June.'

'You could be right.'

'When I was a girl, we had to work in the holidays. We helped out on the farms or helped our mothers in the house.'

'Things then were different then, I suppose.'

'An' you see, I was out of school and working proper by the time I was fourteen.'

'Really?'

'Oh yes. None of this staying on for O Levels or whatever they are. None of that in my day.'

'That's a shame.'

'No use to anybody, that's what I say. That's what my husband, Mr Hughes, used to say. No use to a working man.'

'But these days, surely—'

'Some things never change. Money comes from hard work and good ideas. Flippin' O Levels have got nothing to do with it.'

'You may be right,' John muttered, feeling increasingly downcast.

'Definite.'

He attempted a couple more slow and difficult slurps of tea and wondered what his hostess might have in store for him later.

'What time would you like me to come for dinner?' he asked in his most obsequious manner.

'Dinner?'

'Yes. In the evening.'

'Half past six is the time I'll be doing the evening meal. But only on days when you've been to work.'

'So, does that mean…?'

'You'll have tea at tea-time on Saturday and Sunday, and of course, I will give you a Sunday dinner as well. I go to a lot of trouble with that, mind.'

'I'm sure—'

'My gravy is praised from here to Timbuktu. I've never had a bad word said about my gravy.'

'Well, I'll very much look forward—'

'And there'll be pudding after. You'll be spoilt, mind.'

'Oh, thank—'

'Apple tart, blackberry tart, rhubarb tart. A fine lot of beautiful tarts.'

John eyed her nervously, unsure whether her skills lay in cookery or procurement.

He put his cup down carefully on its saucer. 'And, er, will dinner be at half past six tonight?'

'Tonight? Don't be daft – you've just had tea!'

Dismissed from the middle room so that Mrs Hughes could watch the six o'clock news, John shuffled up to his rose-bower and sat on the edge of the bed. This wasn't at all what he had envisaged when he'd applied for a teaching job in Trecadno. He had imagined green hills, sea views, freedom, peace… He had looked forward to accommodation that was delightfully old-fashioned yet equipped with new millennium conveniences. Tiny floral rooms governed by bossy goblins had not featured in this vision.

He checked his mobile phone and found that it could detect no signal whatsoever. There was no way around it:

he would have to beg the use of Mrs Hughes' home phone if he needed to speak to anyone. Though the only candidate for conversation was his mother. He picked up a suitcase and put it on the bed. He took out his brown suit, his only suit, and after a struggle with the door of the tiny wardrobe, suspended it on a hanger. The rest of his belongings he left in his suitcase. There was no point in putting his shirts in the drawers of the dressing table if it was only going to be replaced. There was similarly no point in piling his books on top of it, and there were no other places for his books and papers unless he stuffed them under the bed.

He closed his suitcase and moved over to the window. Shifting the thick net curtain, he gazed dejectedly down onto the backyard, and the tired-looking vegetable patch. The tortoiseshell cat was now stalking beneath the privet hedge that separated Mrs Hughes' territory from the garden it backed on to. The two rows of narrow gardens resembled a mediaeval enclosure system in miniature. They were bathed in sunshine and quite devoid of human life.

The stillness of the back gardens was strangely overwhelming. Already weary from his journey, he felt compelled to lie down on the bed and close his eyes. But if he'd hoped to sleep, he was disappointed, for his room was directly above Mrs Hughes' middle room, and hence above her television. She had the volume turned right up, making it impossible to miss even a syllable of Moira Stuart's reportage, Michael Fish's weather forecast ('continuing warm in the south'), and a sequence of unremarkable items of local news ('city-centre supermarket infestation'; 'local councillor seen leaving massage parlour').

Before 7pm, Mrs Lavinia Hughes switched channel to a Welsh-language programme, the high volume of which in no way compensated for its unintelligibility. John's brow developed anxious creases. He had completely ignored the fact that another language was spoken in his new home

9

area, and wondered whether this inadequacy on his part would affect his teaching. Perhaps he could go to Welsh classes, he thought. Perhaps just going to the classes would endear him to the locals even if he failed to master the language, which was likely.

His stomach started to gurgle, its only sustenance that day having been a squashed ham sandwich and two unwanted garibaldi biscuits. Action was clearly required: if dinner wasn't to be forthcoming from Mrs Hughes, he would have to venture out of Chapel View in quest of food.

He tip-toed down the stairs and across the hall. Given the volume of her television, he'd assumed that his landlady must be a little deaf.

'Where are you going?' boomed the doughty lady over the television, but as John gently, carefully turned the front door handle, Mrs Lavinia Hughes' ears proved more than a match for even the quietest of mice.

'Oh… yes… well…'

'Are you going *out*, by any chance?'

'I felt like some air, Mrs Hughes,' said John, shuffling like a scolded schoolboy up to the doorway of the middle room. 'I didn't want to disturb you.'

'I see. Though you will disturb me when you come back in.'

'Oh… I hadn't thought…'

'No, men never do. I usually go to bed at nine.'

'Right, well, er… perhaps you could give me a key?'

'A key?'

'To let myself in?'

'I barely know you, Mr Simmonds. Do you really think that a single woman all alone in a house is going to give you a key for you to come in any time you like?'

'But that's what normally happens, Mrs Hughes. In every hotel I've ever been into…'

'This, Mr Simmonds, is not London. We do things

10

differently here.'

'I'm sorry, Mrs Hughes, I just wanted to take a walk. Surely that's not a problem?'

Mrs Lavinia Hughes surveyed him like a dog about to bite.

'Just don't be late. I'll bolt the door, mind!'

He escaped into a town square that had grown much dimmer and cooler than when he had arrived. He turned left, following the gently curving road eastwards away from the chapel, heading for the far end of the church grounds. At that point, just outside the high church wall, there was a small flowerbed of French marigolds with a wishing well in its centre. The marigolds stank, but over them his nose detected an altogether superior niff – the hot and fatty fumes of chips! Gratefully John followed the seductive aroma down a lane lined with grey-walled houses identical to the ones in the square. Turning a corner, he was rewarded with the bright and steamy window of a chip-shop. A small mongrel was tied to a drainpipe outside, while inside there were two small boys and a young couple with dreadlocks. John supposed the dog was theirs.

He joined the queue and nodded at the dreadlocked man.

'Lovely smell in here,' he said, close to dribbling.

'Yeah,' replied the hippy with a gormless grin.

'Good chips, do you reckon?'

'Yeah,' answered the man again.

'Fish OK?'

'Yeah.'

Close inspection revealed that the man's eyes seemed to lack the ability to focus. With a sigh, John turned his attention to the contents of the hot cabinet, wondering when he might enjoy his first normal conversation in his new home.

The hippies cleared out the last of the chips, and John endured a tortuous wait while a fresh batch was prepared. When she eventually got round to dishing out his fish and chips, the woman serving eyed him suspiciously.

'I'll bet you're the new teacher,' she said, plonking his fodder on some newspaper.

'How did you know that?' asked John, taken aback.

'We don't get many Englishmen around here this time of year,' she said, adding liberal quantities of salt and vinegar. 'In fact, we don't get any.'

Leaving the chip shop at last, John looked around for a quiet spot to eat his dinner. He could hardly take it back to Chapel View Guest House. Something as irregular as a bag of chips might send Mrs Hughes over the edge. After a bit of dithering outside a newsagent's, he decided to retrace his steps back to the square in the hope that he might find a bench.

The church clock struck the half-hour as John walked back down Heol y Carlwm into the square. After some fruitless wandering, he decided that the wishing-well was his only option. He tip-toed through the marigolds with his hot and soggy parcel and positioned himself as best he could on the metal grille covering the well.

The light was fading now, and little bats flitted around at roof level. In the darkening eastern sky, a star twinkled, and then another. John smiled at them as if they were new friends. He could never properly pick out the stars when he had lived in London. He thought a little about the life he'd left behind, about the busy streets lined with shops selling everything, anytime. He thought about the job that he'd turned his back on and the school he'd worked so hard for. He thought about Marcia, the woman he had loved and lost. The last few months in the metropolis had been sweaty and painful. Escape had become essential. He knew there would be challenges in Trecadno, but they would be different, better. He took a great breath of cool, clean air and stared up at the stars. He had done the right thing, he was sure. Fairly sure.

Absorbed in his thoughts – and his chips – John failed to notice a heavy footfall approaching him. He jumped at the sudden presence of a tall, gaunt man staring fixedly at him from the edge of the marigold bed. The man had stringy grey hair down to his collar, and very thick round glasses. Despite the warm weather, he wore a raincoat and robust-looking boots. Surprise caused a chip to stick in John's throat, and he started to cough.

'What's the matter with you, then?' asked the tall man in a gruff baritone.

'A bit of… food… went down… the wrong way,' John spluttered. 'I think… I need… a drink.'

'This early?'

The man watched as John recovered his breath. 'Hey!' he said eventually, his thin mouth breaking into a sly smile. 'I know who you are, boy. You're the new school-master fellow, aren't you?'

'Yes, I am. I suppose everyone—'

'I know your name, too. Hang on, don't tell me: Simple Simon. Something like that.'

'Simmonds.'

'Funny sort of name, that.'

'Do you think so? What's your name, then?' asked John, peeved.

'Williams. Everybody knows who I am. William Williams, Deacon of Moriah.'

'Moriah?'

'The chapel'

'Oh? Where is that?'

'*Where* is it? It's behind you, boy! Behind the church – you can't miss it.' He shook his head disapprovingly. 'You'll have to have your eyes tested.'

'My eyes are fine.'

'You'll be no good to the children in the school if you can't see them!'

'I'll see them perfectly well.'

'An' you're risking it, too, sitting there.'

'And why's that?'

'Well for one thing, no one is allowed on that flower bed except Fred Evans, gardener. And for another, that grille is badly corroded and it's a long drop down.'

John shuffled his posterior to the very edge of the well and fingered the bars of the grille nervously.

'Can't have a newcomer falling down there on his first day, eh?' The deacon chuckled. 'It would be like the Iron Age.'

'Pardon?'

'I'm told by people in the know that back in the Iron Age our ancestors used to chuck people down that well as an offering to the gods.'

'Really?' John peered anxiously into the gloom below the grille.

'An' you'd be perfect, of course.'

'Me? Why?'

'Cos you're a Saes… English. Fair game for sacrifice!'

John frowned at him and wriggled off the well, back onto his feet.

William Williams pulled his lapels up to his neck and looked up at the darkening sky. 'Autumn will soon be upon us,' he announced. 'Season of mists and mellow funerals.'

'Pardon?'

'Not as productive as winter, but there's a definite increase compared to spring and summer.'

'Sorry?'

'Funerals, boy! There are a lot of elderly people round here, see. As it happens, there's a funeral tomorrow.' He tilted his head back proudly. 'I will be reading the hymns.'

'Will you?' John looked into the thick lenses, which seemed to magnify the malign quality of the deacon's eyes. 'That's, er, interesting.'

'The thing is, young Simon, we are short of bearers.'

'Bearers?'

'You know, to bear the coffin.'

'Oh, right.'

'So,' said the deacon, starting to slope off, 'I can say you'll be there, can I?'

'What?'

'Eleven o'clock start, but you'd better be at the vestry ten minutes early.'

'Hang on....' John stumbled after Mr Williams, inadvertently crushing a marigold.

'Hey! That's criminal damage, that is!'

'Sorry, I didn't mean...'

'Never mind. We'll say no more about it. Ten to eleven tomorrow morning, all right?'

'But where am I supposed to go?'

'Where?' William Williams stood over him and glowered. 'What sort of damn fool question is that? Moriah Chapel, of course, boy! Don't be late!'

CHAPTER TWO

Moriah Chapel

When John opened his eyes the following morning, the first things he noticed were the knitted brows of Mrs Lavinia Hughes.

'Oh, er, good morning!' he spluttered, pulling the bedclothes up to his neck.

'Morning? Only just. Some of us have been up three hours.'

'What time is it?'

'Nine o'clock.'

'That's not so late.'

'No? Well, all I can say is that if you want your breakfast you'd better start shifting.' With this, she stomped out of the room and commenced an awkward descent of the stairs.

John sighed and struggled out of bed. He managed to take no more than ten minutes to attend to his toilette, and then dashed down the stairs to Mrs Lavinia Hughes' middle room. He sat down in an armchair, painfully aware both of a distinct absence of breakfast and of the smell of old chips emanating from his shirt. After a minute or two he got up and went looking for his hostess. He found her in the kitchen, a dim place with a low ceiling half-covered by a many-runged clothes airer. A large cast-iron boiler sat alongside a cooker at the far end of the room, and a wooden table occupied most of the remaining space.

'I went to your middle room first,' he said, his face

apologetic.

'That was a waste of time, then, wasn't it? Breakfast is served in here.' She pointed at the table. 'You'd better sit down, hadn't you?' John dutifully pulled up a grimy wooden chair. 'I cooked this two hours ago,' Mrs Hughes continued, removing a plate from the oven with a tea-towel. 'I've tried to keep it warm for you, but it's not going to be as good as when it was fresh.'

'Ah.' John's spirits crumpled at the sight of wizened sausages sitting in a puddle of congealing lard.

'You see,' she continued, 'I was under the impression that you would be in work by now.'

'Normally, of course, I would be, but—'

'And that you would want your breakfast by seven at the latest.'

'Indeed, but as I say—'

'But maybe things have changed at that school.'

'The thing is—'

'So, you'd better let me know what time you do want breakfast.'

'Right. Seven o'clock, then.'

'Just as I thought.'

'But tomorrow is Saturday, of course.'

'Another day. The same as any other to me. It wouldn't be fair to expect me to remember different times for different days, would it?'

'I suppose not,' John relented, applying his knife and fork to a limp piece of fried bread.

Mrs Lavinia Hughes started to fuss with her kettle, humming a tune that sounded like a hymn. John was reminded of his conversation with the deacon.

'I met Mr William Williams last night,' he said as Mrs Hughes stirred the teapot.

'Oh yes?'

'He asked me to be a bearer at a funeral. It's in Moriah

Chapel.'

'Well, it wouldn't be anywhere else, and that's a fact.' She waddled over to the table with the pot. 'And you agreed, did you? I suppose you realise who you'll be carrying?'

'Well, no, actually…'

'Emanuel Parry, the butcher.'

'Oh?'

'He was a *very* big man.'

John cast a timid glance at Mrs Lavinia Hughes' substantial girth and felt a chill creeping into his heart.

'And,' continued his hostess, 'he had gangrene.'

'Gangrene?'

'He had circ-uw-late-ory problems,' she said slowly and not without a little pride, 'and he got gangrene.'

'Ah.'

'So I hope Joss Edwards the undertaker has done his job well, that's all.'

John tried not to follow this train of thought as he still had one and a half cold sausages to chew through. He accepted a cup of tea with thanks and tried to wash down his breakfast with large sips. But even Mrs Hughes' sweet tea could not disguise the full horror of the lukewarm mass before him. He pushed the fatty remains hither and thither across his plate, finally forming them into a thick ribbon in the centre, over which he strategically folded his knife and fork.

Mrs Lavinia Hughes stared at the arrangement in dismay.

'Didn't you like my breakfast?' she asked as red blotches of outrage erupted over her chubby cheeks.

'Certainly. It was a fine breakfast. I would have gulped it down normally, but I'm a bit anxious about the funeral.'

'Nervous type, are you?'

'No, but you see …'

'I see perfectly well, Mr Simmonds.'

Mrs Hughes shuffled away, and John listened with a heavy heart as her footsteps resonated on the stairs. After a suitable interval he left the table and proceeded hesitantly up to his room. A black suit had been spread out on his bed.

'I thought you would appreciate that,' said Mrs Lavinia Hughes to the lumbar region of his back. John jumped, turned, and knocked over a bedside lamp.

'Clumsy clot!' exclaimed his landlady. 'That came all the way from Aberystwyth!'

'It's not broken,' John stammered.

'It better not be. I'll test it later. Anyway, I hope the suit fits. Mr Hughes was about your size.' Mrs Lavinia Hughes beamed coquettishly and sidled away along the landing.

John picked up the trousers and held them up against himself, noting a reek of camphor. The waist was clearly far too big and the legs about three inches too short. The jacket was at least two sizes too large. But his own brown suit was not appropriate for the imminent occasion, so he supposed he would have to make do.

At a quarter to eleven, John left Chapel View Guest House wearing his own grey trousers (un-ironed) and the late Mr Hughes' black jacket and headed over to Moriah Chapel. In contrast to the previous night, the square was now filled with gossiping people. He had to struggle to reach the vestry, which was located around the back of the chapel next to an arc of tall oaks. The vestry was a barren place, though now filled with black-garbed townsfolk. To John, the scene resembled a court of law. Each dour face turned to stare at him as he took tentative steps into the building.

A small man with a very tight-fitting jacket scuttled up to him and started speaking in Welsh.

'I'm here as a bearer,' John ventured, at what seemed like an appropriate juncture. 'Mr William Williams asked me.'

Upon hearing his name, Mr Williams emerged, ghost-like, from a corner. 'At last, boy. I thought you'd forgot.'

'Here I am. As instructed.' He fiddled with a button on the late Mr Hughes' jacket. 'I just hope I'm up to the job.'

'You'll have to be, won't you? Now then, here's my son Idwal, who's also a bearer. You stick with him.'

Mr William Williams sidled back into the shadows, leaving John to consider 'son of deacon'. There could be no doubt of this young man's paternity. He was stockier than his father, but equally tall, and had the same limp hair hanging in greasy strands over his ears. The face was much the same too – gaunt and faintly grey – though it possessed the smoothness of youth. Both father and son looked distinctly dangerous.

'You're the English chap, then?' remarked Idwal in an off-hand way while trying to discipline his tie.

'I'm the new biology teacher.'

'Aye.' He sniffed loudly. 'I never liked biology.'

'That's a pity.'

'What use is bloody biology except to find out about women's insides? An' I knew all about them already.'

'Biology is important for all sorts of things, especially in an agricultural area like this, and—'

'Agriculture? You must be bloody joking. D'you think I'd want to get up before dawn every morning to wade through cow shit?'

'Well, er…'

'No, I bloody wouldn't.'

'So, er, what do you do, then?'

'What d'you mean what do I *do*?'

'What's your job?'

Ignoring the question, Idwal Williams sniffed again and tucked the back of his shirt into his trousers. 'Hey, we'd better get going,' he said. 'The undertakers will be here any minute.'

He led the way through the vestry into the chapel. Opening the main door, they encountered a hoard of expectant faces topped with an assortment of black hats. John turned to Idwal.

'Was Mr Parry a local celebrity?' he asked, somewhat alarmed.

'He was just a bloody butcher.'

'So why the crowds?'

'Doesn't everyone come out for funerals where you come from?'

'Actually no,' John replied as an enormous hearse turned into the square. Four young men attired in ill-fitting black suits emerged from the crowd, and all six bearers lined up on the chapel steps in readiness. The rear door of the hearse was opened by a bent old man attired in black tailcoat and top hat, and John and his fellow bearers grappled with the remarkably wide coffin. When this grim receptacle was eventually placed before the pulpit, the bearers retreated to pews in a dim corner at the front of the chapel. By his comrades' pale and sweaty faces, their twisting in their seats and muffled groans of discomfort, John gathered that they too would be spending the service dealing with spinal column displacement. The minister and his deacons soon trouped in, and everyone stood to attention.

The minister was a small man with cropped white hair that stood up like the bristles of a toothbrush. He put on a pair of half-moon spectacles and stared down at the packed pews with an expression of intense fury. A verbal bombardment followed, all in Welsh. A fair amount of spittle was involved.

'He's been watching the videos again,' Idwal Williams whispered into John's left ear.

'Sorry?' John whispered back.

'Hitler at Nuremburg,' Idwal replied. John perspired a

little more.

The minister continued to rant until Mr William Williams advanced with leaden gait onto the platform just below the pulpit. He opened his hymn book and read out the first verse of a hymn. As everyone stood up to sing, Idwal whispered to John:

'Don't forget, we've got to carry old Parry back out as well.'

With that happy thought lodged in his mind John took up his hymnbook. It very rapidly became apparent that he would contribute little to the singing, since even if he could have worked out the hymn being performed, let alone which verse thereof, he would have had no hope of pronouncing the words. He resorted to opening and closing his mouth soundlessly like a fish. This unusual mode of hymn singing meant that he was free to survey the scene around him. Rays of sunlight reflected off a large glass vase of gladioli and the winged spectacles of a large woman nearby. The pews themselves did not shine, for their old wood had been dulled by years of handling.

The front pew contained a row of crow-like black-hatted females, presumably the kin of the deceased. They were all small, stout, and aged about fifty. Mrs Lavinia Hughes looked as if she could have been related, but was seated four pews back. She met John's gaze with a girlish smirk, and he promptly looked back down at the pages of his hymnal, only coming up for air on the fifth verse. He glanced furtively up at the gallery, which was also packed to capacity. Here, the age range seemed different, and John realised that a large swathe was female and dressed in identical navy dresses. The group launched into an exclusive rendition of a verse, and John inferred that they constituted the chapel choir.

He scanned each of the choral faces, pausing longer on the younger ones. One had lank-looking long hair and pointed nose: John decided that she must be a Williams. Next to her was a short woman lacking a neck who had to be a Hughes. But alongside her was a sight wonderful indeed: a young woman with wide eyes and a cupid's bow mouth set in flawless skin. Her face was framed by auburn hair that cascaded down her shoulders like a fiery fountain.

The singing stopped and everyone sat down except John. He remained standing, his eyes fixed on the heavenly vision in the gallery. Idwal grabbed at his sleeve, or rather at the sleeve of the late Mr Hughes, and yanked his fellow bearer back down onto the pew. The minister resumed his position (on a box) in the pulpit, and began what John assumed to be an extensive and detailed account of the deceased and his many virtues. John had no way of confirming this for he understood none of it. But he didn't care; his attention was completely held by a certain member of Moriah Ladies' Choir. Trecadno was starting to look up a bit.

When the last hymn had been sung, the bearers stood in readiness to restore the ample remains of Mr Emanuel Parry to the hearse.

'Who's that girl up in the choir,' John whispered to Idwal, 'the one with the long red hair?'

Idwal didn't bother to look up. 'That's Elisabeth-Mai,' he said, 'and you can forget about *her.*'

Once the hearse had pulled away, and the mourners had departed in the direction of the crematorium, the deacons, choir, and other assorted hangers-on trooped back to the vestry for refreshment. Mr William Williams advanced on John with heavy steps and patted him on the back.

'Good work, boy. Good work. You'll help us again, I hope?'

'I'll be teaching at the school every weekday from now on, Mr Williams.'

'There's always Saturday, boy. But today is Friday, of course, and Friday night is quiz night.'

'Quiz night?'

'Aye. Down the Wanderers' Club. A fine night we have, don't we, Idwal?'

'Definite,' mumbled Idwal, halfway through a large yawn.

'You'll join us, won't you, boy?'

'Perhaps,' said John, 'though I don't know where the club is.'

'Mrs Hughes will tell you.'

'I'm not sure if it's wise to ask,' muttered John nervously.

The deacon's gaunt face cracked into a smile.

'Don't you worry about her, boy. She'll be all right about tonight. Like a lamb, she'll be. You be there at seven sharp.'

Idwal dawdled off and John started to do likewise, but his progress was impeded by a large obstacle below eye level. Mrs Lavinia Hughes had found him.

'That jacket looks *very* good on you,' she said, her head tilted in judgement. With some anxiety, John remembered the excessive perspiration that the jacket had had to endure, not to mention the tearing sound he'd heard when Idwal had yanked him down onto the pew.

'I must get it dry-cleaned before I give it back to you,' he said hoarsely.

'Don't you worry about that, Mr Simmonds.'

'Oh, but really…'

'There's no dry-cleaners in Trecadno.'

'Oh, well then…'

'Just leave it on your bed,' she instructed, eyes gleaming.

CHAPTER THREE

The Wanderers' Club

'Boys will be boys,' announced Mrs Lavinia Hughes, as she inspected the jacket once owned by her departed spouse. John could barely believe it. The tear in the lining had not seemed to elicit fury, nor had the unmistakable whiff of sweat produced sarcasm. Indeed, the worthy lady's response to the return of the garment was to produce a ham sandwich and a piece of Battenberg cake.

John might even have enjoyed the sandwich if Mrs Hughes hadn't hovered over him the whole time. He decided that a visit to his new place of employment was in order. Trecadno High School was easily reached by following a narrow lane called Heol y Dyfrgi that ran westwards, parallel to a small stream edged with oak and ash trees. A squat, two-storey block with a flat roof formed the main part of the school. It looked like it had been constructed in the seventies, and going by its flaking paint and chipped plaster, it didn't seem to have been touched since then either.

An aged school secretary greeted John with an expression of mild distaste and informed him that Mr Ivor Kane, the head, was in.

'Does he actually have one?' asked John with a giggle.

She rolled her eyes and turned back to her paperwork. John knocked on the door of the headmaster's office but received no response. Though he could hear noises within. Muffled giggles, in fact. He decided to look for his laboratory, and advanced uncertainly down a long corridor, stopping every so often to peep through the small windows set in each of the classroom doors. He eventually located the biology lab, only to find the door locked. He stood there deliberating, wondering if there was any other part of the school worth exploring, or whether he should head back to Chapel View. He was put out of his misery by the appearance of a little man wearing an overall.

'You'll be Mr Simmonds,' said the figure with a castrato-like squeak.

'That's right,' replied John. He had become resigned to everyone knowing about him in advance.

'I'm Dai, the caretaker. I'll let you into the lab, shall I?'

'Thanks. You've arrived at just the right time.'

'No trouble.' He turned the key and backed off into the dim corridor. 'I'll see you later,' he called from the shadows.

'Oh?' said John.

'In the Wanderers' Club,' squeaked Dai as he disappeared out of view.

The biology lab was a large space containing six dark wooden benches that straddled the room like enormous coffins. Windows covered one of the long laboratory walls but faced the wrong way to let in much sunlight. John sighed, knowing that dimness equates to doziness, especially last lesson, and especially in that nocturnal species the sixth-former. The opposite wall bore an array of cupboards. John opened the door of one of them only to be immediately overwhelmed by the stench of formaldehyde. A nervous grope into the cupboard's dusty interior revealed specimen pots of blackened cockroaches, yellowing dogfish, and curled masses of earthworms. He closed the cupboard door in disgust and opened a drawer in one of the benches. It contained three toffee wrappers, and a couple of rat dissection guides covered in off-putting reddish fingerprints. He moved forward to the teacher's desk to see what treasures might await him there. All he found was a box of chalk, a board duster, and an old textbook of mycology.

John walked along each bench, occasionally looking into the cupboards beneath. They contained little other than scraps of paper and a lot of dust. He sat down on a stool at the back bench, steeped in despond and weariness. Recent carvings on the benchtop informed him that 'Alison Francis loves Malcolm Bowen' and 'Beynon James is a wanker'.

He turned his gaze to the cold windows and tried to think through his priorities. The first thing he needed was a timetable, and then he should try to get his hands on a set of syllabi for the examination classes. This would enable him to plan lessons for the first week, which would lead on to checking the whereabouts of apparatus for practical sessions, and any other resources he might need.

He looked at the wall above the teacher's desk, at the curling posters around the blackboard. The chambers of the heart had become faded and perforated, and the cabbage-white butterfly's wings were almost brown. He really ought to smarten up this room, he thought, and he really must find a way of removing the solidified chewing gum plugging the gas taps. There was a vast amount to do, far more than he had imagined, and a significant chunk of it had to be done by Monday. John had been thrilled by his appointment at Trecadno High School, but now he felt daunted and unprepared.

Problems came thick and fast into his mind but none of them found any solution there. He just couldn't concentrate at all. Perhaps he was tired from the previous day's travelling. Or perhaps the formaldehyde was affecting him. It didn't help that every time he glanced at the empty blackboard a face seemed to appear on it. It had glowing eyes and seductive lips, and hair the colour of fire.

After an hour inside the lab, he felt as pickled as the

dogfish and decided to go in search of the headmaster again. He had advanced about fifty yards along the dim corridor when he noticed a plump, ruddy-faced man plodding towards him. The man appeared to be in late middle age, with wisps of grey hair swept over the top of his head. His shirt was undone almost to the waist. He clearly hadn't noticed John advancing from the gloom and started visibly when he realised that he was not alone.

'My God!' he cried, staggering back a little. 'Who the hell are you?'

'I'm John Simmonds. Don't you remember me, Headmaster?' He had little trouble in recognising the man who had interviewed him two months earlier. 'I'm the new biology teacher.'

'Are you? Good God. What on earth are you doing here?'

'Well, I thought—'

'Oh, never mind.' The headmaster looked down at himself and gave an embarrassed laugh. 'Very hot today, isn't it?'

'Yes.'

'I get overheated very quickly,' he added, struggling with a button. 'Anyway, my boy,' he continued, 'glad to see you're settling in. See you on Monday.' And with this he hurried off with a conspicuous air of relief.

John made his way to the school entrance with a deep sigh. Passing the headmaster's office, he once again heard rustling and smelt perfume.

Walking back towards the town, John was grateful for the greenery and the gentle swaying of lace-like ash leaves. Reaching a sunny gap in the trees, he sat down on a hillock and gazed down at the stream and the patchwork of green fields beyond. A small tortoiseshell butterfly flew past his nose followed by a huge dragonfly. In the trees above him a cluster of bluetits chastised each other as they jumped from branch to branch. After a few minutes, John saw what looked like a ginger tomcat drinking from the river, but soon realised that it possessed a bushy fox's tail. His spirits were raised by the sight of the fine creature finishing its drink, and he beamed happily at the greenery around him. This was what he'd wanted when he'd planned his escape from London. He had surely made the right choice.

Feelings of contentment were maintained even through Mrs Lavinia Hughes' evening meal, an indeterminate stew containing misshapen dumplings.

'I done it special for you,' she announced. 'An' I've given you bread rolls.'

John decided it would be prudent to eat first and then work out why Mrs Hughes was being so nice. In the event, she volunteered the information.

'You'll want to go to quiz night, I daresay,' she said as she settled herself on a chair next to him.

He broke off chewing a dumpling and looked up in alarm. 'Mr Williams suggested it,' he said.

'Of course. It's a good evening out.'

An uncomfortable thought shuddered through John's mind. 'Do *you* usually go, Mrs Hughes?'

Mrs Lavinia Hughes smiled expansively. 'It's kind of you to ask,' she cooed, 'but no. The Wanderers' Club on a Friday night is no place for a respectable widow.'

John couldn't stop a gleeful grin spreading over his face. 'I'm hoping it will be enjoyable,' he said quickly.

'I'm sure it will be,' she replied, folding her arms under her ample bosom. 'And what do you plan to do tomorrow?'

John anticipated another threat. 'Er,' he began, as he gulped down a fragment of gristle by mistake. 'I was thinking of going exploring if the weather holds.' He glanced at Mrs Lavinia Hughes' bulging midriff. 'I thought I might go for a really long walk. Uphill.'

'You're thinking of Bryncadno, perhaps?'

'I'm not sure yet. I need to study a map.'

'Indeed. Were you thinking of heading off early?'

'Possibly.'

'And returning quite late?'

'Around teatime I should think,' he said hesitantly. What was she getting at?

'Well, do you know,' she said conspiratorially, 'I thought that's what you might say! I thought that a nice, fit young man like yourself might fancy a long walk.' She licked her lips.

John blanched. Surely with her build she could hardly be a walker.

'And you see,' continued Mrs Hughes, 'that fits in very well with my plans.'

A little wave of nausea began to advance up John's oesophagus. '*Your* plans, Mrs Hughes?'

'You see, if *you* go off first thing – let's say half past eight, shall we? – then *I* can catch the ten to nine bus to Carmarthen with the girls. That means that we can be there by ten. And then, see, if you don't need to be back before tea-time – let's say six o'clock – then we can catch the five o'clock bus back and I'll still have plenty of time to cut you a sandwich.'

'That sounds a good arrangement,' he said, brightening.

'I like a good day out. All the winter fashions are in the shops now, see.'

'Oh, right…'

'It's just wonderful that our plans agree so very well.' She smirked at him.

John put down his cutlery and picked up the remaining half roll. 'Of course, if you were able to give me a key,' he ventured, foolhardily, 'you could go anywhere you like at any time, and you wouldn't have to worry about me.'

Mrs Lavinia Hughes' bonhomie drained away at once. 'We've already discussed that,' she hissed.

'Really, Mrs Hughes, it would be so convenient for you.'

'For *me*? To give *you* a key?'

'Yes, a front door key.'

'The door is immaterial, Mr Simmonds. My answer is the same every time. Mrs Myrtle Evans in Bryn Mefus gives people keys, but she has inferior poly-cotton sheets and ready-sliced bread. Mrs Ariadne Davies in Tŷ Heulog would probably give you a key, but then you'd have to put up with damp cornflakes every morning, and the smell of her three manky cats.'

'I'm sorry, Mrs Hughes. I didn't mean to offend you.'

'Didn't you, now? Well, a key is quite out of the question, whatever. I am a woman living alone.'

'I understand.'

'Good. I hope you will agree, then, that I could not possibly give you a key.'

'Of course you couldn't.'

The Wanderers' Club turned out to be on the opposite side of the town from the high school, though the river John had seen that afternoon ran close to both buildings. Mrs Lavinia Hughes equipped him with directions and a torch, and at about quarter to seven he headed off in an easterly direction.

The walk was a lot longer than he had anticipated, and he soon found himself amongst shadowy hedgerows and shimmering birches with no buildings in sight, nor people. Just staring cows and birds singing shrill songs of reprimand. John stopped and surveyed the narrow road before him, wondering if he had taken the wrong route. He was on the verge of turning back when he heard a familiar dragging gait some distance ahead of him. He trotted forward to catch up with its source.

'Hey! You again!' exclaimed Mr William Williams, the owner of the plodding feet.

'Yes indeed,' replied John. 'I thought I'd take your advice and give quiz night a try. I'm sure it's better than sitting in Mrs Hughes' middle room.'

Mr William Williams chuckled.

'You'll break the poor woman's heart, you will. Watching TV with her young men is almost as good as shopping to her.'

'You make it sound as if she only ever has young men at Chapel View.'

'She only ever does, boy,' William Williams said with a sly grin.

They walked along in silence for a little while.

'That's lovely birdsong,' John remarked. 'Though I don't know which bird produces it.'

'No? An' you a biology teacher, too? Kinnock, that is.'

'Er, do you mean dunnock?'

'Maybe. Both make a lot of noise, whatever.' He suddenly grabbed John's arm. 'But here we are at the Wanderers'!'

Despite the Wanderers' being a large building, John would have walked straight past it if Mr Williams hadn't pointed it out. It was completely hidden by trees, as if to keep it the preserve of locals only. William Williams led the way to the entrance of this great concrete box and pushed John into a hot cloud of smoke and babble. All those gathered around the many tables fell silent immediately, and cold eyes fixed on the stranger as if he was a prisoner being led to the dock. The deacon diffused the situation by putting an arm around John's shoulder and raising the other in general salute. By the time he'd steered the newcomer to the bar, everyone had turned back to their drink and banter.

They were aiming for two middle-aged gentlemen positioned on stools. One was thin, with thick grey hair, intellectual glasses and a smart summer jacket. The other had a bald head, red face, bulbous nose, and a tatty check shirt that hung over an overflowing gut. A pipe drooped from his mouth.

'Evening,' the deacon bellowed at them as he undid the top buttons of his raincoat.

'Greetings, William!' exclaimed the thin man.

The deacon positioned himself on a stool next to the two drinking companions.

'I got a friend tonight,' he said, and motioned to John to sit next to him.

John attempted to squash himself into the confined space Mr Williams had indicated. 'I'm John Simmonds,' he said, sucking in his stomach.

'Very pleased to meet you,' declared the thin man, offering a hand. The red-faced man also shook hands.

'Hey!' cried the deacon. 'What d'you mean, "John"?'

'That's my name,' said its owner.

'"John" is a Baptist's name. You're not a Baptist, are you?'

'Pardon?'

'John the Baptist. Lover of water. Loads of 'em around here. You can't move in Penymynydd swimming pool for Baptists.'

John stared at Mr Williams, speechless with incomprehension.

'See, we're *Annibynwyr*. Independents,' continued the deacon. 'We don't hold with dunking.'

'Would it make any difference if I was a Baptist?' asked John.

'I'll say. We get enough riffraff in this town without more Baptists.'

'You've been at the communion wine again, William,' said the red-faced man.

'That is a slur, Jonesy, a bloody slur. Anyway,' the deacon continued, turning back to John, 'what about it now? Are you a Baptist?'

'No. I'm not an anything. Not that it's any of your business.'

'It certainly is my business. I am a deacon in this town, and I am entrusted with the maintenance of morals. We don't want people coming in and brainwashing us!'

'For goodness' sake, William!' muttered the thin man in exasperation.

The red-faced man withdrew his pipe again and called out in the direction of a curtained door behind the bar. 'Maldwyn, get us a round. William will pay once he's aired all his prejudices and picked out the moths from his wallet.'

A troubled look came over the deacon's dour visage, and he tapped his pockets with alarm. 'On this one occasion, as we have a visitor, I will agree. Mind, buying rounds can cause intoxication. People should buy their own. That would make 'em drink less.'

'I haven't noticed you rejecting the drinks bought for you, William Williams,' said the thin man.

'Waste is sinful,' announced the deacon.

A little man with curly white hair suddenly appeared behind the bar. 'Gentlemen,' he said in a sleepy voice, 'what will it be?'

'The usual,' said the red-faced man, pipe in hand.

'Right you are,' replied Maldwyn the bartender, reaching for a large bottle filled with liquid the colour of sunset.

The thin man leant forwards to address John. 'You're the new biology teacher, I imagine?'

'I think someone must have put an ad about me in the local paper,' replied John.

'Alexander knows everything,' commented the deacon with a wink. 'Heck, I haven't introduced you!' he suddenly exclaimed. 'This is Daniel Jones, general practitioner,' he said, indicating the rubious man, 'known to all as Doc Jones. And beyond him,' he continued, pointing at the thin man, 'is Mr Alexander Pritchard, history master and know-all.'

'Pleased to meet you both,' said John politely.

Maldwyn put a glass of amber liquid in front of each of them and beamed expectantly at the deacon.

'I should clarify, John,' continued Alexander, the thin man, 'that I know about you because I share your imminent place of employment.'

'The comprehensive school?'

'*High* school, if you don't mind,' responded Alexander. 'Yes indeed. I took up my post there as head of history twenty-four years ago.' He took a sip of his drink and sighed wistfully. 'It was Trecadno Boys' Grammar School when I started. In those days the place still seemed bright and new. Such good boys we had back then. They used to win competitions, get into Oxford. The school rugby team even beat Trecadno Wanderers once.'

'That was a well-known fix,' muttered William Williams.

'But what about now?' asked John. 'Is it still a reasonable school?'

Alexander Pritchard pulled a face. 'What can I say? We try. We do our best. But you can't fashion good furniture from damp wood, nor can you make good bread from contaminated flour.'

'Contaminated? What do you mean?'

'A recent influx of wild children. Families living in fields.'

'Though farming doesn't interest them,' added the doctor.

'Farming is too advanced for them, more like,' said Alexander. 'They constitute a pre-agricultural aggregation. Proto-Neolithic, if you like.'

'No, I don't bloody like,' commented the deacon, putting his empty glass down with a thud. 'Can't you just use simple words?' He turned to John. 'He's talking about the flamin' crusties.'

'I saw a couple in the chip shop last night,' said John.

'They're always in there,' said William. 'Too bloody lazy to cook for themselves.'

'Plenty of money for chips and takeaways though,' said Alexander. 'Rich parents, you see.'

'They live in tents below our beloved Bryncadno,' hissed William Williams.

'It's a hill a few miles away,' explained Alexander. 'They camp there because of the ley lines. Three of them meet at Bryncadno, apparently.'

'Really?' John was impressed but mystified.

'Lines of magnetic variability,' continued Alexander. 'Some people believe that the Celts would only build on ley lines.'

'They don't just come for ley lines,' muttered Doc Jones.

The deacon interrupted before any further reasons could be clarified. 'What d'you think of your whiskey, then, boy?' he asked.

'Very good,' answered John, and it certainly was, though his focus was still on the ley lines.

'That stuff is the best tonic money can buy, isn't it, Jonesy?'

'Never come across a better one.'

'Do you have a practice in Trecadno, Dr Jones? John asked him.

'Yes, Ffordd y Cadno.' He didn't sound enthusiastic.

'You won't see him there,' said William Williams.

'No?' replied John uncertainly. 'Do you mean that I'm too healthy to go there?'

'I hope you are, boy,' replied the deacon, 'but that's not the main reason. Which is that our Jonesy is never there.'

Doc Jones scowled. John maintained a polite but nervous silence.

'I'm not stuck on a golf course all day if you're wondering,' Daniel Jones said. 'It's just that these days I am less tolerant of my fellow man than I used to be.'

'I'm less tolerant of children than I used to be,' Alexander Pritchard remarked. 'Five more years until retirement. But enough of us,' he said turning to John. 'I hope you are starting to settle in.'

'Oh yes,' said John, with an enthusiasm he did not feel.

"Course you are,' decided Mr Williams. 'We'll make sure of that. We can do all sorts of things to you. *For* you, I mean.' He coughed.

Alexander Pritchard raised his elegant eyebrows. 'How are you taking to Chapel View, John?' he asked.

'Mrs Hughes is quite a character.'

'That's a polite way of describing her,' said Alexander.

'I don't think I'd have chosen Chapel View Guest House if I'd known quite how much of a character she is,' said John. 'Though there wasn't much choice.'

'Neither of our two other guesthouses come with glowing recommendations,' said the know-all. 'Though they'd be less perilous for you than Chapel View.'

'Why's that?' asked John.

'You're a smart young man,' said Doc Jones, with a broad grin, 'and Mrs Hughes is a lonely widow.'

The three older men broke into a chuckle.

'Hey,' interjected Mr William Williams, 'you *are* single, aren't you? You haven't got a little woman tucked away somewhere?'

'Not anymore,' replied John, inadvertently blushing.

'Chucked you, did she?' asked William.

'My marriage broke down,' he said, giving Mr Williams a black look. He raised his beer glass to his face as if wanting to hide behind it.

'Sorry to hear that, my boy,' said the doctor quietly. 'Same thing happened to me many years ago.'

'Was that why you left your job in London and came here?' Alexander asked John.

'Pretty much.'

The three gents nodded in sympathy.

'The house was put up for sale, so I needed a new home. I needed a new life, you could say. I came across an advert for Trecadno High School. It seemed perfect. Far away from Marcia, my ex. Far away from the bustle of the city and all the talk about politics and Iraq. And I knew a bit about the place because my grandmother lived here.'

'Well, well!' exclaimed William Williams, hitting John on the back. 'You're not so bad after all, even if you are a Baptist!'

'Look, Mr Williams—'

'I'm very glad, boy. Who was your grandmother, then?'

'Ada Jenkins. My mother's mother. Her husband, my grandfather, died before I was born. His name was—'

'Bryn,' interjected Mr Williams. 'Carpenter, if I remember correctly.'

'That's right,' said John with surprise.

'Good man, he was. Good singing voice, as I recall.'

'Really?'

'Shame he died so young.'

'That's why my grandmother—'

'Went to live with your mother in England. Yes, very sad.'

John was unsure whether William was sad about the bereavement or the move to England.

'How do you know all this?' he asked.

'This is a small town,' said Doc Jones, 'and some people like to keep tabs on everyone.' He squinted at William Williams.

'I am a deacon, a borough councillor and a magistrate. It is my responsibility to know everyone.'

'And know all their business,' said Alexander.

'Nothing to do with you, Alexander Know-All Pritchard, seeing as you come from Penymynydd.'

'I moved here ten years ago, for goodness' sake!'

Alexander muttered.

'But you got no ancestors here, see, Pritchard,' continued the Deacon, 'no roots in Trecadno. Not like John here.'

'I've never heard anything so petty,' declared Alexander, taking another swig of his liquor.

'Maldwyn!' called the deacon. 'Another round over here. Pritchard's turn.'

'I'm very glad I've met you,' John said to Alexander. 'It'll be good to know someone at the school on my first day.'

'I'll show you the ropes as best I can,' the older man replied, 'though of course we're all busy at the start of term. Unfortunately, your laboratory is at the opposite end of the school from the history room.'

'I went into school this afternoon. I was hoping to prepare a few things before Monday. The place was almost empty. And the biology laboratory was, er…'

'Disappointing?' suggested Alexander.

'Exactly.'

'I don't suppose you met the head of science?'

'No. That would have been helpful.'

Alexander made a face that implied the opposite. 'And what about our esteemed headmaster?' he asked.

'I knocked on his study door but there was no answer. I saw him in the corridor later. He seemed distracted. Actually, he was buttoning up his shirt.'

The other two men pricked up their ears.

'I was on my way out,' continued John. 'We almost collided.'

'You didn't notice any females?' Doc Jones asked.

'Just the secretary.'

'Miss Morse. She doesn't count,' said Alexander. 'Not in the fumbling stakes.'

'Fumbling?' said John, wide-eyed.

39

'Now there's another immigrant for you,' declared Mr Williams. 'Ivor Kane comes from Bridgend. Doesn't go to chapel either. Bloody shocking, it is.'

Alexander chuckled. 'Kane is a shocker, I agree. Actually, a few on the staff are from even further afield than him. Cardiff and Edinburgh, for example. Betty Wontsmey, our cookery teacher, comes all the way from Canada.'

'Curious name,' said John.

'Especially the way she says it,' replied Alexander with a raised eyebrow. 'Probably Old Dutch, I'd say.'

'Double Dutch more like,' retorted the deacon. 'Her husband Andy will be here any minute, poncing about with his bloody martinis, telling everyone where to sit.'

'He's a fan of feng shui,' clarified Mr Alexander Pritchard.

'Feng my arse!' declared Mr Williams. 'He prances in here with his poncey pals, talking posh an' polluting the air with scent. This is a local club for local people.'

'You have to admit that he's an asset in the quiz,' said Doc Jones.

'Only if the bugger turns up. Where was he last week, I'd like to know?'

'Had to go to a lecture. That's what he said.'

'Bloody rubbish. He leaves that lovely woman on her own all the time and goes off with his—'

'Never mind that, William,' cut in Alexander. 'Though now that you mention it, Andy should have arrived by now. The quiz starts soon.'

'If he doesn't turn up maybe John here can help. Educated boy, see, even if he is a Baptist.'

John gritted his teeth. 'Is it worth telling you yet again that I am not a Baptist?'

'Ignore him, John,' said Doc Jones, nose aglow. 'But it wouldn't be a bad idea to have a reserve. What do you think, Alexander?'

'Capital idea. Capital.'

There was time for another round of drinks, and for the assemblage to realise that Mr Wontsmey was going to let them down again. Thus it was that John found himself ascending a flight of steps to the stage located opposite the bar, on the far side of the vast clubroom. His team took their seats on one side of the stage, with the opposing team, the King's Headers, sitting opposite. John was unhappy about the exposure but could hardly refuse to help on his very first day.

By this time, numbers had swelled and there was barely any space between the tables. John looked down at the leery townsfolk with trembling hands and guts. Why had he let himself be dragged into this? This was the second time that day that he'd been press-ganged into doing something he didn't want to do. But one benefit of his elevated location was that he could see exactly who was in the audience, and he paid particular attention to females with red hair. He was unable to discover the perfect form of Elisabeth-Mai, which was disappointing until he realised that she wouldn't see him making a prat of himself.

A small, ageing man who looked as if he might have been a brother to the minister of Moriah Chapel (and was) soon hobbled on to the stage to commence the proceedings. He had a squeaky, nasal voice suggestive of chronic catarrh.

'Good evening, ladies and gentlemen!' he announced. 'Here we are again, for another of our famous quizzes! I, Edgar Evans, have the pleasure of your patronage.' This was received with polite applause. 'Once again, we thank the Wanderers' Club for havin' us, and supplyin' us with good drink at a good price!' The audience emitted cheers and wolf-whistles. 'Now then! Now then!' he exclaimed. 'We have with us tonight our resident Cubs,' more cheers, 'and our visitors, the King's Headers, who have come all the way from the King's Head, North Angle.' Polite applause. 'Now

41

then, we begin with round one. As usual, I'll start with the resident team, and I'll ask each team member a general knowledge question. No conferring.'

As team captain, Alexander had to answer the first question.

'Mr Pritchard, who wrote *The Old Man and the Sea*?'

'Ernest Hemingway,' responded Alexander without hesitation.

'Quite correct,' replied Mr Evans, to cheers. 'Next question to our medical man, Dr Daniel Jones. Dr Jones, what is the name given for the regions of the earth's crust that drift slowly over the planet?'

Doc Jones thought for a moment. A hint of tension entered the large room.

'Tectonic plates,' he replied eventually.

'Just in time,' said Edgar Evans, 'and quite correct!' Delighted clapping.

'Now we come to our newcomer. Standin' in tonight for Mr Andy Wontsmey is the new biology master at the high school. All the way from swingin' London, we welcome Mr John Simmonds!' Polite applause. 'Now then, Mr Simmonds. Can you tell me the capital city of Uzbekistan?'

John cleared his throat. He hadn't even heard of the country, let alone its capital.

'Er, no. Sorry, I don't know.'

The audience grumbled discontentedly.

'Shame,' said Edgar Evans. 'I can pass it over to the King's Headers for a bonus point.'

'Tashkent,' growled a large man with a broken nose who had once been a prop in the Angle Irons rugby team.

'Quite correct!' announced Mr Evans.

The King's Headers answered almost all their questions correctly. Indeed, everyone seemed to be highly knowledgeable. Except for John. Not only was he ignorant of ex-Soviet republics, but he went on to show inadequacies

42

in the fields of astronomy, Scandinavian literature, and the Industrial Revolution. But to his relief he managed to redeem himself on a team round by giving the correct answer to an esoteric question on ferns. This put the Cubs neck and neck with their opponents.

Last of all was a 'fingers on buzzers' round, not that there were any buzzers. Competitors had to put their hands up to signify their readiness to answer. There were nine questions in this round: four were answered correctly by the Headers, and four by the Cubs. Then came the last question.

'Now then,' said Mr Evans grandly, 'the whole game depends on this last question. Whichever team gets this right wins the quiz!' Whoops of expectation filled the room.

'No conferring, mind. Are you ready? Where is the Annual Welsh Bog-Snorkelling Championship held?'

Silence. The Headers' captain glowered, and the man with the broken nose looked down at his knees with shame. Alexander Pritchard sucked on his lower lip in an agony of attempted recollection.

John put up his hand.

'Yes?' asked Mr Evans.

'I can't pronounce it properly, but I think the place is Llanwrtyd Wells.'

'You are right!' cried Mr Evans. 'The Cubs win!'

'Hey!' said Mr William Williams to a jubilant John when they were all back at the bar. 'How come you knew that, then?'

'The bog-snorkelling, you mean? There was an article about it in a newspaper someone left on the bus I came in yesterday.'

'Bloody good job you read that.'

'And a crying shame that we didn't,' said Doc Jones. 'This newcomer knows more about Wales than we do!'

'Embarrassing,' replied Alexander with a hang-dog

43

expression.

'John here saved the day,' said the doctor, 'and that's a damn good reason to have another round.'

'May I join you?' asked a female voice as Maldwyn doled out more liquor.

'Betty!' cried Alexander. 'Good to see you, my dear. Where did that husband of yours get to?'

'I must apologise for him,' intoned the lady with a mild American accent. 'He had to go to London today. His train home was delayed.'

'Is that right?' muttered Mr William Williams, glancing at the lady with a mixture of annoyance and admiration.

'Never mind,' continued Alexander. 'We had a stand in tonight, a good one, too. May I introduce our new colleague, Mr John Simmonds?'

The woman shifted from behind the Know-All, allowing John to see that she was tall with trendily cropped blonde hair and piercingly blue eyes. She was also in possession of an ample bosom and legs that stretched up to her leather miniskirt. He was too stunned to speak.

'Betty Wontsmey,' said the fine woman, sidling up to him. And he certainly did.

Alexander winked at Doc Jones. They were well-used to this reaction. 'Mrs Wontsmey teaches cookery at our school,' he said.

John had assumed that nothing could surpass Elisabeth-Mai, and yet in a crummy clubhouse in a backwater of deepest Wales, was a golden goddess beyond his wildest dreams. His mind was quite taken over by the idea of her legs entwined around him.

'Well, boy?' boomed the deacon. 'Aren't you going to say hello to the lady?'

'Hello,' John squeaked.

'I'm very glad that you'll be joining us on the staff, John,' Betty said.

'Ah. Thanks. Thanks very much.'

'We'll see each other every day.'

'Will we?' John was beginning to feel faint.

'Won't you join us for another drink, Betty?' asked the doctor.

'I don't have time, alas. I just came over to tell you about Andy.' She cast a sizzling smile at John. 'But next Friday, I'll come all night.'

It was late when they left the Wanderers' Club, and there was an autumnal chill in the velvet darkness around them. This was barely noticed by the revellers, distracted as they were by chatter, drink, or visions of glorious women. But they couldn't ignore a sudden, unearthly shriek from somewhere to the right of the road. The men stopped in their tracks and John shone Mrs Hughes' torch around him with dread. Opening scenes of *An American Werewolf in London* came unbidden into his mind.

'What on earth is that?' he whispered, terrified.

Another blood-curdling shriek rang out, though this time it seemed to come from behind them.

'We'd better run,' gasped John, beginning to hyperventilate.

'Haven't you ever heard that sound before?' asked Doc Jones, catching his arm.

'Only in horror movies.'

'But there are thousands of foxes in London, surely?' said Alexander.

'Foxes?' replied John, thoroughly confused. 'But...'

'Surely you've heard them call to each other? It's especially noticeable during the mating season.'

'I've never heard *that* noise,' said John.

'Maybe it's too noisy to notice in London,' suggested the doc.

'I saw a fox this afternoon,' John said. 'Quite close to the school. It was quite a surprise.'

'Surprise?' growled the deacon, '*Surprise*? You do realise where you've come to, don't you?'

'What d'you mean?' asked John nervously.

'But my dear boy!' exclaimed a bleary Alexander. '"Trecadno" means "town of the fox".'

CHAPTER FOUR

Bryncadno

A t twenty-five to nine on Saturday morning John was
bundled out of Chapel View Guest House clutching an
unpromising pack of sandwiches. His landlady came out
after him sporting a tight blue coat, bright pink lipstick,
freshly curled hair, and an ominously large shopping bag.
A posse of women had gathered at the bus stop next to the
chapel where John had alighted two days earlier. They all
looked more or less like Mrs Lavinia Hughes, and all
seemed to be engaged in a form of verbal knitting, with
each woman conversing with several others in an
unintelligible staccato.

'Right,' announced Mrs Hughes, as she locked the front
door. 'You set off on your walk, and I'll see you back here
at about half past six.' She waddled across the road to her
companions. 'Enjoy yourself!' she called back to him. 'We're
going to, and that's a fact!' She laughed and gave a farewell
wave. 'When you come back, you're going to get a real treat
for your tea. Liver and kidney beans washed down with a
nice Tovali!'

The females turned towards him and laughed. With his
eyes set firmly on the pavement, John set off in an easterly
direction. As he reached the far side of the square, beyond
the church, he saw the bus approach, and stopped to watch
the score of rotund females hoisting themselves into the
dusty single-decker. At least he'd be spared the company

47

of Mrs Lavinia Hughes for a few hours.

John decided to purchase a map and a drink before heading for the hills. He also wanted to locate Trecadno's pharmacy. In the midst of the chatter and whiskey at the Wanderers' Club, he'd learned that the lovely Elisabeth-Mai worked there. He imagined her surrounded by rainbow arrays of cosmetics and mists of fine perfume.

He headed to the newsagent's shop, thinking this would be a good bet for a map. He vaguely remembered where it was from his explorations on Thursday evening, and he arrived at Hopkins for News at ten to nine to find a large man with prominent whiskers, presumably Mr Hopkins, manhandling bales of newspapers.

'I'm very glad to see you open,' said John amiably to the man's rear. 'I thought that perhaps none of the shops around here open before nine.'

'That is quite correct,' replied the whiskery man without turning round.

'Your door is open, though.'

'Yes. It is. That is how I get in and out.'

'Yes. Well. Could I possibly come in? I do intend to buy a few things.'

'I'm not open yet.'

'But it's *almost* nine o'clock.'

'The time is six minutes to nine. And in those six minutes I have to lug all these ruddy papers inside. So to you, I am not open.'

John carried on up Lôn y Gwenci in a huff, determined that he would take his custom elsewhere. So irritated was he that he walked straight past a shop window containing a huge old medicine bottle in front of faded red curtains. He plodded on, hoping to see other shops, but all he noticed was a cobbler's squeezed between the huddle of grey residences either side. He went in, just for something to do, and found himself in a tiny space surrounded by shelves of ageing boots that smelt of glue and decomposing feet.

'Aha,' said a deep voice from below the counter. A tall, thin man with protruding grey eyes uncurled himself. 'Worn your shoes out already, have you?'

'Er, no. Though I intend to do a lot of walking, so I expect to bring you quite a lot of custom eventually.'

'What do you want, then?'

'Help, actually. I wondered if you could direct me to a shop that sells maps.'

'Maps? Not in Trecadno, boy.'

'Oh.' John gave him a withering look. 'You wouldn't be related to Mr William Williams, by any chance?'

'William Williams, deacon?'

'That's the one.'

'I am his brother, Emyr Williams.'

'That figures.'

John left the claustrophobic confines of the shop and continued a hundred yards or so to the end of the lane. He found himself facing a junction graced by a large public house, the Brush and Mask. He stood in a state of indecision as the church clock chimed nine, wondering whether to turn left or right. In the end, he did neither, for it was clearly folly to go either way without the aid of a map. With a heavy heart he retraced his steps down Lôn y Gwenci, and within a few minutes was once again at Mr Hopkins' door.

No barrier to entry was in evidence, and so, swallowing his pride, John wandered through the cramped and cluttered aisles, hoping to locate a fizzy drink and a map. He had almost given up on the latter when he caught sight of a cylindrical stand on which were positioned post-cards, paperbacks, and – joy! – a small handful of pink OS maps. Most of them were for parts of Wales outside Trecadno, but the last one he picked up had 'Penymynydd and District' on its cover. John happily advanced to the counter with his find.

'That will be eleven pounds and twenty pence,' said Mr Hopkins.

'That much? Are you sure?'

'Look at the till, then.'

'The Pepsi can't be much more than a pound.'

'No, but the map doesn't come cheap. That's a proper Ordinance Survey map, that is.'

'The last one I bought was four pounds fifty.'

'I don't give a toss about maps you bought in the past. What I care about is rent, rates, heating, lighting, and transportation costs. If I didn't charge ten pounds twenty pence for that map, I'd make no profit on it whatsoever.'

'But that's well over double the normal price.'

'It *is* the normal price in this shop, right? Now, do you want to buy it or don't you?'

With reluctance, John handed over the amount requested and crept out. He chastised himself for giving in, and for forgetting to ask directions to the pharmacy. The day had not started well.

He found a patch of bright sunlight and unfolded the map. Trecadno was depicted as a small, grey blob of conurbation with four roads heading out of it like the legs of a basking amphibian. Around it was endless green and white rurality including a cluster of concentric relief rings that had to be Bryncadno. Furthermore, it looked like the road he was standing in would take him there directly.

He re-folded the map with a newfound confidence but did not start walking, for his attention had been caught by a large window containing a strange bottle. Further inspection showed that there was a peeling wooden sign above the window bearing the word '*FFERYLLFA*' in large capitals, with 'Pharmacy' in much smaller letters beneath. To one side of the door was a brass plaque that read, 'E.M. Glyndwr, B. Pharm.' John's heart leapt, and the vision of his idol changed into a knowledgeable scientist busy with scales and vials.

He tried the door, but it was very firmly locked. A little yellowing, hand-written note taped onto the inside of the window bore the words. '*Ar gau yn ystod y penwythnos*'. Fortunately for John, this mysterious rune was followed by the message, 'Post prescriptions through letterbox for Monday collection'. He concluded that hanging around would be a waste of time and resolved to find an excuse to pass the pharmacy after school on Monday.

With a spring thus put into his step, John set off down Lôn y Gwenci once again, confident that he was en route for Bryncadno. As he passed the cobbler's shop he heard a cry:

'You again? Lost your way, boy?'

'Bog off,' John shouted back, continuing down the road. After all, most of his shoes were new.

Within a couple of hundred yards, houses had been replaced by bramble hedges laced with cobwebs. He paused by a gate to take a swig from the bottle of Pepsi he'd bought from troublesome Hopkins, and to let the sun warm his face. To the south-east, he could see a neat, jelly-mould hill that reminded him of Silbury in Wiltshire. This had to be Bryncadno. He lingered a while, listening to the hum of bees on a nearby clump of ivy and savouring the scent of blackberries and newly mown hay. He congratulated himself once again on choosing to relocate to a place of such tranquillity, a place where grass came in many varieties and lengths and stretched far beyond the limits of a fence. This was a wondrous contrast to the human monoculture that was London.

A nearby blackbird gave a sudden chirrup of reprimand, and someone laughed. Stirred from his reverie, John looked around but could see only grazing cows. Though two fields away, a plump man strode into the distance with surprising swiftness.

51

John walked on, down the hill, and soon found himself in the dappled shade of an oak wood. Sunlight fell in shifting spangles like dancing yellow eyes, and robins and wrens sang sweetly. At the bottom of the hill, the road met the river at a fording point. Six large, flat stones had been placed across the river close enough together to allow a small child or an animal to cross without fear of wetting their feet. Beyond the ford the road climbed a little, then levelled off, but remained surrounded by trees. One section seemed unusually straight, prompting John to consult his map to see if it might be Roman in origin. The map did not provide this information, though it did indicate that a footpath led from the road right up to Bryncadno. As he packed the map away, John glanced backwards and saw a large red fox sitting in the middle of the road, staring straight at him. Given that this was Trecadno, he supposed this was not unexpected. But for some reason it made him feel rather uneasy and distinctly alone.

By late morning he had reached the Bryncadno footpath, which took him from shady woodland to sunny moor. The sun had strengthened, and John was soon sweating. Three large birds of prey circled high overhead and cried to each other with strangled shrieks. He knew they were buzzards, but in the hot air they seemed like vultures surveying an imminent meal.

Bryncadno was larger than he'd expected, and far from being smooth, he could now see that its sides were knobbly, with clumps of bramble, gorse and hawthorn dotted over rough grass. On reaching the hill, the path skirted around it in a corkscrew fashion. From its northern side, John could see a group of wigwams in the field below, wisps of smoke drifting up from their apices. Was it the smoke that gave the air a heady, sweet smell? The encampment was silent, with no one in sight.

Another spiral of the path took John to the summit,

which was roughly circular in shape and about the size of a tennis court. As predicted, the views from this spot were wonderful. John slowly turned through 360°, wishing he had binoculars. To the south-west were low, green, undulating hills; to the north-west, he could just make out a few of Trecadno's rooftops and the church tower. Distant mountains could be seen to the north-east, and due east he could see a large river which the map revealed as the Afanc. This widened down to the sea to the south-east, providing the finest view of all.

He found a sheltered spot next to some gorse bushes and sat down to consume his lunch. Mrs Lavinia Hughes had packed spam sandwiches, an aging apple, and an exceedingly dry scone. By the time he got to the scone, a small group of foxes had gathered beneath a hawthorn tree a little way down the hill to his right. They seemed hot and sleepy, just like him. In fact, he felt very tired indeed. This was a little puzzling since he hadn't been pushing the pace and had covered barely more than three miles. But it was a hot day, and the last stretch of his walk had been completely devoid of shade. He contemplated moving on, but his head felt heavy. So did his eyes. The distant sea had become blurred, and the river was somehow merging into the fields. His eyelids soon drooped closed, and his muscles gave up, making him collapse into a weary mass between two gorse bushes.

He dreamt of a troupe of foxes advancing from the woods up Bryncadno. They followed the circular path up the hill, one behind the other, and formed a ring around him, watching him with bright eyes. And then, suddenly, they disappeared, leaving a single red fox sitting in the very centre of the hilltop. It approached John slowly, coming right up close.

'You shouldn't be here,' it whispered in his ear.

'I'm sorry,' replied John, in his dream.

The fox laughed and leapt high in the air. As it landed, it transformed into Elisabeth-Mai. She was wearing a red dress, and her hair flamed wondrously down her shoulders. She knelt down beside him, and John smelt lily of the valley. She pulled his mouth open and poured into it a milky fluid that tasted of mint. She dabbed his brow with some sheep's wool dipped in cold river water. He tried to smile.

'Don't stay here,' she said. 'Go from here.'

'I can't move,' John murmured.

'You are very sleepy,' she said.

'Very sleepy,' echoed John.

Elisabeth-Mai walked away, but the scent of lilies lingered in the still air.

Two hours later John awoke to find branches of gorse above his face and a dock leaf in his mouth. He was annoyed with himself for such doziness, though glad that he'd managed to avoid sunburn. He sat up blearily, and took a swig of his Pepsi, now warm, and looked down at the hawthorn to his right. The foxes were gone, though the buzzards were still gliding overhead, lower than before.

He stood up to find that his head ached terribly. Haltingly, he made his way straight down the slope of Bryncadno, ignoring the path. At the bottom of the hill, he sat down on a large rock shaded by oak trees to compose himself, knowing that he could go no further that day. Eventually, he gathered his resources and got back to the road to commence the long march home.

He hadn't gone far when he heard a faint roar approaching. A large brown Rover soon came into view, heading towards Trecadno. John decided that a lift into town was a damn good idea and waved at the car. It slowed down, and the driver laboriously wound down his window to reveal that he was Mr William Williams, deacon.

'Hey! What are you doing here, boy?' he said, peering

at John through his thick lenses.

'I've been walking.'

'What, to Bryncadno?'

'That's right.' John tried to look amiable. 'Actually, I'd be grateful for a lift back. I don't feel so well.'

'I suppose you can have a lift,' said the deacon reluctantly. 'Get in.'

A substantial yank was required to open the heavy, rust-edged passenger door.

'Got a headache, have you?' Mr William Williams gave him a sly, sideways glance.

'My head is really fuzzy.'

'Hey, you're not sickening for something, are you? I'll drop you off at Doc Jones' place if you like.'

'No need for that,' replied John, though he did wonder if he ought to get himself checked over.

'I'll take you straight to Chapel View, then.'

The car ascended out of the trees and into harsh sunlight.

'Oh, I've just remembered, Mr Williams,' exclaimed John as they reached the edge of town. 'Chapel View is all locked up. You see, Mrs Lavinia Hughes—'

'She's on a shopping trip. Of course she is. They all are, including Mrs Williams. Bloody nuisance. She won't be back to do my tea.'

John looked at his watch. It was just past three o'clock. About three hours to kill before Mrs Lavinia Hughes' return, and no obvious place where they might be killed.

'Mr Williams,' he said as they approached the square, 'would any pubs be open now by any chance?'

'You're not after a drink at this time of the afternoon, are you? You're turning into an alcoholic, boy. You want to watch your step. No wonder you're getting headaches.'

'I'm not an alcoholic, Mr Williams. I just need somewhere to spend the next three hours.'

'Well, no problem there. You can come and have a cup of tea with me.'

John's spirits sank further, but he had nowhere else to go. Besides, the thought of an armchair plus a mug of tea was quite appealing.

The grey folds of Mr William Williams' face almost glowed with pride as he steered the car around Moriah Chapel.

'Fine building,' he muttered to himself. 'Solid.'

Passing Chapel View Guest House on their left, they turned into Lôn y Llyg, where the Williams residence was to be found. Like most of the other streets in Trecadno, this was a terrace of little grey houses with no front gardens or driveways for cars, and no space for on-street parking. Mr Williams had to manoeuvre his tired old vehicle down a back lane and then into his dilapidated garage. The deacon made sure that he had enough space to lever himself onto *terra firma*, but was not so accommodating of his passenger.

'How does Mrs Williams manage?' asked John, through the driver's-side window, of an oblivious Mr Williams.

'Eh?'

'How does she manage to get out?'

'Mrs Williams doesn't come in this car. Only at Christmas, if we go visiting.'

'Don't you ever go shopping with her on weekends?' asked John, attempting to wriggle across the driver's seat.

'Do you really think a deacon has the time or inclination for *shopping*?' He spat the word out as if it were contaminated. 'Shopping is for women.'

After much contortion, John eventually escaped from both car and garage, and followed William Williams along a brick path running up the centre of his little garden.

'Not such a good time of year for vegetables,' remarked the deacon. 'Mind, the cabbages are still going strong, and there are still tomatoes in the greenhouse.'

'Excellent.'

'Are you a gardening man at all?'

'Well, to be honest—'

'Ah. People from the city don't understand about growing things.'

'As a matter of fact—'

'But here we are at my back door,' said the deacon before John had a chance to continue. 'Now wipe your feet carefully, or Mrs Williams will have something to say about it.'

John was led into a dim middle room that seemed an exact replica of the one at Chapel View. The same two armchairs, old television, and sixties tiled fireplace plus electric fire.

'Shall I put the fire on for you?' asked Mr William Williams to John's utter disbelief.

'It's a really hot day, Mr Williams.'

The deacon squatted down to switch on a bar. 'Hey, don't mention it. You don't want to catch a chill on top of everything.'

'I'm very hot already. Honestly.'

'But you'll cool down, see. Nothing worse than going from very hot to very cold. That's how old people get hypo... hypo-something.'

'Thermia.'

'No, no. It definitely starts with "hypo".'

The deacon switched on the lamp above the TV. Its shade displayed the message 'I am the Light of the World'. John stared at it until his eyelids closed again.

'Hey, have you nodded off?' inquired his host as he lurched into the room some minutes later with a trayful of tea-things. 'It must be the drink, boy. You'll have to be careful.'

'I'm sorry,' mumbled John, shaking his head. 'I'm just incredibly tired.'

'Well, here is just the thing for you. A nice strong cup of tea.'

Mr William Williams poured out a cup of tea for John and, without inquiring whether he might like sugar, stirred in two spoonfuls. As it turned out, the intense sweetness seemed to be helpful.

'Did you see any of those damned crusties up at Bryncadno?'

'Just their tents.'

'Ah.'

'It was all very quiet. No sign of life. Though there was some smoke, so someone must have been there.'

'Well, see, you don't make much sound when you're stoned out of your brain.'

'I don't suppose they're stoned all the time.'

Mr Williams smirked cannily but said nothing as John tucked into his slice of cherry genoa.

'You got an appetite, boy. They say drinking a lot gives you a good appetite.'

You should know, John thought.

'You were doing all right last night, I can tell you,' continued the deacon.

'I don't normally drink that much. But last night was my first time in the Wanderers' Club, and we won the quiz.'

'Aye, fair play. We all drank to that.'

'So,' said John after more tea and cake, 'was Bryn Cadno some chap who worked with foxes, then?'

'Eh?'

'The chap the hill was named after.'

'What are you talking about, boy?'

'Isn't "Bryn" a man's name?'

'It can be. It means "hill". Bryncadno means "hill of the fox".'

'Ah. Thank you. It's difficult working out the meanings of local places when you know so little Welsh.'

'Aye, it must be.'

'And there are so many of them. Take your road, for example.'

'Lôn y Llyg?'

'Yes. That's a bit of a mouthful. What on earth does that mean?'

'Lane of the shrew.'

'Really? And what about the road down to the school?'

'Heol y Dyfrgi?'

'That's right.'

'Road of the otter. Named after the river.'

'The river of the otter?'

'Aye. Otters live in rivers. I thought you'd know that, boy, you bein' a biology teacher, an' all.'

John tried not to look annoyed. 'Yes, I did know that. So, what about the one that sounds like "belly"?'

'Lôn y Bele. Pine-marten Lane.'

'Good grief.' He paused to think of other bothersome street names. 'And the road with the newsagent's shop in it?'

'Lôn y Gwenci? Weasel Lane.'

'Weasel?'

'Small thing. Nasty bite with it.'

'This whole town seems to be named after predatory mammals.'

'I don't know about that, but they're all fine Welsh animals, and that's for sure.'

'It's quite unusual, don't you think?'

'Seems perfectly normal to me.'

'I've never heard of a place where *all* the streets are named after mammals. Usually you find names like "High Street" and "Station Road". Animals hardly ever get a mention.'

'They do here.' The deacon started to put all the tea-things back on the tray. 'Oh bugger,' he declared as he replaced the tea-cosy, 'I'm supposed to be peeling spuds.'

'Oh?'

'I've got to peel 'em and put 'em on to boil at half-past five. We'll be having them with a bit of ham when Mrs Williams comes in.'

'It's probably best if I leave now, then.'

'Don't be daft. The ladies won't be back for at least three-quarters of an hour. Later, if they've got that daft bugger from Swansea driving the bus.'

'Ah.'

'Come with me into the kitchen.'

Resistance was pointless. John followed his host like a dejected dog, and sat as directed on a small wooden stool. He watched Mr William Williams wrap a frilly pink pinny around his waist and set to some dirty potatoes with a peeler.

'Things we do for the women, eh?'

'Oh, er, yes.'

'Bloomin' liabilities, they are.'

'Mmm.'

'You'd know all about that, of course.'

John sighed, and William Williams surveyed his guest with pity.

'Ran off, did she?'

'Pardon?'

'Your wife. Ran off?'

'In a manner of speaking,' John said with a scowl.

'Another man?'

'Since you raise the subject, there was another man.'

'Ha! I thought as much. Frailty, thy name is woman!'

'Pardon?'

'Famous quote. From, er, *"Saint Paul's Letter to the Corinthians"*. Very apt.'

John shifted uncomfortably on his stool like a little boy in school.

'Look, er, Mr Williams, you've been very kind, but I

really must go now.'

The deacon peered up at a plastic plate-shaped clock with the words "The End is Nigh" arched over the top.

'It's still too early, boy.'

'Well, the thing is, I need to get some, er, mints.'

'Mints?'

'Yes. Good for the digestion.'

'Looking ahead to Mrs Lavinia Hughes' evening offering, are you? Well, well! But you'll be out of luck for mints. The only place you'd get mints on a Saturday afternoon would be Hopkins', and he'll be closed now.'

'But surely there must be a supermarket here somewhere. I mean, after all, Trecadno is not a tiny place. I've seen smaller that at least have a *Spar.*'

'A *Spar*? Not here, boy. Mrs Probert keeps the Post Office Stores just up Terras y Ffwlbart, but she's closed on a Saturday afternoon. You'd have to go to Penymynydd to find a shop open now.'

'Oh.' John gently rubbed his temples with his fingertips. 'Well, I really think I ought to get a bit of fresh air anyway.'

'It's turning cold, mind. You've got to watch out this time of year.'

'Right. I'll watch out.' John foisted his bag onto his left shoulder. 'Thank you for the tea, Mr Williams. I'll see you soon.'

'All right, boy. Hey, I won't see you out, all right?'

John turned tired eyes away from the deacon and his feminine attire.

'Don't worry. I'll see myself out.'

As John stepped out of Mr William Williams' front door, the church bells solemnly informed the populace that six o'clock had arrived. The sun had started to sink, and the heat of the day was fast departing. He decided to stroll down to Lôn y Gwenci in a leisurely manner, hence providing another chance to inspect the pharmacy. Perhaps, just perhaps, Elisabeth-Mai might appear. He imagined her face pressed up against a windowpane waiting for Mr Right to turn up.

As he turned out of the square, enticing wafts of hot vinegar hit his nostrils, but he resolved that he would not be tempted. He had just had two large pieces of cherry genoa, and then there was Mrs Lavinia Hughes' liver dinner to come. Alas.

But the chip shop's lights were on, and the teenagers spilling out of the open door looked deliriously happy as they cradled their greasy bundles… John walked over. He went in.

It had not been part of his plan to walk past the pharmacy brandishing chip-filled newspaper, but that is what he ended up doing. And despite having some misgivings about his over-consumption of stodge, he was not overly sorry. The chips were delicious and reviving. He was trying to survey the pharmacy windows without appearing to stare, and the chips were key to this. His strategy was to glance nonchalantly, take a chip, then to sneak another quick look at the window.

Lôn y Gwenci's aged female population were not so easily duped. There was much twitching of curtains. But no such activity was evident at the pharmacy, and John soon gave up on his vigil.

Turning into the square, he heard the rumble of a diesel engine. It had to be the bus from Carmarthen. He dumped the remains of his chips in a litter bin and headed for a shady spot near the front of the chapel, which he hoped would conceal him from the alighting ladies. But shade was no challenge to Mrs Lavinia Hughes' laser-like eyes, and she waved at him and called him over. Peals of boisterous laughter came forth from the other ladies as John obediently plodded towards her.

'Here he is, girls! Here's my handsome Mr Simmonds!'

The ladies shrieked.

'He's been out walking. I'm sure he could do with a nice lie down!'

A chorus of 'OOO's came forth, as if from a flock of lewd pigeons. After all the banter had come to end, Mrs Lavinia Hughes headed over to her blue front door followed by a sheepish John. She gazed up at him fondly from her cluster of carrier bags.

'Would you go in first?' she asked, coyly.

'Why?' replied John, puzzled. She'd already put the key in the door.

'Just go ahead of me through the porch, will you? I don't feel safe till I get the lights on.'

The sun was in the west and streaming straight into Mrs Hughes' hallway. John sighed and edged into the porch.

'Go up the stairs for me,' she urged. 'It's always dark up there.'

'All right, Mrs Hughes. If you insist.'

'I do.'

'I think I'll have a lie down, Mrs Hughes,' he called down when he reached the landing, immediately regretting his choice of words.

'Good idea. I'm coming up now.'

A lump formed in John's throat.

'I've got to put all my things away,' she added.

John gave a great sigh of relief. Of course. She had shopping to sort out. That was surely far more interesting than any man. He lay down on his bed and fell sound asleep for the third time that day.

Mrs Lavinia Hughes spent an hour sorting through her carrier bags, just enough time for John to reach a phase of sleep a few steps away from death. Indeed, by the time Mrs Hughes was ready to serve her liver dinner, he had advanced too far into the Land of Nod to turn back. In vain did his landlady shout up the stairs about gravy and onions.

In vain did she bellow outside his door about the sins of turpitude and food-wasting.

'Bloody men,' she muttered as she hobbled back down the stairs. 'Never mind. The dinner will keep until tomorrow. Gravy might be a bit lumpy though.'

CHAPTER FIVE

Trecadno High School

For a teacher, there is no time quite as bad as 7am on a Monday morning on the first day of term. Though for worrying types, the previous Sunday night might be even worse. John was exceedingly anxious, so absorbed in planning the week ahead that he quite forgot about attending the evening service at Moriah Chapel. Not that he really wanted to go, though he would have appreciated another glimpse of Elisabeth-Mai to take his mind off things.

Panic gripped him early the following morning, specifically his abdomen, and he was up and occupying the bathroom well before seven. Unhelpful frying smells were wafting up the stairs when he emerged. Once dressed, he opened the rose-covered curtains and blinked. He pulled the net curtain to one side to confirm his initial observations. He was not mistaken: despite the dustbowl conditions of the weekend, rainwater was now streaming down the windowpane.

Mrs Lavinia Hughes tut-tutted in a knowledgeable way when he expressed surprise in the change in the weather.

'You can borrow an umbrella from me,' she said. 'I'll give you Mr Hughes' nice big black one.'

'Thank you.'

'No trouble. Mind, you'll have to take care of it in *that* school.'

'Of course I will.'

'And you'll be wanting your wellies.'

'I haven't got any. And it's not so far to the school.'

'Have you seen what it's like out there? And it's set now, see.'

'Set?' John forced himself to ingest some rigid bacon.

'Set to stay.'

'What, for the week?'

'Oh no, it'll be set wet until April. We might get the odd dry day, I suppose.'

John spluttered out some of his over-hot, over-weak coffee. 'You make it sound as if Trecadno has a monsoon season.'

Mrs Lavinia Hughes' porcine visage took on a huffy expression. 'I can only tell you what I know about this town, which I think you will agree is more than *you* know.'

'Oh, er, of course…'

'And I know that the rain comes in at the beginning of September and goes at the beginning of April.'

'I see.'

'Mind, there are some summers when it never quite leaves.'

'Ah.'

'Which is why you need to visit Mr Emyr Williams. Soon.'

John tried to wipe coffee off his tie.

'Emyr Williams?'

'The cobbler. He's the only one round here that sells wellies. And repairs them. You can't get by without 'em, so everyone keeps on the right side of Emyr.'

Breakfast over, John opened the front door to be greeted by vertical sheets of water. They hit the ground like a multitude of fountains and formed rivulets flowing westwards towards Stryd y Dyfrgi. Which just happened to be the road to the school. It was clear that Mrs Hughes' advice about wellies had been sound. The late Mr Hughes' unwieldy black umbrella protected John's upper body from the worst of the drenching, but from the knees down he had no chance. He squelched into the main school entrance, taking some comfort from the sight of several pupils suffering the same problem.

The dripping throng had an adverse effect on the school floor, and Dai the caretaker scurried around anxiously with a large mop.

'Good morning!' said John in the general direction of the little man. 'Which way should I go for the staffroom?'

The caretaker, who was known by all as Dai Pinter, stopped mopping and stared at John's legs. He seemed to be on the verge of tears.

'Down there,' he said with a strangulated squeak, pointing towards the corridor that contained the headmaster's office.

John shuffled, wetly, along the corridor and found a door marked 'staffroom'. The sight that met his eyes when he pushed the door open was shocking indeed. The room contained several sofas, across which were draped female bodies in various states of alertness. There were no men at all.

'Hello, love,' said an aged specimen near the door. 'You're a bit wet, aren't you?'

'Yes. Er, I'm really sorry, but—'

'Don't be sorry,' said a younger woman. 'It's not your fault that the heavens opened.'

'No. Um, I was looking for a staffroom. One *I* can use.'

'You've come to the wrong place, then, haven't you?' said the aged lady. Giggles rippled through the room.

'Put him out of his misery, for God's sake,' said a hoarse voice from the back.

'The men's staffroom is just past the headmaster's office,' said the aged lady with a touch of disappointment. John backed away nervously. He soon found the room he needed, which turned out to be a smoke-filled den full of dark shapes reading newspapers.

'New boy!' someone called as John squelched in.

'Poor sod,' muttered someone else.

'Hey, stop dripping all over our floor,' intoned a genteel and learned voice.

John was much relieved to see that Mr Alexander Pritchard, Know-all, was approaching him.

'How on earth did you all manage to stay completely dry?' John asked.

'Combination of car and wellie-boots, my boy. And a waterproof coat that goes down to the ankles.'

'Ah. I made the stupid assumption that the weather here would not be so very different to London.'

'Never make assumptions about Trecadno, John.'

'Look, er, is there any chance of borrowing some trousers while these dry out?' He looked down at his legs with remorse.

'I'm sure we can find something. But you might not manage to get yours dry by the end of the day. I'm afraid the heating doesn't get put on until the beginning of October. You'll have to ask Dai Pinter if you can put them in the boiler room. Or you could ask Mrs Wontsmey if you could put them in her drying cabinet. She uses it for tea-towels and suchlike.'

'Is that the lady who was at the Wanderers' Club last Friday night?' John asked with a gleam in his eye.

Several eavesdropping gentlemen chuckled.

'I see she made her usual impression. Anyway, I'll see what I do can about trousers.'

Twenty minutes later, John followed Mr Alexander Pritchard into the assembly hall and seated himself in an ancient metal-framed canvas-backed chair that seemed designed to accelerate vertebral degeneration. He was now wearing a jogging outfit supplied by the rugby coach, probably not the best attire to make a good impression on one's first day unless you happen to be a rugby coach. A mass of disgruntled pupils sat cross-legged on the hall floor nattering to each other. And staring at him. This was to be expected, though it was still disconcerting. The uniform of the little watchers didn't help, for their black trousers and skirts and deep scarlet shirts made the assemblage look like a gathering of the Junior Vampire Society. John scanned a sample of faces and noticed that many were pale with dark rings beneath their eyes. Perhaps they *were* members of the Junior Vampire Society. Nothing about Trecadno would surprise him.

The headmaster eventually advanced into the hall and staggered up the little wooden stairs to the stage. His face was very pink and his eyes watery. He looked down at a prompt sheet on the lectern and surveyed his audience with the air of someone who very much wanted to be elsewhere.

'Hymn number forty-six,' he grunted.

A sudden piano chord made John jump. He had seen no one sitting behind the upright piano (Mr Fuster, music, was a very small man). The little vampires all got to their feet clutching their hymn books, the teachers followed, and all began to sing 'Bread of Heaven'. It was all a little too much like Moriah Chapel for John's liking, but at least he understood the words this time, and vaguely knew the tune. When the last verse came to an end, all re-seated themselves, and the headmaster studied his notes.

'We start a new school year,' he intoned. 'Another year when you have the opportunity to learn and to do your best. Another year when I'll expect good behaviour and excellent performances on the rugby pitch.' Murmurs of approval.

'You may have noticed that we have lost the services of Mr Pugh, biology. In his place we have Mr John Simmonds, from London.' A faint murmur of 'oooo-s' came from the sixth-formers at the back of the hall. 'We welcome you, Mr Simmonds!' This prompted a round of muted clapping. 'The first day of term is a bit strange for all of us, so listen carefully to what I have to say about the day's arrangements. Presently, Miss Ewer will announce the form rooms. Last of all, she will tell the first formers – Year Sevens, I mean – which classes they are in. Then we will have a ten-minute break while all boys – I mean pupils – go to their form classrooms for an extended tutorial session. Lunch will be early today.' A cheer broke out at that. 'And you will start lessons this afternoon. Now remember: I insist on best behaviour this term. I do not expect to have to mete out discipline to boys, or others, in the way I was compelled to last term…'

'What was all that about "boys or others"?' John asked Alexander as they trooped out.

'It's one of Mr Kane's many quirks. He can't quite reconcile himself to little girls. He was only ever in charge of boys in the past.'

They arrived back at the staffroom, and John gratefully sat down on a pleasantly compliant sofa.

'Sorry, chum,' came a voice. 'My seat, I'm afraid.' John got up with apologies and found another patch, only to encounter the same problem two minutes later. He meekly trooped over to Alexander.

'Where can I sit without causing some sort of offence?'

'The chair over there is free, I think,' he said, pointing at one of the metal-framed, canvas-backed chairs that had caused John such discomfort in the hall. 'Mind you, there's no point in getting settled.'

'Oh? I thought the head said that lessons weren't starting until this afternoon.'

'Indeed he did, my boy. But he also mentioned that forms were assembling with tutors.'

'Yes. But I still don't see—'

'Didn't anyone tell you?'

'What?'

'That you'll be a form tutor. You'd better go and see Miss Ewer, the deputy headmistress.'

Mindful of the difficulties associated with re-visiting the ladies' staffroom, John decided to head back to the hall, aiming to intercept Miss Ewer as she made her way out. The disadvantage of this plan was having to run a gauntlet of pupils giggling at his over-large replacement trousers.

Miss Ewer brought up the rear at a fair lick and would have marched straight past him. She was a tall woman with a grey basin-cut and pronounced calf muscles.

'Miss Ewer!' shouted John. She looked around, eyeing various pupils suspiciously.

'Miss Ewer!' repeated John, rushing up from behind. He was compelled to tap her on the shoulder, and she turned sharply.

'What on earth?' she began.

'I am so sorry to bother you, Miss Ewer. I am John Simmonds, the new biology teacher.'

'What is that to me?'

'Ah. Well, I was told that I might have to take on tutorial duties, and that you would be able to tell me all the details.'

'Mr Simmonds, it would appear that you are male. I take charge of the ladies. I advise you to speak to Mr Burrows-Morgan.'

'Mr Burrows-Morgan?'

'Indeed. He is the deputy head responsible for male staff.' She started to walk off.

'But, er, where will I find him?'

'In the men's staffroom, of course.'

John dragged himself back to his starting point and located Alexander. By that time, the learned gent was on his second coffee and well on the way to completing *The*

Times crossword.

'Alexander!' cried John in plaintive tones. 'I found Miss Ewer. She wouldn't speak to me. I am the wrong gender.'

'Ah.'

'She said I must consult Mr Burrows-Morgan.'

'Oh.'

'So, where is he?'

Mr Pritchard put down his cup and looked up from his newspaper.

'You have a problem there, my boy.'

'That comes as no surprise. This place is just one big problem.'

'Now, now, John. You really shouldn't be so negative on your first day.'

'I don't see how to be positive. Anyway, where is this Morgan-Burrows fellow?'

'Burrows-Morgan. See the armchair in the corner by the window?'

'Next to the shelves with all the empty bottles?'

'Indeed. Its occupant is the man you want.'

'He appears to be asleep.'

'Yes.'

'Is that the problem?'

'Yes. And he's unlikely to wake up before lunchtime.'

John flopped down on the sofa next to Alexander.

'Not there, my boy! Old Mr George sits there.'

'How many years of service are required before one is entitled to a decent chair?'

'Oh, at least five.' He wasn't joking.

'So, what shall I do about being a form tutor?'

Alexander looked at him with the first signs of annoyance. 'I was hoping to finish this by the end of break,' he said, indicating the crossword.

'Sorry,' replied John. He looked around at the recumbent bodies in the gloom. 'But the thing is, Alexander, thirty children will soon be in pursuit of me. I don't know which room to go to, or which form I'm taking, or anything about their timetables.'

'You're a worrier, aren't you?'

'I don't think I am. I'm just trying to justify my salary.'

'Salary, eh? You're an optimist as well as a worrier.'

John closed his eyes in despair.

'The answer to your problem is clear as day.'

'Is it?'

'Certainly. And I'm surprised you didn't think of that yourself. Just visit the school secretary, Miss Morse. She has all the registers and timetables.'

On reflection, it was obvious that John's tutor group would meet in his laboratory, and that all the information he required would be on two sides of A4 in a drawer in the school office. It also made sense that he would be assigned a selection of the new intake.

The tutorial session passed without any major mishaps. John started by asking his twenty-five wards to write out all their details on a sheet of paper, and he wrote out their timetable on the blackboard for them to copy. Being new, they were still enthusiastic and so had brought paper. Administrative tasks soon completed, John let them play hangman and battleships for most of the session, so long as they were quiet. Being new, they obeyed. Older pupils would have rapidly progressed to throwing paper aeroplanes and soggy boiled sweets.

At lunchtime John locked the lab door with relief and headed in the general direction of the men's staffroom. He hadn't gone very far when a female voice called to him. It was slightly husky and distinctly American. John turned to see Betty Wontsmey standing in the doorway of the cookery room, legs up to her neck.

'Hi, John. Remember me?'

'How could I possibly forget you?'

He approached closer. The visage before him was rather different to the one he remembered. It was handsome for sure, but with the benefit of good light and vision unimpeded by alcohol he was able to see the wrinkles around her eyes and the sagginess about her neck. In the smoke-filled dimness of the Wanderers' Club, Mrs Wontsmey could pass for thirty, but now John could see that she was at least ten years older.

'Come in, John. Come and see my little domestic science empire.'

'Oh. Well, the thing is—'

'I have your trousers,' she purred.

'You do?'

'The caretaker brought them. He thought I'd be able to dry them quicker than he could. They're in here,' she pointed at a large, cupboard-like structure that John supposed was the drying cabinet.

'Ah, thank you. Are they dry now, do you know?'

She opened the cabinet door and slowly ran a hand down a trouser leg. 'They're just fine.'

John coughed. 'Well, thank you. Er, I don't suppose you know anything about my shoes?'

'Oh yes.' She went over to the other side of the room and removed the shoes from an oven. 'There, now. All cosy for your toesies.'

'Great. Thanks. Well, I suppose I'd better get these on. Then it will be time for lunch.'

'Perhaps you'd like to accompany me down to the refectory?' asked Betty.

'Ah. OK.'

'You can change in here if you want,' she said with a smirk.

'In here? Oh, no. I mean…'

'There's a screen next door in the needlework room.'

'A screen?'

'The pupils have to try on the things that they sew.'

'I see. Well. All right then.'

'I'll show you, shall I?'

Betty indicated a wicker-work screen and retreated a short, though not quite respectable, distance. As John grappled with zips and buckles, he could just about see through little gaps in the wicker-work that Betty had seated herself on a table. She was swinging her golden legs.

'You know, John,' she said, 'I often make myself lunch in here.'

'Really?'

'I have all the facilities, you see.'

'Of course.'

'My meals are simple and pleasant.'

'I'm sure they are.'

'Especially compared to what the refectory serves up.'

'Ah.'

'Perhaps you'd like to join me some lunchtimes?'

'Oh, well…'

'It's good to have lunch away from the pupils. Away from everyone, in fact.'

'That sounds, er, reasonable.'

They were soon walking down the long corridor that led to the refectory. After they'd obtained their food from the self-service counter, Mrs Wontsmey directed John to a corner table. It had one other occupant, a large man with hollow eyes and a bald head.

'Hi!' said Betty as she put down her tray.

The gentleman grunted.

'Frank, this is John Simmonds, another member of your science team. He teaches biology.'

The large, dark head looked up briefly. 'Biology isn't a science.'

'What is it, then?' asked John as he moved his plate from

his tray to the table.

'Bloody good question,' came the reply.

'You're in a bad mood today!' said Betty good-humouredly. 'We'll just ignore you, shall we?'

'I bloody well hope so,' muttered Frank Erskine, physics teacher, as he removed a small bottle of whiskey from his jacket pocket. He poured some of it into his orange squash, causing the drink to take on an excretory hue, and promptly got up to leave.

'Perhaps the macaroni cheese depressed him,' said John, looking down at his own plate. 'It looks rather solid.'

It was indeed, and not very warm. By contrast, the blancmange that John had chosen for dessert was formless and strangely hot. John soon gave up on his repast.

'I think I'd better get myself sorted for the afternoon,' he said to Betty, pushing his chair back. 'A class will arrive at one thirty; I can't remember which one. Thank you for your company over lunch.'

'What about tomorrow?'

'Tomorrow?'

'Would you like to join me in the cookery room at lunchtime?'

'I'm not sure,' he replied distractedly, as he tidied his tray.

'I see…' she said, with an unmistakable note of displeasure. Without another word, she rose and walked away.

Why was it that his every move in Trecadno seemed to go wrong?

A short, burly woman in a once-white overall advanced towards him at a rate of knots.

''Ave you finished with that, or what?'

At one thirty a class did indeed turn up, announcing themselves as 9F. No one explained the significance of the

'F' and John thought it unwise to ask. The boys were child-like and grubby, but the heavy hand of adolescence had touched most of the girls. Several were tall and slim, with immature curves beneath their black skirts and jumpers. Some of the eyebrows were plucked, and several eyelids decorated. John dreaded what the year eleven girls would be like, let alone the sixth-form girls. He pictured a troupe of pouting vamps.

Once they had finished thwacking each other, fiddling with bags and muttering expletives, 9F arranged themselves untidily along the dark laboratory benches, and stared at him.

'Right then,' announced John with as much confidence as he could muster, 'what did you do in biology at the end of last term?'

'We didn't do biology last term,' responded one of the front row boys.

'No? You did general science, then?'

'It was *integrated science* that we did, sir,' said a girl from a middle bench.

'Ah. Right,' said John, gratified by the 'sir'. He contemplated the options. They would probably have studied cells, and the heart, and maybe enough physiology to understand the basics of puberty. Food might be a suitable topic for them, especially as it provided scope for some simple practical work, which would hopefully keep the little buggers occupied.

'Have you studied food substances?' he asked.

A faint twitter passed around the class.

'We 'aven't *studied* nothing, sir,' announced one of the boys proudly.

'Really? Well, have you covered the topic?'

A girl with curly fair hair put her hand up. 'Sir, have you got a *particular* interest in food?'

John frowned. What on earth did the silly girl mean?

'A particular interest?' he inquired.

The boys on the front bench laughed.

'What she means is,' a brave one piped up, 'are you having an affair with the cookery teacher?' A peal of raucous laughter circled the room.

John could feel prickly heat ascending his neck. 'What a stupid thing to say! I suppose you saw us sitting together at lunch, did you?' More twitters. 'Well, I think you need to know, form 9F, that people often have lunch together without having affairs.'

'Yeah, but you *are* interested in food, sir,' called out someone from the back of the class.

'An' Mrs Wontsmey is *very* interested in you,' said another voice from an indistinguishable corner of the room. The class erupted into a cacophony of laughter.

'Right! That's enough!' John shouted. 'Take your science exercise books out.'

The laughter diminished but didn't stop, and no exercise books were forthcoming because the class didn't have any. John scrabbled about in a cupboard, looking for bits of paper to hand out as a temporary measure. Many disrupted minutes elapsed as he went from cupboard to cupboard, and eventually from child to child, handing out supplies.

At long last, when he was sure that they all had something other than the benches or each other to write on, he began to write on the blackboard.

FOOD SUBSTANCES

The main types of food are:

'Now then, class,' he said, 'what *are* the main types of food? Can you write down three important categories of food for me? Write them down in pencil first so that you can rub your answers out if they're wrong.'

'Please, sir, I haven't got a rubber,' came a plaintive cry from a middle bench.

'Use the girl's behind!' came the quickfire response from the whole of the back bench. The class erupted again.

'Very funny,' responded John, 'though hardly original. You, what's your name?' He pointed at a small, dark-haired boy with glasses on the front bench.

'Royston, sir.'

'Right, Royston. Tell me one of the food substances you have written down.'

Royston fumbled with his bit of paper, which was already torn and covered in thumbprints.

'Jelly, sir'.

The class exploded again.

John took a deep breath. 'Well now, Royston. Jelly is, of course, a type of food, so you're not wrong. But it's not one of the *main* types of food, is it?' He looked forlornly into the body of the class. 'Who can give me a good example of a food *type?*'

'Dinner!' came a cry.

'Breakfast!' came another.

'No!' shouted one of the bossier girls in exasperation. 'Types of *food*, you idiots, not types of meals.' She looked up at John. 'Chinese, sir!' she declared with much assurance.

John sighed.

'OK, 9F, just copy down the list I'm going to put on the board.'

He was halfway through writing the word 'carbohydrates' when the laboratory door suddenly opened and a whirlwind came in. It came to a stop next to the teacher's bench, revealing a short, fat woman with tight grey curls at its epicentre. The whole class got to their feet in an instant and stood in deathly silence.

'You, I take it, are Mr Simmonds?' inquired the epicentre, peering through horn-rimmed glasses.

'Yes,' replied John uncertainly.

'Why aren't you at my meeting?'

'Your meeting?'

'Yes. My meeting. I think it a bit rich that on your first day you can't manage to attend an important meeting.'

'But I didn't know—'

'We always have a meeting at the beginning of term.'

'I'm sorry, but who are you exactly?'

Faint sniggering came from the pupils.

'Who am I? Good gracious, Mr Simmonds, you *have* got a lot to learn, haven't you? I am Mrs Perrig. *I* am the *head* of science.' She held her head as high as it would go, and surveyed John disdainfully from the end of her squashed nose.

'Oh. Right. Sorry. But, er… what about these?' He pointed at his pupils.

'You mustn't worry about them. They can have a break.'

A quiet, courteous 'hurray!' rippled through the room as the whirlwind gathered itself up and surged out of the laboratory door. Within seconds, the class had done likewise. John was left staring at wooden benches occupied only by a forlorn collection of tattered sheets of paper, all bearing the same, sad, solitary heading.

John locked the laboratory and hastened to the secretary's office, where he hoped he would learn the location of the meeting. Miss Morse eyed him with suspicion.

'You again?' she asked.

'Yes. Sorry. Apparently, there is a meeting of all the science staff. Would you happen to know where it is taking place?'

'I have not been informed of the meeting, but I would imagine that it is taking place in Mrs Perrig's laboratory.'

'I see. And where exactly is that?'

'It's the chemistry laboratory. At the far end of B Corridor.'

'Thank you.' He backed out of the room. 'Thank you very much.'

Five minutes later he had located B Corridor and knew he was approaching the chem lab by the threatening odour of sulphur and miscellaneous crystals. John opened the door nervously to find five pairs of eyes directed at him. The most piercing of the gazes was indisputably that of Mrs Perrig. She greatly resembled Mrs Lavinia Hughes, John thought. But then, if the bus queue for the shopping trip was anything to go by, all adult females in Trecadno resembled Mrs Hughes. Except for Betty and Elisabeth-Mai. A little beam of brightness momentarily lifted his heart, and he smiled.

'Do you think it's amusing to be so late to my meetings?' inquired the hobgoblin.

'No. I'm very sorry.' He edged towards the stony row of colleagues. 'As I mentioned earlier, I wasn't told about the meeting.'

'Mr Simmonds, I seem to recall telling you myself.'

'Yes, just now, but otherwise—'

'And that has never been necessary during the whole time I have been at this school.'

John sat down next to Frank, who kept his jowly head well down like a chastised bulldog.

'We were talking about problem pupils,' announced Mrs Perrig. She commenced a diatribe on children John had never met, allowing him the opportunity to scan the assembled scientists. In addition to Mrs Perrig and Mr Erskine, there was a short man of middle years with little hair and a colourless face. The scorch marks on his off-white shirt indicated that he taught chemistry and lacked female companionship. John smiled at him pityingly. The other two teachers were females, both youngish but careworn. One of them would surely teach biology, John decided, and he hoped she'd be an ally. Neither showed the slightest sign

81

of friendliness.

The rant about inadequate students continued for ten minutes, after which the head of science paused to shuffle her papers. John decided this would be a good time to ask a pressing question.

'Mrs Perrig, could I ask you about timetables?'

The esteemed lady swivelled her eyes towards him like a vulture eyeing a potential carcass. 'What did you say?'

'Timetables, Mrs Perrig. I was not consulted about the classes I have to teach. Furthermore,' John continued with reckless bravery, 'I have no syllabuses, nor any schemes of work. There seem to be no textbooks, worksheets, or indeed anything that might assist in the teaching of my subject. I could not even find exercise books this morning.'

Mrs Perrig seemed to expand, as if filling with super-heated steam. Which was not far off the mark, for when she opened her mouth, a torrent of hot air came forth. 'Timetables are nothing to do with me! Miss Ewer and Mr Burrows-Morgan deal with timetables!'

'I think you'll find that Mr Burrows-Morgan deals with nothing very much at all,' replied John, delighted at his manifest courage.

'Damn right there,' muttered Frank.

'Who said that?' screeched Mrs Perrig.

Frank turned his eyes back down towards his hands.

'I approached Mr Burrows-Morgan this morning,' continued John. 'I was told that he was in charge of timetables, so I made a point of going to see him. He was asleep. Actually, going by the various bottles arranged around him, I would say that he was in a drunken stupor.'

Frank started to quake with suppressed laughter.

'Mr Burrows-Morgan has many onerous duties,' hissed Mrs Perrig through clenched teeth. 'Sometimes things get on top of him.'

The bench started to vibrate.

'That's no comfort to the staff, is it?' replied John cockily. 'The poor secretary has to cover for him.'

Mrs Perrig's eyes opened a quarter-inch wider and glittered with spite. 'Mr Simmonds,' she said. 'You seem to have made some rather unfavourable judgements about our school despite the fact that you have been here for less than a day.' She drummed her fingers on the desk in a meaningful manner. 'I am surprised you wanted to come here at all. Did you, perhaps, have some particular problems in your previous employment?'

'Certainly not. I wanted a complete change for personal reasons.'

'Oh, *personal* reasons, were they? It is often difficult to separate the personal and the professional when it comes to education. I must acquaint myself with the content of your references. I am beginning to wonder whether a slip up has been made.'

'A slip up?'

'An error of judgement. It would appear that we have selected someone whose temperament is not in keeping with the school.'

'Now hang on a minute—'

'We are not discriminatory here, Mr Simmonds,' she said, oozing doom. 'We employ suitable candidates of any race or gender. But our teachers need to be able to identify with our pupils and conform to our systems.'

'I am perfectly prepared—'

'We *believed* that you would do your best for us, Mr Simmonds. Perhaps we were deceived.'

'Deceived? Now look—'

'And if that was the case, then of course it behoves us to rectify the situation, and the quicker the better.'

'Rectify? What do you mean?'

'Give you notice of unemployment, or of redeployment elsewhere in the county.'

'But you can't—'

'Can't what, Mr Simmonds?'

His throat was becoming dry. 'I mean, even *in extremis,* you'd have to give me a term's notice.'

'Not for re-deployment, Mr Simmonds. Did you not read the small print on the letter you were sent? The appropriate period of notice for that event is one week.'

'A week?'

'Just so.' She spread a chubby hand before her and studied her almost non-existent fingernails. 'But we are digressing from our agenda. The next item is accident duty. We need to set up a rota to deal with laboratory accidents, and if last year was anything to go by, there will be plenty of them. Mr Simmonds, would you like to volunteer to take the first turn?'

By the time Mrs Perrig called the meeting to an end, all pupils had left for home and John had a headache. It felt as if two small drills were boring into his skull just above each eye-socket. He followed Frank towards the men's staff room, and when he was sure that the chem lab was well out of earshot, turned to his companion.

'I haven't got off to a very good start, have I?'

'Best to keep out of her way,' grunted Frank.

'But she's the head of science! She should be directing what we teach, whom we teach, and what resources we have. Everything, really.'

'Is that what it was like at your last school?'

'Yes.'

'It isn't like that here.'

'Does anyone pass an exam in this school?'

Frank shrugged. 'It's been known.'

'What are Mrs Perrig's grades like?'

'For Chemistry A Level? Good. But then, students enter the A Level class by invitation only. Her invitation, that is.'

'What sort of size is the biology A Level class?'

'Interesting question.'

'Do you know the answer?'

'No.'

Alexander was in his usual seat in the men's staff room, clutching a mug of coffee and a copy of *Private Eye*. 'Very droll, very droll!' he muttered to himself. John went over to him.

'Where does the coffee come from, Alexander, and don't say "Brazil".'

'It's by the sink. If anyone asks, say it's coming off my allowance. But you'll need to put a couple of pounds in the kitty soon or you'll be banned.'

Armed with a reviving mug of dark brown water (all the milk had gone), John found his tube-framed chair and pulled it up close to Alexander.

'How has your first day gone, then?' asked the latter, feigning innocence.

'It was one of the worst days of my life. This place is old-fashioned, ill-equipped, badly organised, and run by dictators.'

'You make it sound like Italy in the 1930s.'

'It's not funny, Alexander. I've had a hell of a day.'

Mr Pritchard reluctantly put down his esteemed literary organ. 'What exactly went wrong?'

'I don't know where to begin. I have no syllabuses or exercise books. The head of science has threatened to sack me. And I think I've offended Mrs Wontsmey.'

'Really? Surely some mistake?'

'Lots of mistakes, Alexander. Mrs Perrig has no business threatening me with anything. I have done nothing wrong. On the contrary, I've just been trying to teach efficiently.'

'Such is life. Perrig by name, Perrig by nature.'

'Sorry?'

'Her name is a modification of the Welsh word "perygl", meaning "danger".'

'Bloody hell. You know, I'm tempted to see the headmaster about her.'

'Not a good idea,' replied Alexander, eyebrows raised. 'Mrs Perrig has a great deal of influence over Mr Kane. A very great deal.'

'Ah.' John swigged his coffee as if it were gin.

Alexander patted his hand. 'Don't worry, my boy. All will be well. And all manner of things will be well.'

'Humph.' John stared down into his chipped red mug.

'Actually, the object of your immediate worries should be Mr Emyr Williams.'

'Emyr Williams?'

'Are you not in need of waterproof footwear?'

The clouds were thinner and higher than they had been that morning, occasionally spitting out the odd bit of drizzle as if to assure John they hadn't forgotten about him. He decided that an open umbrella would slow him down, so he ran with it tucked under his left arm. He had to run because the cobbler's shop was due to close at half-past four. He hared up Stryd y Dyfrgi, rushed past Chapel View Guest House (a plump hand quivered at a curtain), and darted up Heol y Carlwm, turning into Lôn y Gwenci. He sprinted past the newsagent's shop and the pharmacy, wishing he could loiter.

Mr Emyr Williams was seated in a corner of his shop when John arrived, panting, at twenty-five past four. The cobbler raised his eyebrows. 'Someone's in a hurry.'

'Yes.' John stopped to get his breath back. 'You see, I must have Wellington boots.'

'You *must*, must you?'

'I need them. Desperately.'

'You weren't so desperate to see me last Saturday.

86

Walked straight past me, you did, when I called you.'

'Oh dear.' John leant against the old wooden counter in limp resignation. 'I apologise. I was in a hurry and didn't notice you.'

'No?'

'No. Anyway, I should be most grateful, Mr Williams, if you would kindly sell me a pair of Wellington boots, size ten.'

'Size ten? Big feet you've got.'

John closed his eyes in despair. 'I suppose you're going to tell me that no one around here has feet that big.'

Mr Williams reached under the counter and produced a pair of black Wellington boots wrapped in transparent plastic. 'Size ten is one of my best sellers. I got plenty.'

'I don't suppose you have waterproof macs also?' asked John, trying his luck.

The cobbler sniffed. 'Matter of fact, I 'ave. Here, look.' He produced a mac from under the counter in the manner of a triumphant magician.

'But it's bright yellow.'

'What's the problem? You'll show up, won't you? In the dark, like.'

The mac was bound to be the butt of many a joke, but overall, things were looking up. John had acquired robust anti-rain gear, and the lights were still on in the pharmacy.

The interior of that establishment was reminiscent of a bygone age. A single lightbulb dangling from the centre of the ceiling emitted a weak amber light, and the faded red curtains in the window produced liverish shadows. Rows of wooden shelves covered the walls, bearing antiseptics, anticolics, antitussives, and diverse other liquid antidotes. Also on view were dressings, soaps, talcs and tissues. On the far side of the room, set at right angles to the window, an enormous wooden counter languished like a tired old rhino. Behind it, many little wooden drawer-fronts could be seen, presumably concealing myriad pills and ointments. The place smelt like the inside of an empty paracetamol bottle, musty and medical, though as John approached the counter, he was aware of another far pleasanter scent: lily of the valley.

As he drew level with the counter, the vision of which he had dreamt suddenly appeared before him. She was smaller than he'd expected, but every bit as beautiful. Her hair was pinned up in a bun, with charming stray curls escaping around her ears and neck. Her eyes were green and luminous and looked directly into his.

'Can I help you?' she asked.

'Oh. Yes. I would like, er, a pack of aspirin.'

'What dosage?'

'Dosage?'

'250mg tablets, or 500mg?'

'Um...'

'And how many? I have packs of twenty or fifty.'

'Ah. Right. A pack of twenty of the 250mg tablets, please.'

'You don't suffer from gastric ulcers?'

'No.' John grinned nervously. 'Not yet anyway.' He cleared his throat. 'I, er, have just taken up a post at the high school.'

'Yes,' replied Elisabeth-Mai with her back to him.

'You know who I am?'

'This is a very small town. News spreads very quickly.'

'You probably know my name, then?'

'I do. And I imagine you know mine.'

John felt prickles of confusion heat up his face. He thought of the nameplate outside the pharmacy door.

'Er, yes. Miss Glyndwr. It is "Miss", is it?'

'It is,' she said, handing him a brown paper bag containing a small box of aspirin. 'That will be forty pence.'

John couldn't hide his delight as she put down his

packages and fumbled around in his jacket. As he checked through his small change, he tried to think of something appropriate to say, something that might aid his pursuit of this glorious female. But nothing came to mind. He handed her a fifty pence piece.

'Thank you,' she said, and opened the till.

'I saw you singing,' John said, in a sudden burst of inspiration, 'in Moriah Chapel.'

'Ten pence change,' replied Elisabeth-Mai, suppressing a snigger.

'Thanks. Right.' He picked up his waterproofs. 'Goodbye, then. I daresay I'll be needing something else soon.' But she had gone.

CHAPTER SIX

At the Wontsmeys'

What a week. Endless rain, endless lessons, and endless difficulties, including no opportunity to re-visit the pharmacy. Still, Friday arrived soon enough.

Mrs Lavinia Hughes greeted the last day of the working week by yelling up her perilous staircase to awaken her recumbent guest. John heard the screech and rolled over. He tried to convince himself that he was on holiday. In Greece, maybe. No, the Maldives. It didn't work. In neither place was the refrain 'Get up, Mr Simmonds!' commonly heard, nor were windowpanes lashed by rain.

John wriggled himself up into a semi-seated position and gazed morosely at his crumpled clothes. Before long, those cold garments would be doing battle with 7B. They would re-group and sally forth into the midst of 10D, covered with sweat, and most probably tears. But such soiling was unlikely to deflect the lunchtime assault of Mrs Wontsmey. On the contrary, these manly musks would probably entice her out of the cookery room all the more quickly.

Was that what he wanted? Betty Wontsmey was attractive in an American, older woman sort of way. Especially when drunk. The fact that she was married seemed to be no barrier to her, but it certainly worried John. Anything remotely related to marriage worried him. He also suspected that she might have leech-like qualities, that she was the clingy type that caused pain. It was clear from the sniggering in the men's staffroom that the lady had already attempted to adhere herself onto other male teachers. He would resist, he decided. He would keep himself for Elisabeth-Mai.

John dragged himself out of bed. Within forty minutes he was trudging along Stryd y Dyfrgi in his black Wellington boots and brilliant yellow mackintosh, holding aloft the late Mr Hughes' black umbrella.

7B surprised him by being bright and enthusiastic. But they'd only been in the school as long as he had. They'd soon learn. 10D, by contrast, were old hands at the good old game of 'bait the teacher', and it took all John's energy and ingenuity to deflect their evil intentions. But he managed it. He sorted them into six groups, and with the aid of miscellaneous books and newspapers (gleaned at some cost to his time) each group investigated a different sort of infectious bacterium. The groups were each instructed to select a scribe to write down their findings on transparent film, and to choose a reporter to explain them when displayed to the class via the overhead projector. He supposed 10D did not really need to know about the gory details of tuberculosis, typhoid fever, and plague, but deadly diseases were always good for keeping children amused. John decided that he'd catch up with the syllabus after October half-term, by which time he hoped they'd all be friends.

Lunchtime soon arrived, and he collapsed into his tube-framed chair, barely noticing in his exhaustion the protesting twinge that shot up his spine.

Alexander looked at him with pity. 'Come on,' he said. 'Let's eat. I'll pay.' John stared at him, baffled by this magnanimity. 'Come along, lad,' urged Alexander again. 'Generosity doesn't overcome me often.'

Alexander led John, and a tray of chicken curry and

pineapple pudding, over to a table with a charming view of the bins.

'Well, my boy,' said Alexander, as he tucked a serviette into his collar, 'you've started off very well.'

'Have I?'

'It's always a gamble, taking on a new member of staff, particularly in a small school. And, if I may say so, when the new member of staff is from England.'

'Hmm.'

'Not that old Kane had much choice in your case. I think there was just one local applicant, and she is known to frequent certain insalubrious streetcorners in Penymynydd.'

'Good grief!'

'Quite. Anyway, you're doing a good job.'

'Thank you, Alexander. I'm trying very hard. But Trecadno High School is not easy to get to grips with. I pity any newly qualified teacher who happens to come here.'

'That's modern education for you. Not for the fainthearted.'

'Frankly my biggest problem is Mrs Perrig. She's a waste of a good salary. There are plenty of unemployed graduates who could do a better job than her with their hands tied behind their backs.'

'I couldn't possibly comment, though I think you'll find that chemistry graduates are not thick on the ground. Those who can teach *our* pupils are few indeed.' He forked in some rice. 'But I do have a tip for you with regard to your resource problem.'

'Really?'

'Write a list of the things you need – don't go overboard, mind – and take it to Mr Burrows-Morgan.'

'The inebriate deputy head?'

'The very same. And make sure it's accompanied by an offering of strong drink.'

'Pardon?'

'Make it a large bottle.'

'But the man's already—'

'He's not quite as sozzled as he looks. Not all the time, anyway. Just do as I say, and you'll have your exercise books and textbooks without bothering Mrs Perrig.'

John stuck his spoon into some congealing custard. 'Is there an off licence around here?'

'The nearest place selling strong drink is the pharmacy.'

Light appeared in John's weary eyes. 'Really?'

'Indeed. Very good for whiskey.' Alexander put down his knife and fork with delicacy and pushed his plate away from him, simultaneously pulling his bowl of dessert to the fore. 'Now then, my boy. Will you join us once again at the Wanderers' Club tonight?'

'Certainly. I need an evening out.'

'And can we rely on you to help us out with the quiz if Andy lets us down again?'

'I suppose so.'

'That's settled then,' Alexander declared.

When the bell rang for the end of the day, John's A Level class trouped out of the lab with the demeanour of those resolved to enjoy Friday night. He, by contrast, was spent. He would have to be more careful in his lesson preparation. The pupils needed to be more occupied, and he needed to do less talking. There was a lot to think about, and it would keep him going for hours. Days, actually. But for now, educating Trecadno's youth would have to take second place to the evening's first and most crucial mission – a visit to the pharmacy.

He left the school at four and squelched along Trecadno's flowing roads in his boots and yellow coat. At this time of day, there were no pupils left to shout 'banana!' behind his back, but he wouldn't have cared if there were. His thoughts were on Elisabeth-Mai. Drizzle wormed its way down his collar and up his cuffs, and hovered dangerously around his knees. Despite his anti-rain gear he was soaked through by the time he arrived. But he barely noticed. The object of his desires was behind the counter, speaking slowly and carefully in Welsh to a small, shrivelled old woman.

John edged forwards once the aged lady had departed. 'Hello again,' he said, tripping over the late Mr Hughes large, sodden umbrella. 'Sorry.' He straightened himself out as best he could, becoming blissfully aware once again of the fragrance of lily of the valley. 'I don't seem to be able to cope with all this rain paraphernalia.'

'No. Well, how can I help you today?'

'I need to buy a bottle of spirits.'

'You *need* to buy one, eh?' She smiled superciliously and removed a large, interesting-looking key from a pocket.

'Yes. That is, *I* don't need it. Well, I do. But not to drink. It's for, er, a friend.'

'A gift, perhaps?'

'Exactly. It's a gift.'

Elisabeth-Mai opened a large cupboard which contained three shelves packed with bottles. The reddish light within the shop made them glow like embers.

'Good grief!' stammered John. 'I didn't expect you to have such a good range of liquor.'

'It's not as extensive as it looks. It's all whiskey.'

'No gin or rum?'

'There's no call for them.'

'Good grief!' he repeated, surveying the bottles. 'This must be paradise for a whiskey-lover! I had no idea that there were so many distilleries in the British Isles.'

'Mmm.'

'Strange, when you think of it, that Scotland and Ireland are awash with whiskey, yet there seems to be nothing from Wales.'

Elisabeth-Mai raised a mischievous eyebrow. 'Well now, would you like to purchase any of these bottles?'

'Yes indeed. But I really don't know which one.'

'May I recommend this new product from the Black Valley Distillery in Connemara?' She removed a bottle from a shelf and handed it to him. 'It's a single malt distilled from a wort made from black treacle.'

'A wort?'

'The mixture that is fermented prior to distillation.'

'Oh.' He noticed the price-tag and gulped. 'Do you recommend anything else?'

'I think the one you have there would be the most acceptable gift.'

John stared at her, confused. Was she trying to extract the maximum amount of cash out of him?

'Famous names aren't always the best choice,' she continued, and took the bottle from John's hands.

'Perhaps not.' He had no idea *why* not, though.

'Not for certain people, anyway,' she remarked, amusement dancing in her eyes as she wrapped the bottle in green tissue paper.

John stared at her. 'You know, don't you?'

'Sorry?'

'You know who it's for?'

'I'm not completely certain.'

'Yes, you are. Do you know everything about me?'

She grinned. 'As I mentioned before, this is a small community. And there are certain traditions in the town that are well-established.'

'Like buying whiskey for certain people in the hope that one's life becomes easier?'

'Mr Burrows-Morgan didn't get the way he is overnight. That will be twenty pounds and sixty-two pence.'

John gulped and struggled with his anti-rain

impedimenta in the effort to find some cash.

'At least you won't need all that tomorrow,' said Elisabeth-Mai as she watched the performance.

'What do you mean?'

'It won't rain tomorrow,' she said. 'So tomorrow would be a good day to see our stone circle.'

He stopped fumbling and stared at her. 'The stone circle?'

'It's a scenic spot. I'll show you the way if you like.'

When John eventually managed to reverse the rapid descent of his lower jaw, it formed itself into a wide and joyful smile. 'You mean, you…?'

'If you're free.'

'Most definitely!' He'd have paid double, treble, the price of the whiskey bottle for this outcome.

'Well then, meet me here at two.' She raised an eyebrow at him. 'Your whiskey is ready for you if you have the means to pay for it.'

John got back to Chapel View Guest House at five, beaming with a sense of victory. Despite being half-drowned by rain, sweat and tears, he had never felt happier. Elisabeth-Mai had actually asked him out! Hadn't she?

Mrs Lavinia Hughes smirked at him lovingly as she opened the front door. 'I've got eggs Florentine tonight,' she announced.

Was she confessing to some gynaecological oddity? 'That sounds really, er, interesting,' he said.

'I thought I'd try it with potatoes dauphinoise.'

'Please don't go to any trouble,' responded John, struggling with a wellie boot. 'Ordinary potatoes will be fine, I'm sure.'

Mrs Lavinia Hughes adopted her most profoundly offended expression. 'I am trying to do my best for you, Mr Simmonds.'

'Oh, yes, and I appreciate—'

'I thought you'd like something a bit different. Like they get in London.'

'Oh, right.' He pulled off the other boot.

'That's settled, then. It'll be ready at half-past six.'

'Oh, um...'

'What?'

'You couldn't make it six o'clock, could you?'

Mrs Hughes harumphed. 'Don't tell me. That bugger Pritchard has wheedled you into that flippin' quiz again, hasn't he?'

'Yes. Sorry.'

'He doesn't know everything, you know, that one.'

'Hmm. Look, the thing is, the quiz starts at seven.'

'It's a low priority, isn't it, my food? All this effort I'm putting into feeding you, and you still prefer some smoke-filled den.'

'Mrs Hughes, your cooking is wonderful. Truly.'

A mist of pleasure coated her piggy eyes. 'Is it?' she asked coyly. 'Is it *really* wonderful?'

'It's superb.'

'*Superb*, eh?'

'Definitely. But I have to go out tonight. It's been a long week, and I need some recreation. I'll crack up if I stay in.'

'Hmm. Typical man.'

John did his best to drool over the eggs Florentine. Every time Mrs Hughes turned to look at him he 'ooohed' or 'aaaahed' in mock delight. He crammed in the last dollop of spinach with a heavy stomach but a proud heart. Today, he had vanquished all: the schoolkids, the adorable Elisabeth-Mai, and even the stodge served up by Mrs Lavinia Hughes.

But the self-satisfied grin was soon wiped off his face when she plonked a bowl of dessert in front of him. It contained a mountainous portion of spotted dick smothered in custard with the consistency of scree.

Despite his heavy internal load, John almost pranced towards the Wanderers' Club that night. The drizzle had become much lighter, and in a fit of optimism John abandoned both wellies and umbrella. The overcast sky had dimmed to a point at which puddles were difficult to spot, but not even wet feet could dampen John's spirits.

Dr Daniel Jones was just ahead of him as he entered the clubhouse.

'I see we have a convert to Quiz Night,' declared the doctor.

'I'm not specifically coming for the quiz,' replied John. 'I just wanted to get out, to be honest.'

'Of course, my boy. It must get very claustrophobic within Chapel View Guest House.'

'I'll say. I'd really like to find my own place. A flat or something.'

'To rent or buy?'

'To rent, for now.'

'Not much available around here.'

As Alexander had anticipated, Andy Wontsmey did not turn up, and John found himself on the stage once again, sandwiched between the doctor and the Know-All. Once again, he was too ignorant to make much of a contribution. But he did know that the male seahorse gestates young rather than the female, and he managed to remember that Henry VIII's fifth wife was Catherine Howard. It was just enough to give the Cubs another victory. All in all, it had been a good day, and the next promised to be even better. It was therefore easy to accept a drink from Alexander, another from Daniel, and another gallantly proffered by Mr William Williams.

'Hey,' said that gentleman, 'hope you can see to get home. You'll be walking into the hedge the rate you're going.'

'Don't be daft,' said John glibly. 'I'm used to alcohol.'

'Are you? Perhaps that's why your wife left you, eh?' suggested the deacon. 'Drink drove her into the arms of another man. Frailty, thy name is woman.'

'St Paul might have been right, but drink had nothing to do with it.'

Alexander turned his head in John's direction. 'St Paul? That quote is from Shakespeare. *Hamlet.*'

John frowned. William Williams pretended not to hear.

'Where was your local in London, then?' the deacon asked.

'Just to repeat, Mr Williams: I am not a heavy drinker.' His voice had become slurred, which did not help his argument. 'But I did have a local. Not that I went there often. Once a week, maybe, to meet friends. The Carpenter's Arms.'

'Where in London would that be, then?'

'Finsbury Park. Just along Seven Sisters Road.'

'Is that right? The ladies will want to know about that.'

'The ladies? Which ladies? Why?'

'Oh, you know. Ladies. They want to know everything.' Mr William Williams put down his empty glass with a thud. 'Right. Now then, whose round is it?'

It was Alexander's. The Know-All sidled up to John.

'How about half a shandy this time?' he asked.

'I'm drinking whiskey tonight, Alexander. I'm celebrating.'

'Fair enough. A quiz victory is worth celebrating.'

'I'm not celebrating the quiz result,' said John, bringing everyone's heads turning towards him. 'I'm celebrating Elisabeth-Mai!' He beamed into his whiskey glass.

Doc Jones turned to the deacon, whose scowl sagged a little further.

'What about her, boy?' asked Mr William Williams

slowly.

'We're going for a walk together. Tomorrow. Just her and me.'

'A walk, eh? And whose idea was that then, boy?' asked the deacon again.

John smirked. 'I was trying to pluck up the courage to ask her. I mean, she's a stunner, isn't she? But she beat me to it. She said it would be dry tomorrow. Hope she's right.'

'Elisabeth-Mai is usually right,' remarked Doc Jones, re-lighting his pipe. 'Where are you planning to go for your walk?'

'To a stone circle, she said. I didn't know you had one. Sounds a bit like Stonehenge.'

Doc Jones glanced over at Alexander and seemed relieved to note that the latter was deep in conversation with a man in a flat hat.

'Not quite in the same league,' responded the doctor.

'You're getting around, boy,' said William Williams. 'Seeing our sights.'

'I suppose I am. Though I won't go to Bryncadno again in a hurry.'

The deacon exchanged glances with the doctor again. 'No?' he inquired.

'I was ever so tired after going there, and I had a terrible headache. I was glad of the lift back.'

'It was a hot day,' said the Deacon.

'No heat now,' muttered John groggily. 'Never seen so much water. Must be some quirk of the topof… topol… er…'

'Topography,' pronounced Alexander, re-joining his companions. 'Trecadno is considered a meteorological oddity. Something to do with stationary clouds over the Afanc during the Autumn Equinox.'

Their geographical discussion was cut short by the appearance of Mrs Wontsmey.

'Good evening, Betty. Let me buy you a drink,' said

Alexander.

'Thank you. I'll have a large vodka.'

'Me, too!' announced John. 'I will join this lovely lady with a lovely vodka.'

Ten o'clock became eleven o'clock, and eleven soon slipped towards twelve. People slowly drifted away, but the bonhomie at the bar continued unabated. As the church clock in Trecadno began to strike midnight, Mr William Williams got up and put his coat on in a meaningful way.

'It's time to go home, boys,' he said.

'Quite right,' said the doctor, draining his glass and knocking the tobacco from his pipe into an ashtray. 'Mustn't overdo these things.'

'Some people don't know when to stop,' said the deacon, grimacing at John. 'That boy has a drink problem, an' no mistake.'

Alexander pushed his chair back. 'How on earth are we going to get him home? Look at him!'

'Definite absence of muscular tone,' commented the doctor.

'Jelly-like,' added Alexander.

'Mrs Lavinia Hughes mustn't see him like that,' said Doc Jones.

'No indeed,' agreed the Know-All. 'Perhaps he'd better stay somewhere else tonight.' He giggled and glanced over at Mrs Wontsmey, who seemed remarkably sober despite her substantial intake of vodka.

'I'm off,' announced William Williams. 'I'll let you sort out the boy.'

Alexander saluted him and turned to his Canadian colleague. 'Mrs Wontsmey,' he began. 'Betty. You are a woman of the world. Have you any suggestions as to what we do with our junior colleague?'

Betty grinned lazily. 'Taxi?' she suggested.

'Enoch Pratt likes a pint on a Friday night,' said Doc

101

Jones. 'He'll have parked up hours ago.'

'Aren't there any other taxis in Trecadno?' asked Betty.

'Just the one,' said Alexander. 'Taxis are an innovation around here, you know.'

'I suppose he could come to us,' said Betty with feigned reluctance. 'Seeing as our house is close by.' She grinned at the doctor. 'You'd better let Mrs Hughes know where he is. I'll get him back there by lunchtime.'

Doc Jones looked at John's slumped form. 'Midday sounds about right. Alexander, take an arm.'

As the lights were switched off in the clubhouse, Daniel and Alexander draped John's floppy form over their shoulders. The good doctor, being considerably more robust than his friend, took the bulk of the burden, and one irreverent observer spread it around town that Alexander just held John's hand.

But no one could question John's manliness, for he would be spending the night *chez la* Wontsmey. Whether his manliness would be able to take advantage of the situation was another matter, since it was clear that John was approaching anaesthesia. His emetic reflexes were still intact, alas, and a little way down Lôn y Bele the crab-like triumvirate came to a dead halt to allow John to be sick all over the road.

'It was the spotted dick,' he mumbled as Alexander found him a handkerchief.

'The vodka, more like,' said Daniel Jones.

'What a mess!' hissed Alexander with up-turned nose. 'I just hope it rains in the night.'

'No, it won't,' John moaned.

Sometime well after dawn, John rolled over and opened an eye. The light that entered caused a stab of cerebral pain, and he closed it again, fast. Waves of sleep swept over him again, taking on a spasmodic quality when they reached his bladder. John pictured scenes of fountains. Persistent, tingling ones.

He sat up, far too rapidly. To his horror he was abundantly sick all over Betty Wontsmey's smart blue duvet. He rubbed his aching forehead with a clammy hand and tried to move a leg. He had just managed to get a foot free of the polluted duvet when he heard a knock on his door.

'Are you OK?' asked a female voice.

'Er… urgh,' he replied.

Betty stuck her head around his door. 'Oh, you poor thing!' she crooned. 'I'll bring you some coffee and a clean duvet.'

'Er… no… ug… don't bother. Betty, I'm so sorry…'

'It's no bother.'

He let his head fall back onto the pillow and shut his eyes, in the faint hope that if he couldn't see, he wouldn't feel so desperately embarrassed. Five minutes passed but Betty had still not returned, and the urge to urinate had become overwhelming. Very gingerly, John raised his throbbing head and propped himself up to a seated position. Very carefully, taking due care not to dislodge the foul pool nestling in the duvet, he shifted his left foot and encouraged it to move to a spot on the floor. Once it was firmly planted on the carpet, he felt more confident about shifting his torso sideways. A goodly chunk of his body was thus released from the duvet before John discovered another problem. He had nothing on.

He looked down at the floor for some discarded apparel but saw none. With much difficulty – for the morning sun was now shining straight into his eyes – he scanned the whole room for evidence of last night's outfit. Not that he could remember what he had been wearing, but there must have been trousers and a shirt. And underpants.

He was still in this state – with his right leg respectably

covered but the rest of him exposed – when Betty entered the room with a large mug and another duvet. She showed no inclination to bother with privacy.

'Oh – arrgh!' he exclaimed, shooting back under the sodden duvet.

'Sorry, John. Did I surprise you?'

'Uuuh…'

'I've brought you some coffee. I'll put it here.' She put the mug down on a small table and deposited the new duvet at the bottom of the bed.

'Fanks,' muttered John through the excruciations of his head. 'Er, ugh, Betty, where, er, is the bathroom? And where are my, er, clothes?'

'They had to be washed, I'm afraid. They're almost dry, but I'll bring you something of Andy's for now. The bathroom's the first door on the left.' She left the room, leaving John wondering about the circumstances in which he had been parted from his attire.

Five minutes later, neither Betty nor clothes had appeared, and John's situation was becoming desperate. He had no choice but to lever himself out of bed once again and make his way to the bathroom. But how could he retain his modesty? He decided to wrap the new duvet around his waist as best he could. Thus it was that he staggered towards the door with a long and rather unwieldy train flowing behind him. But all was well: he opened the bedroom door without a problem, pulled the duvet through it, and soon spotted sea-blue tiles that bespoke of a bathroom. It took a while to persuade his voluminous robe inside this room, hampered as he was by blurred vision. But eventually he made it inside, closed the door, and obtained blessed relief.

Unbeknown to John, the bathroom was L-shaped, with an invisible corner containing a shower cubicle. As he turned to leave, he caught sight of the cubicle and its unexpected occupant: a middle-aged man with a crew cut wearing nothing but a medallion. John froze.

'Hi!' said the damp torso, with a Canadian accent. 'You must be John.'

'Uh… yeah,' he mumbled, clinging to his duvet.

'Pleased to meet you,' said the torso. 'Andy Wontsmey.' John most definitely didn't. Mr Wontsmey started walking towards John and stretched out a hand in greeting. To John, in his bewildered state, the arm appeared to target a region below his waist.

'Ah… Oh!' cried the addled teacher, lurching towards the exit. Alas, the duvet had less momentum, and he tripped over it, falling heavily into the door.

'Don't worry, fella, I'll help you up,' said Andy.

'Argh!' exclaimed John with alarm, gathering sufficient of his inner resources to get himself off the floor, through the door, and into the hall. He found Betty standing before him with a coffee pot.

'I was going to bring a top up,' she said, unfazed, 'but you haven't even started the first cup. Don't you like my coffee?'

'Ohhh… Betty!' he cried and collapsed onto the floor.

Betty put down the coffee pot and rushed over to him. 'You poor thing! Are you unwell?'

'Yes!'

With great confidence and not a little relish, she grasped him under the armpits and somehow managed to guide him back onto the bed, from which the despoiled duvet had been removed. She sat down next to him. 'Perhaps you need another sleep?' she suggested, smoothing his brow.

'Oh… Ah… yes. An' water.'

'Of course. I'll bring you a large glass of water and a fresh cup of coffee.'

'Mmm. Fanks.' He closed his eyes. Then he opened them

and surveyed his ventral aspect. 'Betty, the duvet!' he cried, in distress.

'OK,' she replied, and giggled.

John drank his water and his coffee and sank back into the depths of slumber. At ten to twelve he stirred and reached out an arm. 'Darling!' he murmured. 'You are so, so beautiful. And so clever.'

Betty, who was hovering nearby, came closer.

'I want to kiss you,' continued the recumbent form. 'I want to hold you.'

Betty went up close to him and took his hand.

'You are so beautiful,' he repeated, as his hand was squeezed gently but firmly.

This simple mechanical act re-activated the small part of his brain that was not pickled, and his eyelids managed to creak open. Bloodshot, nervous eyes looked up at Mrs Wontsmey in a misery of vulnerability. But things could have been worse. He might have been holding the hand of Mr Wontsmey.

'John!' exclaimed Betty lovingly. 'You were having such a lovely dream!'

'Er… Yes,' he muttered, withdrawing his hand.

'Are you feeling better now? Could you cope with some lunch?'

John massaged his brow and attempted to sit up. 'Lunch?' he inquired, baffled.

'I have pea and ham soup. Could you cope with that, do you think?'

'Pea and ham?'

'Do you like it?'

'Yes,' he said, truthfully enough, though at that moment he couldn't think of anything worse. 'What time is it?'

'Midday. Time for lunch.'

John clapped his hand to his mouth. 'Oh God!' he cried.

'What's the matter?'

'I have to go somewhere.'

'When?'

'At two.'

'That's two hours away. Don't panic.'

'But I need to shower.'

'You can shower here.'

John had a vision of Andy waiting for him in the bathroom. 'Mrs Lavinia Hughes will be expecting me. I'll have to go back there.'

'She knows where you are. Doc Jones phoned her.'

'He phoned Mrs Hughes?'

'You were a little unsteady on your feet last night. We all decided that you should come here, and the doc said he'd let Mrs Hughes know where you were.'

John groaned. 'I made plans to go walking. Hill walking. I need to get my boots.'

'What size feet do you have?'

'Ten.'

'Big, eh?' Betty raised an eyebrow.

John coughed. 'Average, I'd say.'

'The same size as Julian, actually. He's Andy's friend. He won't mind if you borrow his boots. He has several pairs, all in different colours.'

John tried to take this in but failed. 'I don't want to cause any further bother,' he said.

'It's no bother, John.'

'Yes, it is. I've been a dreadful nuisance. I'm so sorry that you've seen me in such a state.'

She smiled generously. 'It happens to us all. Don't worry. Stay for lunch, eh? You'll feel much better.'

John closed his eyes in a gesture of defeat. 'OK. But I have to leave at one thirty at the latest.'

CHAPTER SEVEN

The Stone Circle

Pea and ham soup was not an ideal repast for someone in John's delicate state, and his digestion was further impaired by the thought of being late for his rendezvous with Elisabeth-Mai. Still, the soup tasted good, and seemed to revive him. John had soon mustered enough energy to contribute a sentence or two to the lunchtime conversation.

'Which part of Canada are you from, Andy?' he asked.

'Western Ontario.'

'I'm from Toronto,' Betty explained. 'We met at university there. A long time ago, huh, Andy?'

'Sure was.'

She looked at her husband wistfully. 'So much has changed since then.'

'How did you end up here?' asked John, gently wafting a spoonful of soup to help it cool.

Betty looked over at Andy again.

'We wanted to see the world,' he explained. 'And I wanted to paint. So we went to Paris.'

'Very romantic,' said John, nibbling some bread.

'We were very poor,' said Betty. 'Andy had to teach. I was a waitress. After a couple of years, we shifted to London.'

'I ended up teaching art again,' Andy said.

'In London? I used to teach there,' John said.

'Betty told me. My school was a private school, or a public school as you would say.'

'*Oddershaw's School for Boys*,' muttered Betty.

'Never heard of it,' said John. 'You decided not to stay there, obviously.'

Andy looked a little uncomfortable. 'We wanted more space,' he said, at length. 'I wanted time to concentrate on my paintings.'

'We came to Wales,' Betty said, 'and we found this place.'

'It's perfect for an artist,' said Andy. 'And it was cheap.'

'Not quite cheap enough,' said Betty sadly. 'One of us had to get a decent job. It was my turn.'

'It's charming,' said John, trying to be polite. In truth he thought the house was ramshackle and the decor eccentric. 'Very peaceful.'

'Too peaceful sometimes, eh, Andy?' said Betty.

At twenty past one John put down his teacup and announced that he would have to leave. He thanked his hosts for their hospitality and the loan of clothing and lied that he looked forward to seeing them again. Courtesy also prompted him to promise Betty that he would join her for a little private lunch at school the following week.

Once released into the fresh air, John's instinct was to run, but neither his head nor his legs would oblige. Julian's pretty but uncomfortable pea-green boots wouldn't have let him anyway. At least, he told himself, he didn't need to call at Chapel View Guest House. But as it happened, Mrs Lavinia Hughes had just visited the cobbler's and was dawdling in Lôn y Gwenci in the hope that she might catch sight of her lodger.

'Where have you been?' she demanded, rushing towards him.

'Oh!' Dismay froze him. 'Mrs Hughes!'

'You deserted me last night.'

'I'm very sorry, but you see—'

'I do see. I thought you enjoyed my hospitality.'

'I do, Mrs Hughes. I really do. But…'

'But you have to get drunk every so often.'

'Not at all, but it just happened that…'

His landlady's nostrils flared with the chagrin of a spurned lover. 'Just a minute. Are you saying that you went to stay with them Wontsmeys when you *weren't* drunk?'

John's face was an agony of perplexity. 'Yes. I mean, no. I was definitely drunk last night. But I don't get drunk regularly.'

'Hmm.' Mrs Hughes allowed a little gleam of affection to creep into her beady eyes. 'You'll be ready for your dinner now, I daresay.'

John cleared his throat. 'Ah. The thing is, Betty – that is to say, Mrs Wontsmey – she had prepared—'

'Hold your breath. I know what you're going to say. That woman thinks she can cook. Cookery teacher, my foot! She might as well try teaching Chinese. Too many allowances have been made for that woman.'

'Mrs Hughes, I am so sorry. I am really looking forward to your tea this evening.'

'Well, of course you are.'

'But I must go now. I'm late already.'

'Late? For what?'

'I'm going walking this afternoon.'

'Walking?' She screwed up her eyes. 'Who with?'

John sighed. Was there any point in trying to conceal his assignation? 'I'm going to the stone circle with Elisabeth-Mai,' he admitted, bracing himself for the explosion.

'Elisabeth-Mai? Good gracious.' Mrs Hughes sniffed, adjusted the angle of her head, and unfolded her chubby arms. 'Well, you better get off, then, hadn't you? Just make sure you give me back my torch.'

John reached the pharmacy just as the church clock rang

out its two o'clock chimes. He stood at the door a few moments to recover from the sight of his landlady, and from the sudden realisation that he must have left her torch at the Wontsmey residence. He didn't notice Emyr Williams, cobbler, staring out of his grubby window, nor did he see the fluttering curtains. All was dim inside the pharmacy, and there was no sign of Elisabeth-Mai. He was about to raise his hand to knock on the flaking red door when he heard piano music. It was quiet, distant, and very beautiful. A complex sequence of notes rose and fell like a myriad little bells carried on waves. Abruptly, the playing stopped and bolts were drawn. A little woman with spectacles looked up at him through the half-open door.

'Come in,' she croaked, and hobbled off.

He stood uncertainly alongside a shelf of disinfectant bottles. Their faint scent of pine formed a fleeting picture of Betty Wontsmey leaning invitingly against a huge Canadian redwood. The image disappeared as a smiling Elisabeth-Mai appeared sporting a casual blue jacket and a youthful ponytail.

'Hello, John,' she said.

'I hope I'm not late.'

'Not by much. I see you're well-equipped in the footwear department.'

John looked down sheepishly at the green boots. He wanted to say that they were not his, but that would involve an admission of drunkenness and a night *chez la* Wontsmey. He emitted a weak titter.

'We don't usually see such smart boots around here,' she continued, as if sensing his discomfort. 'We generally have to make do with ancient old things patched up by Mr Williams.'

John needed to change the subject. 'I heard some music as I approached your door. It was lovely.'

'Chopin,' said Elisabeth-Mai.

'Ah.'

'Are you interested in music, John?' she asked as she zipped up her jacket.

'Sometimes,' he said uncertainly. 'I don't know much about classical music.'

'Hmm.'

They ambled down a series of lanes, eventually arriving at a gate to a meadow. Once they'd climbed over the stile alongside the gate, they tramped along a narrow dirt path that headed uphill following a hedge. Elisabeth-Mai walked confidently, leading the way. It was as much as John could do to keep up with her, especially given the delicate state of his head and intestines. After a while she stooped down to pick a flower.

'Do you know what this is?' she asked.

John looked at the small, yellow blossom uncertainly. 'Is it cinquefoil?'

'Not a bad guess. Tormentil, actually. Very similar to cinquefoil. I'm glad you know about plants.'

'My knowledge of wildflowers isn't great.'

'Well then, you must learn.'

They pressed on in silence, John gazing admiringly at the back of her head, and at the expansive views revealed by the low hedges. He noticed a fox sitting quite still behind one of them; it seemed to be watching them. A hundred yards further along there was another fox, its fur the colour of flames. Precisely the same colour as his companion's hair. They eventually reached another large gate, and Elisabeth-Mai leant against it, gazing eastwards.

'It's absolutely wonderful up here,' John said when he'd caught her up. 'You can see right down the valley. What a glorious amount of green!'

'The Afanc Valley,' she replied. 'The Afanc is a fine river.'

'Is "Afanc" the Welsh word for some sort of mammal by any chance?'

'Beaver.'

'Really?' Mixed images passed through his mind.

'The valley would have looked very different a hundred years ago,' Elisabeth-Mai remarked.

'Would it? What would we have seen back then?'

'Coal mines and spoil heaps.'

'Good grief!'

'Indeed. The river marks the edge of the coalfield. There was a railway alongside it to take coal down to the jetty at Aberafanc, where it was loaded onto ships. You can still find old station platforms if you know where to look.'

John looked around, puzzled. 'So, this pastoral scene is actually quite new?'

'There were always farmsteads between the mine-workings, so some of the fields are old. The larger ones are more recent. The last mine closed in 1973. Nature takes over man's folly with great speed.'

'You're glad that the mines closed?'

'Personally, yes. But back then it was a disaster for many. William Williams was a miner. He'd only just married and bought his house when he was made redundant.'

'Gosh.' John tried to reconcile this lamentable young Williams with the one that presided over Moriah Chapel. He failed.

Elisabeth-Mai pointed to a patch of woodland a little way below them, well above the river. 'We're heading there.'

'I can't see a circle of stones,' he said, squinting into the sun. 'Though I can see a man who looks very much like Dr Jones.' He indicated a field to the north.

'He likes to tramp around the countryside. Says it keeps him fit.'

'Doesn't seem to do much for his waistline.'

They grinned at each other, and John's heart skipped a beat.

'I can see a fox, too,' he added, encouraged. 'There are

loads around here.'

'You've noticed?' asked Elisabeth-Mai.

'You can't miss them. They seem to lack the instinct to run away.'

'They have nothing to fear from us.'

'But they don't know that do they?'

A superior smile flickered across Elisabeth-Mai's now gloriously pink, wind-blown face. 'You think not?'

Twenty minutes later they had reached their destination.

'Amazing!' declared John, when he saw the great stones up close. He looked around at the grassy hills, the shining river, and the mountains rising to the north, all lit with weak, diaphanous sunlight. 'I'm surprised that I haven't heard about this circle.' He reached out to touch one of the great rocks. 'I mean, it's really *very* much like Stonehenge, and plenty of fuss is made about that.'

A strange little smirk played on Elisabeth-Mai's lips. 'The Welsh don't like to make a fuss. We're self-effacing. From an early age we are trained to consider pride a sin, and to endeavour to be humble and quiet. Some maintain that we were trained to be servile.'

'Really?' Distinctly non-servile images of Mr William Williams, Mrs Lavinia Hughes, and Mrs Evadne Perrig flickered unwanted before his eyes. 'I can't say I've noticed a lot of humility around here.'

'Perhaps people are on their guard with you. You are a newcomer, an oddity. A potential threat.'

'A threat?'

'In theory, you've taken a local person's job. You could probably afford to buy houses beyond the means of many who have grown up here. It's likely that you won't patronise our chapel or our festivals. I believe that you cannot use our language.'

'I could learn.'

'Would you really take the time and trouble?'

'Yes,' he said without conviction. 'I could try.'

'I hope you do, John. I really hope you do.'

In the centre of the stone circle was a single square slab laid horizontally at waist height on two primitive rock walls. It looked like an altar, a sacred place where sacrifices to the gods might have been made in ancient times. John was surprised when Elisabeth-Mai casually sat down on it.

'Come and join me, John,' she instructed. 'I've brought a drink.' She produced two small bottles from her backpack and gave one to John. They were unmistakably medicine bottles, made from clear glass with small screw tops and labels on which the word 'cordial' was written in a small, neat script. They looked like something from *Alice in Wonderland*. John sat next to Elisabeth-Mai with the greatest of delight.

'Camomile and mint,' she said. 'Aids relaxation and maintains energy levels.'

'Really?' He took a tentative sip. It was sweet and minty with a weedy tang.

'Do you like it?'

'It's, er, interesting.' He was sure he'd tasted something similar before, though he couldn't think where.

'Well, now,' said Elisabeth-Mai, 'do you fancy walking up the hill just behind us? There's an even better view of the Afanc Valley from there, and you can see Trecadno quite clearly.'

'OK.' He looked around at the long damp grass. 'But the path seems to have ended.'

Elisabeth-Mai got up and began to walk in a north-easterly direction. 'Follow me,' she instructed. 'Not all the paths around here are signposted.'

Just as John caught her up, she bent down to pick another flower-head.

'Do you know this plant? she asked, twirling what looked like a large yellow daisy.

'Sorry,' replied John, bemused.

'This is *arnica*. It's rare in Wales, though there are a couple of spots near Trecadno where it can be found. It has anti-inflammatory properties.'

John decided to change the subject lest he reveal gaps in his botanical knowledge. 'Is this a farmer's path?'

'Farmers may use it, but it was not made by them.'

'Whoever made it didn't do a very good job.'

'The foxes made it,' replied Elisabeth-Mai with a frown.

'Oh.'

'It is Tre-*cadno*, after all.'

'It's not common for towns to be called after animals, is it? Was Trecadno a centre for foxhunting, or something?'

She stopped and glared at him. 'Most *definitely* not,' she exclaimed.

'Oh. Sorry.'

'Foxes are respected around here. Some people even believe that they are the reincarnations of their ancestors.'

'They do?'

'They are never, ever hunted.' She turned back to resume the walk. 'They are creatures of habit, using the same routes. They create tracks in the grass.'

'That's interesting.'

'Foxes are interesting animals. They are the subject of many beliefs and stories.'

'Stories?'

'*Aesop's Fables*, for example.'

'You are very knowledgeable, Elisabeth-Mai.'

'Only about certain things. In Trecadno, we have our own fox story for children.'

'Oh?'

'It's basically a geography lesson. The story tells how a fox cub gets lost and has to work out how to get home. For example, if the cub were here, where we are now, he'd have to go back down to the stone circle. From there he'd

116

need to find his way to the ford in the river – not the Afanc, but the Dyfrgi, Trecano's river – then get to Bryncadno. That's where the fox-paths converge.'

'Alexander said something about paths meeting there. Or maybe lines.'

Elisabeth-Mai ignored the comment. 'Fox stories were useful for children to learn their way around in days gone by.'

'Ah.'

'Especially if they had to walk far from their homes. To get water, or wool. Or tend animals. Or work down the mines.'

'In the mines? Surely not.'

'Until 1842 it was perfectly legal for five-year-olds to work down mines. The minimum age of miners was not raised to thirteen until 1903.'

'That's terrible!' said John, shocked at his total ignorance of such things. 'Kids today don't know how lucky they are,' he added, before cringing at the realisation that this was a favourite saying of his mother's.

Elisabeth-Mai somehow managed to accelerate up the last stretch of hill and John had to run to keep up. She stopped when she reached a gate, and leaning on it, looked back down at the Afanc estuary with satisfied eyes.

'Well, you are right,' John panted as he caught up. 'The view from here is stunning. Is that Bryncadno down there?'

'That's right.'

'Home of the Crusties. Though I didn't see any when I went there.'

'They like to rest.'

'Absorbing the spirituality of the place?'

'Or magic mushrooms, maybe.'

'Really? Do they burn them, I wonder? Something gave me a bad head when I went to Bryncadno last weekend.'

'If you look westwards,' she said, changing the subject

again, 'you can just about see Pembrokeshire.'

'Beautiful!' John collapsed against a gate post. 'You are so lucky.'

'You think so?'

'Of course.'

'You can see all this just as well as I can.'

'But this land is yours. I can only visit and admire.'

Elisabeth-Mai's eyes twinkled. 'How very perceptive of you, John.'

By half past five they were back at the door of the pharmacy.

'Thank you for today, Elisabeth-Mai,' said John, a note of dejection creeping into his voice. 'I really enjoyed our walk. Perhaps we can go on another outing soon. How about next Saturday?'

'It will rain next Saturday.'

'Will it?' John scrambled for something to add to this. Inwardly he was praying to be invited in and offered coffee.

Elisabeth-Mai gave him a condescending look. 'I must go in now,' she said.

'Of course. Goodbye, then. Until next time.' But the door had closed, and the vision had gone.

John remained standing on the pavement, unsure whether the angels had just come down from heaven, or whether the end of the world was nigh. His solitude was broken by the sound of slow steps approaching, the sort of steps made by a resurrected mummy in a horror movie.

'Hey! Is that you, John?' droned the sepulchral figure. John turned slowly, as if in a trance. 'Hey,' continued the figure, 'you're not drunk again, are you?'

John still felt drunk, though no longer because of his alcoholic intake. Mr William Williams soon came into clear view.

'Hey, boy, what you standin' there for?' asked the deacon. ''Ave you been listening to Elisabeth-Mai doin' her archipelagos?'

Having learned of the Deacon's early misfortunes, John tried to remain courteous. 'I was just on my way to Chapel View.'

'You can't face Mrs Lavinia Hughes looking like that, boy!'

Alarm seized John. What horrific sight had his darling had to tolerate for the past couple of hours? 'Like what?'

'Like bloody death warmed up, boy! Your shoulders are drooping, your hair is all over the place, and the bags under your eyes are monumental!'

The shoulders drooped even more, and so did the hair, as William Williams resumed his slow progress down the road. Clouds were thickening, and the light beginning to drain from the sky. Having quite mislaid his own will, John followed the deacon. When he reached the square, he paused to scan the northern arc of houses, now in shadow. One of the few lights visible came from an upstairs window of Chapel View Guest House. Its source was a pale and solitary candle.

CHAPTER EIGHT

The Nature Club

'For shame, Mr Simmonds!'

John had been expecting a rebuke when he appeared for breakfast, for it was nearly ten o'clock – outrageously late for a Sunday morning if you happened to live in Trecadno.

'Don't worry,' Mrs Lavinia Hughes continued, hands firmly planted on her ample hips. 'You've got just enough time for a wash and a cup of tea before we go.'

'Pardon?'

'Before we go out.'

'Where to, exactly?'

'Moriah Chapel, of course.'

'To be honest, Mrs Hughes—'

'Have you got my torch?' his esteemed landlady cut in with a gimlet gaze.

'Er, um, actually…'

'While you're thinking about that, you can get dressed. Did you notice the jacket?'

John had indeed observed the late Mr Hughes' black jacket dangling over the bannisters. He'd assumed that Mrs Hughes planned to donate it to a particularly desperate charity. He plodded back up the stairs and stared at the aged garment with wrath. Then it occurred to him that Elisabeth-Mai would be at the chapel, and the prospect of a quick service suddenly didn't seem quite so onerous.

There was just enough time for him to don his funeral garb, down a cup of tea and attempt to eat some breakfast before heading off.

'I couldn't help noticing the candle in your window last night,' John remarked as he cut into a sad-looking sausage. 'Was it ornamental, or was it there for a particular reason?'

'For the dead,' replied Mrs Lavinia Hughes as she inspected a large brown woollen object resembling a stuffed cat. It was actually a tea cosy.

'Ah. Do you mean Mr Parry?'

'I most certainly do not. That man short-changed me more than once.'

'Hmm.' John studied a leathery fragment of fried egg with uncertainty. 'So, was yesterday the anniversary of Mr Hughes' passing, perhaps?'

'Mr Simmonds, around here we do not need special days to commemorate the souls of the departed,' said Mrs Lavinia Hughes, brandishing the teapot. 'We venerate them at all times. Young people today like to go on at length about the "facts of life" and what the birds and bees get up to. But the most important fact of life remains unknown to them, a grand secret. It is not until you get to middle age that you learn it. And that last, greatest, fact of life, Mr Simmonds, is that we will die. All of us. So, it behoves us to have a bit of respect for the hereafter, don't you think?'

'Oh, er, yes,' he muttered, attempting to gulp down a piece of burnt bacon.

'Right, I'm off to change my shoes,' Mrs Lavinia Hughes declared. John looked down at her enormous pink faux-fur slippers. 'You'd better get a move on.'

Five minutes later, he and his landlady were heading for the chapel, a building that was as stern and grey as the morning sky. Facing them, at the church entrance, other well-dressed Christians were gathering.

'None of *them* come from Trecadno,' Mrs Hughes

whispered to John conspiratorially. 'All newcomers, them.'

John was about to remind her that he also belonged within this condemned category when William Williams appeared.

'Hey, John!' he called down from the top step.

'Hello, Mr Williams,' he replied with little enthusiasm.

'You feeling better now, boy?'

'Yes, thank you.'

'You were in a state yesterday, an' no mistake. You want to watch that habit of yours, boy.'

John gritted his teeth and followed Mrs Hughes into the dim interior of the chapel. His eyes moved upwards, seeking out the sea of navy dresses that would mark out the zone of his beloved. As he stood gazing, his elbow was grabbed very forcibly from behind.

'Over here!' hissed a female voice alongside him. John assumed it belonged to Mrs Lavinia Hughes, but further inspection revealed that its source was Mrs Evadne Perrig. She stretched out a stumpy arm and pointed at a pew.

'Sit!' she commanded.

John was quite unable to disobey and lowered himself into his appointed place. Fortunately, the spot in question had a reasonable view of the choir, though he could not see the object of his desires. Indeed, the neat rows of ladies on the balcony didn't seem at all like the ones he'd seen a week earlier. The deacons soon trouped in, and the minister took up position on his box. Hymns were sung, repeatedly. How his old pals in London would laugh if they could witness this, John thought, especially when the little Gestapo toothbrush of a minister started to spit his customary accusations.

John entered a trance-like state of mock-attentiveness during which his blood flow was diverted to his eyelids. He stayed thus for many, many minutes. At some point, he was disturbed by a scrabbling noise somewhere underneath his feet. He opened his eyes to observe Mrs Perrig's reaction, but her gaze was fixed on the minister, and her mouth was set in an approving smirk. Mr William Williams, up on the deacons' dais, looked as vacant as ever, though when the scrabbling got louder still he seemed to lose control of his hands, which began to flap around like demented seagulls. Without warning, a booming chord vibrated forth from the organ, cutting off Hitler in mid-flow. Instantly the congregation sprung to their feet and started to sing. John looked up at the minister expecting signs of annoyance at this interruption, but he just sang along with the others. A mirror was positioned above the organist's head that allowed her to see the dais. The deacon's hand manoeuvres must have been a signal, John decided. But for what, exactly?

The new hymn seemed interminable. John mouthed nothings at the floor, just as he'd done the previous week, and when the singing finally ended no subterranean scrabbling could be heard. Once seated again, John allowed himself another upward gaze, and to his great joy, saw that Elisabeth-Mai was sitting in one of the rear balcony seats. He was certain that she hadn't been there initially. Perhaps she'd moved so that she could see him. Wondrous thought!

The minister mumbled something, and within a few minutes they were once again in the midst of a hymn, although this time a mercifully short one. This was followed by an announcement from Mr William Williams in Welsh and English. They were instructed to reassemble in the vestry to discuss a secular matter, the sale of Hopkins the newsagent's shop. With much fuss and natter the congregation squeezed themselves into the much smaller room. John felt he had no choice but to go with them.

'Thank you for coming, one and all,' said William Williams. 'We have a matter of some difficulty to discuss. It has come to our recent attention that Mr Hopkins intends to sell his newsagency business.' Mutterings of discontent spread throughout the room. 'This will have immediate implications for the employment of many of our young people, who reduce the burden on their parents by earning a small wage delivering papers.' Clear agreement from the assembly. 'As you will know, Mr Hopkins is not a local man.' Grumbles of disapproval. 'This may account for him wanting to sell his shop to Roger Nash-Thomas.' Low growls. 'Most of us know about that man. He is trying to take over this town. He already has half-shares in the grocery and the chip shop. I wouldn't be surprised if he owns the vicar as well.' The congregation tittered. 'His purchase of our newsagency is a step too far. The man has become a threat to our town, and we need to take action. Us deacons will be making plans this week and we'll be asking you lot for help.'

As far as John was concerned, that was a signal to get out, smartish. But as he made ready for a speedy exit, he happened to notice something bulky in Mr Williams' breast pocket: a rectangular, silver-coloured object. It looked just like a mobile phone.

John set out on Monday morning armed, as usual, with the late Mr Hughes' large black umbrella, plus his wellies and yellow mackintosh. But this fine garment did not reach much below his knees, which left his trouser legs vulnerable to soakings, particularly when cars drove fast through puddles. One such vehicle was large and silver and belonged to the headmaster.

'I hate you, Mr Kane,' hissed John, feeling cold water percolate down his trouser legs towards his toes.

'Soggy banana!' shouted a giggly young voice from somewhere behind him. John didn't bother to turn, despite the urge to dislodge the blighter's teeth.

By the time John arrived, dripping, at the school entrance, Ivor Kane was ensconced in his armchair next to his three-bar electric heater, clutching a mug of tea. All John received upon arrival was a stern glance from Dai Pinter. He had planned to change into his shoes in the staffroom, but the caretaker's evil eye persuaded him to swap footwear immediately. This was no small matter, as socks had to be changed as well as footwear. The procedure took a good five minutes and caused much amusement amongst passing pupils. John was embarrassed and exhausted by the time he staggered into the men's staffroom two minutes before assembly.

'Aha!' exclaimed Alexander Pritchard after draining the last of his coffee. 'We thought maybe you'd done a bunk.'

Nearby gents chuckled. 'No one would blame you, lad,' one remarked.

'I had to change. The headmaster accidentally soaked me as he drove past,' said John.

'Accidentally?' queried Alexander with a wicked grin.

'Are you saying it was deliberate?'

'Don't take it personally. He hates all his staff. All the men, anyway. But this is no time for small talk. We must assemble.'

John dutifully followed Alexander into the hall and took a position on one of the tube-framed canvas chairs. The ladies' chairs were lined up opposite them, and John was reminded of teenage discos before the music started. Though few of those now seated looked capable of jiving.

One who might have been, Mrs Betty Wontsmey, was seated in a position directly facing John. In defiance of the inclement weather, she was sporting blue Capri pants and a shiny white t-shirt which provided a focal point for all male eyes. Mr Kane was not exempt from the lure of lurex and stumbled over the hymns and announcements. But Mrs Wontsmey only had eyes for the newcomer. Which might have explained Ivor Kane's unexpected announcement at the end of assembly.

'This lunchtime,' he growled, 'the first session of the Nature Club will take place. It will be led by Mr Simmonds, the new biology teacher. We are hoping for a high turnout. Meetings will continue every Wednesday until the Christmas holidays.'

Back in the staffroom Alexander Pritchard chuckled contentedly at his younger colleague.

'That's what comes of being young and presentable,' he said. 'Our esteemed head is jealous.'

'Not the desired outcome, Alexander,' John responded, clutching his head in exasperation.

'You should feel honoured. Old Kane is generally far too unimaginative to come up with a revenge strategy like a nature club. You have stimulated what's left of his grey matter.'

'I wish I hadn't. This club will use up a precious lunch hour.'

'It might raise the profile of your subject. Bring you more A Level students.'

John sighed. 'Look, Alexander, I want to be clear about Mrs Wontsmey. I didn't encourage her, and I don't want anyone to think there's anything between us.'

'No need to explain, my boy. We all understand. She'll move on when a new man joins the staff. Though that may not be for some time.'

The first lesson of the day was with the Lower Sixth, all five of them. Sixth-form teaching is often considered by teachers to be a perk, a calm oasis in a storm-tossed sea of lower school hordes. But like most things in Trecadno, the Lower Sixth was atypical. The first of the five that entered the lab that morning was a squat, malicious-looking boy called Dan, whose remarkably thick neck had earned him a pivotal role in the scrum of the Wanderers' rugby team. This gave him near-sacred status in the school, and indeed throughout Trecadno – a status no one was more aware of than Dan himself. He gave John a greasy, fearless leer as he advanced to the second bench and proceeded to kick a lab stool into his preferred position.

Before John could pluck up the courage to comment on this bit of hooliganism, Alec entered the lab and shuffled to the other end of the bench. He was tall, thin and fragile-looking, with steel-rimmed glasses resting on a thin, beaky nose. Three girls soon followed. Following the general model for Trecadno, Eirwen was short and rotund and couldn't stop talking. By contrast, Denise was bony and somehow covered in a film of adolescent grease. But Aimeé was a young version of Mrs Wontsmey. John was well-aware of the danger posed by the girl and made a point of looking down at his notes whenever she entered the room.

'Right,' he announced, when all the shuffling had ceased. 'This morning we're going to look at lipids.' Dan, who was leaning far back on his stool, glanced towards Eirwen's expansive rear and smirked. 'Who can tell me what simple lipids are composed of?' continued John, trying to look encouraging. Silence reigned. 'You should have covered this last year,' he insisted.

Aimeé condescended to tilt her eyes towards John. 'They're oils, aren't they?' she purred, adding a 'Sir' as an afterthought.

'That's right,' John replied. 'Oils are a form of lipids. So, er, class: what are oils made of? Indeed, what are all lipids made of?'

He looked at Dan, who sniffed. 'I don' know, do I?' he replied, looking very bored.

'Obviously not,' John retorted. He looked around, stopping at Alec, though without much hope. 'Anyone?'

'Carbon, sir,' said Alec.

'Well, yes, all organic molecules contain carbon.' He sighed and picked up a piece of chalk. 'You'd better get your files out. Put a heading "Lipids" and copy the following...'

It was Year Eight after break. There were twenty-seven of them. John got them labelling pictures of cells that he'd made on the ancient Banda copying machine in the staffroom. As he perambulated between the scribbling pupils, removing sweets and stopping fights, he tried to come up with ideas for the Nature Club imposed on him by the head. On a dry day he could have led a sedate walk through the school grounds, identifying flowers and birds. If the contents of the biology lab's specimen pots had not been so decomposed, he could have passed them around with a view to promoting fascination, fear, and possibly identification. No other ideas presented themselves by the time the lesson ended. The relief of watching the last Year Eight pupils leaving the room was tempered by the thought of the influx to come. Though it also occurred to him that no one might turn up. After all, to many pupils, a school club was the naffist thing imaginable. Even malleable Year Sevens would surely prefer to dawdle over their lunches than endure further incarceration in his laboratory.

Unbeknown to John, several Year Sevens had already been rounded up and press-ganged into attending. No sooner had the last Year Eight plodded out, than small disruptive faces started to cluster at the glass panel in the lab door, causing it to steam up. John let them in, knowing that he had no more than five minutes to think up something. He could call it the 'Inaugural Meeting', thereby excusing himself from having anything to talk about. He'd ask them for ideas, and if they couldn't come up with any, which was highly likely, he'd send a child to Alexander. He might just swing it for him to borrow the TV and video from the ladies' staffroom.

The little blighters started to settle. Two of them were in his tutor group. He smiled at them, and one gave him a gormless grin in return. The other seemed to take it as a cue for disappearing out of sight below the bench. John cleared his throat.

'Well, now everyone,' he began. 'Well, now... yes. Today, as you know, we are having the first meeting of the Nature Club. I want to emphasise that the purpose of this club is not for me to teach you more biology...' This was a popular sentiment. '...but to give you all a broader and richer experience of nature. This is *your* club. It is for *you* to decide what you'd like to do in it.' The pupils stared at him. This line, coming from a teacher, was eminently untrustworthy. 'So,' he continued, 'what sort of things would you like to do in *your* Nature Club?'

The silence was slowly broken by muffled comments passing between pupils, followed by giggles, general laughter, and eventually intense noise. In the commotion, at first John didn't notice the laboratory door opening. He scrambled for an excuse to explain how slapping each other, shouting, and exploring the cupboards was all part of the Nature Club agenda.

Fortunately, the visitor was not Mrs Perrig but Betty Wontsmey. She breezed in, swinging a small basket on her delightful hip.

'I'm so sorry to be late,' she said. 'Year Nine girls take an absolute age to boil their tea-towels.'

'Oh?'

'I've brought you lunch, John. I mean, Mr Simmonds. And I've brought back your torch.'

'Oh yes! Thank goodness.'

'I knew the Nature Club would stop you getting down to the refectory,' Mrs Wontsmey continued. 'Old Ivor was a bit mean, wasn't he?'

'Ivor?'

'The headmaster.'

'Oh, right. Yes, very mean.'

'I hope you like pizza.'

'Certainly.' John couldn't stop his eyes veering towards the front of her t-shirt. 'Though I may not manage to enjoy it with this lot in attendance.' He reluctantly shifted his gaze to the assembled throng.

'What are you going to do with them?' asked Betty.

'Search me. I've had no time to plan anything, and it's much too wet to venture outside. I asked them for ideas. They don't have any.'

Betty flashed a confident smirk at him and sidled over to a cupboard that he'd never even noticed. To his amazement, she withdrew a sheaf of crisp white paper, and a box of perfect pencils.

'Tell them to draw their favourite pet,' she suggested, and with some precision pelted a piece of chalk at the biggest boy in the room. He yelped, then silence fell, and John was able to issue instructions. Chatter soon recommenced, but that didn't matter to John. The kids were occupied, and he wouldn't go hungry.

Betty cleared a space on the teacher's desk and removed two large blue china plates from her basket, on which she placed pizza, *vol-au-vents* and celery sticks. Last out of the basket were two blue china cups and a bottle of Ribena, which she proceeded to pour. John watched her, bemused.

'Don't you need to dilute that?' he asked.

'Taste it and see,' said Betty slyly.

John took a gulp of a rather good shiraz. 'We can't drink this, Betty!'

'Why ever not? It's one of our best.'

'I don't doubt it,' he said, lowering his voice, 'but we can't drink alcohol in school. Especially not with lessons this afternoon.'

'A cupful isn't going to make any difference.'

'I suppose not.'

He popped a *vol-au-vent* into his mouth. She beamed at him.

By half-past one the Nature Club had been dismissed, but Betty and John remained seated at the teacher's dais. Somehow their cups were still full and their seats quite close together. A child listening at the door, of which there were several, might have heard whispers and giggling. An older, bolder child peeping in through the little window, of which there were three, might have noticed smiling and the occasional brush of leg against leg. Indeed, anyone over the age of fifteen would have concluded that this intimate lunch was tempting fate.

At twenty-to-two, John's Year Seven tutor group was still in the corridor outside the biol lab waiting to be invited in for afternoon registration. It was possible to get away with philandering in Trecadno High School, and certainly boozing, but it was considered a major sin for pupils to clutter up corridors. John's negligence was duly noted by the head of science, who entered the laboratory with her usual force.

'What on earth do you think you are up to, Mr Simmonds?'

John dropped his cup on the floor and started to whimper the beginnings of an excuse. Fortunately, Mrs Wontsmey was neither as addled nor as fearful as her companion.

'Mrs Perrig!' she exclaimed with a very broad and very false smile. 'How nice to see you!'

Mrs Perrig's expression hardened yet further. 'What are *you* doing here?'

'Mr Simmonds was running his Nature Club this lunchtime. He would have missed lunch if I hadn't brought him something.'

'Very good it was, too,' interjected John, finding a little resolve as he put a piece of broken cup into Betty's basket.

'We were just finishing off the last bits,' Betty said. 'It seemed a pity to throw them. We were just tidying up when you came in.'

Mrs Perrig scowled viciously at both of them. 'Next time you decide to have one of these so-called Nature Club sessions, you are to ask my permission.'

'The Nature Club was the headmaster's idea. His instruction, in fact,' said John. 'Don't you remember what he said this morning?'

Behind her impenetrable lenses, Mrs Perrig narrowed her eyes. She looked down at the broken cup, then up to Betty's fulsome chest. 'I recall what the headmaster said. There was no reference to members of staff of the opposite sex partaking of a private lunch with what, if I'm not mistaken, is an alcoholic beverage.'

'You can't criticise us for that,' said John, displaying far more courage than was good for him. 'I mean, what about Mr Burrows-Morgan?'

'Mr Simmonds!' exclaimed Mrs Perrig. 'I think you should look to yourself before trying to pass blame on to others.'

'I wasn't passing blame.'

'Frankly, I didn't expect this of you.'

'But it's not as if we've been—'

'Been what, Mr Simmonds? What have you not been doing?' Muted giggles were heard from the other side of the lab door, and John felt his cheeks heating up.

Betty gathered up her things. 'I must go,' she said.

'Indeed you must,' retorted Mrs Perrig. 'And you, Mr Simmonds, must see to your poor pupils, who have been left to wait while you two enjoy yourselves. I will definitely be discussing this episode with the headmaster.'

'Ah,' muttered John, the fight leaving him.

'Goodbye,' said Betty sweetly, as she made a swift exit.

The afternoon passed in a hot and stressful haze of giggles and badly drawn diagrams. Half-past three eventually arrived, and the last Year Nine left the lab. John slumped onto the teacher's desk and cradled his head on his arms like a mixed infant. He stayed thus for some minutes as the school grew slowly quiet, hoping his brain would empty itself of the dross of the day. This recumbence was remarkably relaxing, and John decided he should aim to repeat it in a more comfortable place. The trouble was, he couldn't think of one. Betty Wontsmey's expansive bed, perhaps. He was still mulling this over when Alexander put his head around the door.

'Busy day, eh?' he asked with a mix of pity and sarcasm.

'Yeah,' responded John, barely moving a muscle. 'Please tell me something, Alexander. How exactly does one become happy in this town?'

Mr Pritchard nodded knowingly. 'Just the same as anywhere else, my boy,' he said. 'Find the company of some like-minded people and engineer your circumstances to suit yourself.'

'Just like that?'

'It's never easy in a new area. But if you like the *feel* of the place – the little streets, the hills and the rivers – then the rest will follow in time. Look at me, I'm an immigrant here, too.'

'From ten miles away?'

'That makes no difference. If you're not from Trecadno then you're from "away".'

'I bet Mrs Perrig doesn't pick on you.'

'She'll come round. She's just doing to you what she does to her new classes.'

'Terrify them, you mean?'

'Pretty much.'

John sighed and started to remove his shoes.

'Are you changing into your Wellington boots here?' inquired Alexander. 'Dai won't be happy if he sees you.'

'Tough,' replied John.

Stryd y Dyfrgi was quiet as John clomped along it, looking like a lost fisherman. The rain had given way to low cloud that blanketed and muffled the grey street, making him feel even more lonesome and dejected. He hurried as best he could in his wellies, sticking to the centre of the narrow, pavement-less road to avoid the rivers of rainwater at its edges.

As he passed the first of the ash trees, a pair of large green smiling eyes appeared out of the mirk directly in front of him. They were at about the level of his knees and moved towards the edge of the road, into the trees. John tentatively followed, and slowly advanced into the grove, the green eyes beaming at him all the while like strange torches. After a little while they flickered and disappeared. John paused, perplexed, and leant against a tree. Had he just seen an unusually bold fox, or was his weary brain playing tricks on him? He was just about to head back onto the road when headlights appeared from nowhere, and a huge soundless car sped up the lane. If John had remained in the middle of the road, he would have certainly been run over. Was it possible that the fox had guided him out of the path of the hurtling limo?

CHAPTER NINE

Back and Forth to the WC

How can one adequately describe the feelings experienced by the average teacher at half-past three on a Friday afternoon? Think of a prisoner reaching the last day of his sentence, or a seedling germinating from subterranean darkness into light. Expressions of sheer joy brightened the faces of pupils and teachers alike as they fled from Trecadno High School at three-thirty on Friday afternoon. A whole weekend of peace, chips and alcohol stretched ahead.

John did not run, nor did he beam with unbridled bliss. As far as he was concerned, he was swapping a prison with kids for a prison with rosebuds. Both could be avoided at the Wanderers' Club, but even that was not without its problems – chiefly the Wontsmeys. He decided to calm his troubled brow by dawdling near the pharmacy. If it was open, he'd manufacture a headache and seek advice. He was bound to have a headache soon, that was for sure.

On reaching the square, he headed for the side opposite Chapel View Guest House, hoping that Mrs Lavinia Hughes wasn't on sentry duty (fortunately for him, Mrs Hughes had a penchant for Cary Grant and *North by Northwest* was on TV). He took a shortcut into Terras y Ffwlbart, and through the large windows of the chip shop he noticed Phyllis Dunn chopping potatoes. It would be a couple of hours yet before the air was filled with the fumes of hot oil and vinegar, but John thought he could smell them. He could almost feel pieces of hot, greasy potato between his fingers and could almost taste salty, fluffy potato. Even after all his years of tapas and tagliatelle in North London, only a huge bag of chips, freshly fried, could satisfy the inner man.

Turning into Lôn y Gwenci, John saw that a large black car was parked outside the pharmacy – the same sort of car that had nearly run him over at the start of the week. Who in Trecadno might own such a car, and who would be foolish enough to park it in such a narrow road? He approached slowly and peered through the dusty pharmacy window. Two figures stood beneath the shop's single lightbulb. One was Elisabeth-Mai, and the other was a smart, stocky man with dark suit and hair. The man took Elisabeth-Mai in his arms and kissed her. On the lips. With passion.

John took a step back, and then another. Could it be true? Was the only attractive, unattached woman in Trecadno already in a relationship? If so, why had she asked him to join her on a walk? Was she a tease? Was his pent-up lust to be wasted, blown away, like the withered oak leaves that rolled down Trecadno's desolate streets? He crossed to the other side of the road and stood immobile, staring at the window. After a little while he began to walk away, though unfortunately in the wrong direction. It wasn't until he reached the cobbler's shop that he realised his mistake. He stopped, rubbed his head and looked up at the sky as if in supplication.

'Hey! You lost, boy?' called the cobbler, sticking his head out of the door.

John turned to him in confusion. 'Pardon?'

'You look lost, boy.'

They both turned at the sound of footfall. The smart man left the pharmacy and got into his fancy car which barely made a sound as it accelerated out of Lôn y Gwenci.

'Bloody nice motor that,' said Emyr Williams. 'Don' see many like that around here.'

'Do you know who owns it?'

Silly question. Of course Emyr knew. 'Penymynydd chap.'

'A professional man?'

'Him? He's a bloody tosser, that's what he is.'

'Pardon?'

Mr Emyr Williams sniffed. 'It's Nash-Thomas.'

John's face blanched. 'But surely Elisabeth-Mai wouldn't have anything to do with him?'

'She got to sell medicines to people if they need them, even 'im.'

He clearly didn't know about the relationship, John decided. Was it a new development? A fragile link that could easily be broken?

'That man's been goin' in there a lot recently,' continued the cobbler. 'Must be something wrong with him.'

John set off again, kicking the odd stone like a chastised schoolboy. He didn't want to go back to Chapel View, for his malaise would be noticed and he would be mercilessly quizzed. As it happened, he was still heading in the wrong direction and hence soon came upon the Brush and Mask. Despite the warm glow in the window, John hesitated at the door. The place looked like a large version of Mrs Lavinia Hughes' house. Indeed, when he eventually plucked up the courage to go in, he found himself in a small hallway that seemed a replica of Chapel View's. Even the stair carpet was the same. He was about to leave when he spotted a bar with pumps and optics and noticed an inviting fireplace. John advanced on it with relief and removed his mackintosh and wellies. Unnoticed and unmolested by barmen, drinkers, cobblers, or heads of science, he sank into a large, soft-cushioned armchair next to the fire and closed his eyes.

'D'you want a drink?' asked a dislocated voice sometime later.

'Whiskey,' mumbled John. Prising open his eyes, he saw a bulky figure shuffling towards the bar.

'Doc Jones!' he called. 'I thought you frequented the Wanderers' Club.'

'I spread myself around.'

John rubbed his eyes and looked up at the wall clock. It was nearly six o'clock. 'Don't you have an evening surgery?' he asked.

'Got a locum to do that,' Doc Jones replied, removing his pipe from a pocket. 'She'll do tomorrow morning's surgery, too. I like a good Friday night.'

'Your poor locum won't be able to have a good night.'

'That's not a problem for her. She's an Evangelist. I only take on Evangelists or Muslims.'

'What?'

'Buck up, boy. They don't drink, do they?' Doc Jones proceeded to prove that he belonged to neither sect by taking a large mouthful of whiskey. He put his glass down and gave John a fatherly grin. 'How are you, anyway?'

'Could be better, Doc.'

Dr Daniel Jones gave a sympathetic nod. 'Is it the job?'

'It's not what I thought it would be. It's an odd school. Odd and static. With little cooperation. And no energy. No feeling of progress.'

'Hmm.'

'In fact, I'd say progress is discouraged. I mean, look at the deputy head!'

The doctor puffed on his pipe. 'I see what you mean. But you have energy, John. You can make things happen.'

'I'm not sure how.'

'Any other issues? Is Chapel View *very* grim?'

John sighed. 'Even in my student days I would have been laughed at if I'd lived the way I do now. I must find somewhere else.'

'And what about your social life?' the doc asked with a sly sideways glance. 'Maybe you don't have enough young company.' John felt a blush creeping up his neck. 'You need some people with more energy than Alexander and I.'

'Don't be silly. I mean—'

'It's not silly,' the Doc interjected between puffs. 'A man needs a companion.'

John sniffed pathetically. 'It would be nice.'

'Like Elisabeth-Mai?' suggested the doctor quietly without removing his pipe.

John's blush intensified and rose over his chin. 'She's a very attractive lady,' he said, doing his best to look unperturbed. 'But I believe she's already attached.'

'Females can be fickle. As our esteemed deacon is fond of reminding us. Give it time.'

'The first time I saw her was inside Moriah Chapel,' John said, all dejection, 'Mr Williams' son was standing next to me. He told me that I shouldn't bother with her. He was right.'

'Faint heart never won fair maiden.'

'Another quotation, Doc?'

'Ask the Know-All. Seriously, though, I'm sure Elisabeth-Mai welcomes attention as much as any of us.'

'She's getting plenty of that at the moment. From a spiv with a dangerous car.'

'Hmm.'

'But you probably knew that.'

'Well...'

John clenched his glass to his chest, his chin jutting out in indignation. 'How could she even consider dating the man who's buying out Hopkins the newsagent?'

Doc Jones removed his pipe from his mouth and rubbed his bald head. 'What can I say? Don't give up. Though there *are* plenty more fish in the sea.'

'But I'm not fishing in a *sea*, am I?' replied John. 'I'm groping around in a small, stagnant pool.'

'Come now...'

'You asked, Doc. You brought up the issue of "young company". Well, I haven't got any, have I? God, I don't know what possessed me to come here. I should have gone to Cardiff or Birmingham. Anywhere that has more to it than a chapel, a chip shop and an abandoned newsagent's.'

'But you did come here,' responded the Doc, smiling benignly. 'Perhaps your Welsh ancestors called to you.'

John gave a sarcastic laugh. 'They must like a joke, my ancestors.'

'Seriously, don't despair. Things might change with Elisabeth-Mai, and you're doing well at the school. You'd be missed if you left.'

'Would I?'

'For sure.' The doctor drained the last dregs of amber liquid from his glass and put it on the table with a clatter.

A small man with very red hair and very blue eyes appeared at the bar.

'Another one, Doc?'

'No, Raymond. Got to go.' He stood up and grinned at John in a fatherly way. 'Mr Simmonds here also has to leave.'

'Do I?'

'Time for the WC.'

'Sorry?'

'The WC. The Wanderers' Club. The quiz will be starting before long.'

The low cloud had lifted, and as the two men walked out of the pub some nervous sunbeams found their way from the western sky.

'Look, John! A fine sunset. That's a good sign.'

'Is it?'

'Maybe we'll have a dry day tomorrow.'

'Elisabeth-Mai said it would rain.'

'Did she? It will, then. Shame.'

John stopped and sniffed the air. 'Chips,' he said, thoughtfully.

'Oh dear,' said the doctor, shaking his head, as if he had just diagnosed something deeply pernicious. 'The economy of large parts of Wales is based on seducing people with vinegar.'

'Maybe. But you can't beat chips if you're starving. And I am. I haven't been back to Chapel View yet.'

'They do basket meals at the WC.'

'Too risky, Doc. I'm going for chips. I'll join you later.'

John went to the trusty old well to eat his chips once again. As he was crumpling up his chip paper, Alexander Pritchard sauntered past.

'Hello again! Were you waiting for me?'

'For you? Oh, for quiz night, you mean?'

'Of course. Come on, my boy. We don't want to be late.'

They were just turning into Lôn y Bele when they heard the booming call of Mr William Williams some distance behind them.

'He's even later than we are,' said Alexander, waving back. 'Come along, John. I don't fancy being preached at.' He turned and cupped his hands back at the deacon. 'See you there, William.'

Behind the deacon, in the darkening town, John noticed little flickering lights appearing, one by one, in upstairs windows. And in the shadows, a large fox stood guard.

The hall was packed by the time they arrived at the Wanderers' Club, and the visiting team had started to assemble on the stage. Even Andy was there, much to John's relief. He hadn't fancied another cross-examination. Doc Jones was on the stage talking to a member of the opposite team, which happened to comprise of medical personnel from the cottage hospital at Penymynydd.

John found the last vacant barstool and ordered a beer, looking forward to an evening of alcoholic oblivion. William Williams sidled up and peered over his shoulder.

'I see you're overindulging again, boy.'

'Yes. I am.'

'I am very shocked.' He turned to address the barman. 'Two doubles over here, Maldwyn, there's a good boy.'

A thin man with touched-up hair approached the deacon. 'Mr Williams,' he began with an accent that was trying very hard to sound English. 'Leaves from the trees around your chapel are blowing all over our churchyard.'

'Well! If it's not Augustus Phillips!' exclaimed Mr William Williams. 'I thought you were dead.'

The deacon shifted and went into a huddle with his brother at the other end of the bar. They were soon joined by two other men and a small, fat woman whose face was concealed behind the cobbler. Their conversation had an intense, secretive quality, as if something significant was afoot. John was mainly listening to the quiz, to questions on Titian, Stalin, and the atmosphere on Venus. But after a while he thought he might sidle up a bit closer to the deacon's cluster to eavesdrop. He changed his mind, fast, when Emyr Williams moved just enough to reveal the face of the woman in their midst. John was looking straight at the fearful visage of Mrs Evadne Perrig.

He turned his head away so quickly that he became slightly giddy. The sensation was not helped by rapidly downing another whiskey. He sat rigid for a few minutes, expecting at any moment to be set upon by the head of science, or the deacon, cobbler, or all three together. But no one came up to remonstrate or gloat. Had Mrs Perrig dropped her glasses? It was not like her to miss an opportunity to harangue. He considered shuffling off to safer terrain, but there were few other seats. He had no option but to sit tight. It would have been better if he'd gone straight back to Chapel View after school, he reflected. Or perhaps he could have caught a bus home to his mother in Surrey. Though he wouldn't have got any further than Cardiff by supper time. Maybe he should have just got on a bus anyway. Any bus, going anywhere.

He ordered yet another whiskey and tried to think about the following day. He was distracted by a botanical question: 'What is the common name of plants belonging to the genus *Lonicera?*' As he mouthed the word 'honeysuckle' in the general direction of Dr Daniel Jones, his felt a hand on his arm. He looked down to see that it was female. Fortunately, it did not possess the chubby yet vice-like fingers of Mrs Evadne Perrig. These were slim and tanned and tipped with silver nails.

'Hello, Betty!' John said. He should have stopped there, but the fact that she wasn't Mrs Perrig made him gush. 'I'm really pleased to see you.'

'Are you, John? I'm so glad.' Her eyelashes fluttered at him slowly, like the heavy wings of an exotic moth. John sensed trouble.

'Would you like a drink?' he inquired, staring down at her velvet-clad legs.

'That would be lovely,' she replied. 'But not yet. I hoped you'd be able to come over to the house and look at a book catalogue.'

'Sorry?'

'A catalogue for biological books. I want to buy a good botany book for Andy's birthday. He sometimes has to draw plants; I thought it would help.'

'Oh. Right.'

'I know you're an expert in botany.'

'I'm hardly—'

'Will you come, John?'

'Now?'

'Now would be best, while Andy is busy with the quiz.

I want his present to be a surprise...'

A large purple orb lit the hall at the Wontsmey residence. It was designed to induce relaxation, no doubt, but John was reminded of a beacon, the sort that warn a populace of pending doom.

'Come this way.' Betty pointed in the direction of the lounge, where the lamps were red and the air fuggy with joss stick smoke. 'Sit down,' she instructed, pointing at a red leather sofa. She disappeared momentarily to put on some music – Donna Summer singing *'I Feel Love'* – and to equip herself with two glasses and a bottle of Merlot.

'That's kind of you, Betty,' John said as she proffered a glass. A bow on her gold lamé top came undone as she leant forward, revealing yet more of her cleavage. 'So, er, where is the catalogue?' he asked, looking around nervously.

'Catalogue?' answered Betty as she sat down beside him.

'The one you mentioned. For biology books.'

'I'll look for it presently.'

'Right.'

Betty leant back onto the sofa, adopting a posture that accentuated her remarkable front.

'What do you think of my outfit?' she asked.

'Lovely. Really nice.'

'It suits me, don't you think? Flatters my figure.'

'Definitely.' He stared at her chest.

She reached out for his free right hand and placed it gently on her left leg. 'This velvet has a lovely texture, don't you think? Soft to the touch.'

'Oh. Yes. Very.'

While nonchalantly sipping her wine, she proceeded to guide his hand towards her inner thigh. 'I really like that, you know, John.'

'Do you?' he groaned.

'Very much. And you?'

Before he had a chance to consider the question, Betty put down her wine glass and began to stroke his right thigh. Both her hands were soon engaged in synchronous rubbing that was not dissimilar to washing clothes on a washboard in days of yore.

'Are you enjoying this, John?' she purred.

Control was ebbing away. 'Err, um…'

'Let me take your glass from you,' she said, doing so with a swift grace. She rapidly found a new position for his left hand underneath her right breast. This was a move too far for gentlemanly restraint, particularly in one so drunk and deprived of female companionship. John leapt forward and planted desperate lips on a choice region of exposed bosom.

'Oh John!' Betty cried in tones of victorious surrender.

'Oh God!' muttered John hoarsely, somewhat affected by the joss sticks, as he tried to unfasten the other bows on the blouse. Alcoholic excess impeded manual dexterity, and by the time Betty's golden garment had come asunder, that lady was well-advanced in her exploration of John's trousers. At the moment of mammary release he emitted a high-pitched 'whoop' – due, in part, to his appreciation of the sight before him, but mainly on account of the firm grip simultaneously applied to a key part of his anatomy. Just as the real action was about to start, the front doorbell rang out.

'Oh-oo…' groaned John.

'Ignore it!' commanded La Wonstmey.

'But Betty,' gasped John, removing his tongue from a nipple, 'what if it's Andy?'

'*He* wouldn't have rung the bell.'

After a couple more knocks, the caller identified himself by yelling through the letterbox.

'Betty!' exclaimed a learned voice. 'Where are you? What have you done with John?'

The pair disentangled.

'Come along!' persisted Alexander Pritchard. 'We need him in the WC for the second half. Your husband has cleared off.'

'I'm drunk,' shouted John, without thinking.

'So long as you can walk, you'll do. Get a move on. We start up again in five minutes.'

Betty's eyes filled with hot tears of humiliation. 'Andy doesn't want me, and now I can't have you either. I so wanted this, John. And now…'

'I'm so sorry, Betty. I also wanted… Yes, well. Look, I'd better go.' He did up his trousers. 'Anyway, what d'you mean about Andy not wanting you?'

'He has Julian, his student.'

'Julian's a boy.'

'Yes.'

'Oh.'

Part of John, the lower half, was devastated by the summons to the WC. But his better parts felt nothing but relief as he hobbled behind the upright figure of the Know-All.

'I hope I didn't interrupt anything, my boy,' Alexander said with a smirk.

'Not much,' John lied. 'All the same, I'm joining you as a pressed man, not a volunteer. Don't expect me to be much help.'

CHAPTER TEN

The Brush & Mask

Teachers often experience strange distortions of time. Each working day seems to drag, interminably, like a lead weight strapped to the neck, and the hands of the classroom clock take an eternity to reach half-past three. But weekends and holidays pass in the blink of an eye. Einstein could have explained it. If anyone ever manages to find a remedy for the phenomenon, they will become very rich and probably be sainted.

October's half-term is one of those joyful, swift to disappear occasions when teachers can pause for breath. John decided that he needed a complete change of air so risked the protracted bus journey to his mother's house in Surrey. He spent most of his holiday week asleep. During his wakeful moments, his mother informed him that he was a fool. According to her, he'd managed to lose a pretty wife with excellent family connections, and in a fit of childish pique had taken himself off to 'a pimple on the backside of beyond', a place she herself had been only too glad to leave. Not only that, he was letting himself be worn down to a shadow of a man. She commanded him to find another job by January. A nice little public school close to home would be good. He could give her his washing and eat her cake, and his favourite beef dinner would be provided every Sunday. Come to that, there was no reason why he shouldn't take himself out of teaching altogether. Mrs Simmonds knew several local councillors who could pull the odd string.

John couldn't deny that he was tempted, *very* tempted, by the notion of a life without recalcitrant children, endless rain, and dour deacons. But his dreams were filled by green hills and bright estuaries, and he bathed in the sunshine of Elisabeth-Mai's smile. Every night the foxes called him.

So, on the Friday at the end of half-term week, John arrived back at Chapel View Guest House. He would normally have found an excuse to escape his landlady, but he was tired from his journey and couldn't cope with quiz night and the perils of the Wontsmeys. Not to mention, another important consideration. Mrs Lavinia Hughes was at last showing signs of agreeing to do his laundry. Negotiations on the issue commenced after dinner in Mrs Hughes' cramped middle room and dragged on for nearly two hours. *From Russia with Love* was on TV at the time, and Mrs Hughes sneaked occasional fond glances at James Bond, the odd drop of saliva dribbling from a corner of her mouth. By the time all villains had been despatched a deal was struck: she would wash and iron John's clothes for an extra £25 a month's rent, and he had to remove all spiders from the bath.

He slept late the following morning, despite getting to bed early the previous night. The nearby drone of a vacuum cleaner eventually roused him, ceasing abruptly the moment he got out of bed. As he washed and shaved, John thought about Elisabeth-Mai. He carried on thinking about her after breakfast as he stretched out on his little bed with his marking. How wonderful it would be if she called to take him on another Saturday afternoon hike. But no visitors turned up to interrupt assessment procedures, or Mrs Lavinia Hughes' baked bean lunch. Nor was John disturbed as he spent the afternoon devising a Year Eleven worksheet on genetic mutations. Though at one point he thought he heard a musical jangle remarkably like the ringtone of a mobile phone.

At five o'clock, Mrs Hughes produced some banana sandwiches and an exceedingly thin slice of currant cake.

'After we've had our tea,' she said, as she stirred the teapot, 'I'll do an hour's worth of ironing to get your shirts out of the way.'

'Thanks.'

'And then I thought we might watch the repeat of *Inspector Morse.*'

John inhaled a crumb of cake and started to cough violently.

'There, there, now,' said Mrs Hughes as she walloped his back. 'You shouldn't eat your food so quick. I'll pour you out another cup of tea.'

That was that. John had to get out.

'I'm afraid I won't be able to join you this evening,' he said on regaining his composure. 'I need to see Mr Pritchard to check on events at school next week.'

Mrs Hughes' face darkened. 'I suppose you'll look for him in the Brush and Mask?'

'Well...'

'Don't you be late. I'll lock the door by ten.'

The afternoon's drizzle had turned into a layer of damp air hovering at chimney level. As John advanced into Heol y Carlwm he noticed a thin plume of smoke rising into this windless stratum and pictured a hearty fire within the Brush and Mask. He was not disappointed. He was also correct about the likely presence of his friends. A bulbous nose turned towards him as he approached the bar.

'Glad to see you back, John,' said Doc Jones cheerily.

'You should have got away while you had the chance,' remarked Alexander Pritchard.

'Maybe a fondness for Trecadno is in your genes?' the

doc suggested.

'My mother and grandmother both left the town, remember?' John said.

'Perhaps they regretted it,' said the doc. 'I certainly did when I absented myself for a few years.'

'You like the countryside around here, don't you?' John remarked. 'You enjoy walking.'

'You wouldn't say so to look at me, would you?' the doctor replied after draining his beer glass.

Raymond appeared on the other side of the bar and peered at the newcomer expectantly.

'What's been happening while I was away?' John asked as he fished around in his pockets for cash.

'The Wontsmeys went to Austria,' replied Alexander. 'Back tomorrow, I believe.'

'You were short-handed on Quiz Night, then?'

'William Williams kindly helped out. At least, he *tried* to help out.'

'Ah.'

'The following day,' added the doc, 'Hopkins shut up his shop for good.'

'No more newspapers in Trecadno, then?'

'Sadly not,' replied Alexander. 'Though periodicals can be sent by post. I have to have my *History Today* every Saturday.'

'It wouldn't actually matter which day you had it,' commented Doc Jones with a grin.

'That's a very old joke,' said Alexander.

'Does anyone know what will replace the newsagent's?' asked John as the next round appeared.

'A hair salon,' said Daniel Jones, fumbling with his pipe. 'It's already set up.'

'Really? Seems a weird choice. Is Roger Nash-Thomas into beauty as well as property?'

'Must have decided to branch out,' said the Know-All.

150

'Surely he won't do well,' suggested John. 'Everyone was so set against Hopkins leaving.'

'There was quite a crowd in there when I passed this morning,' said the doc. 'It's far too tempting for the ladies. They've had to go to Penymynydd for their hairdos up until now.'

'Frailty, thy name is woman yet again, eh?' remarked John. It wasn't a happy thought. For who had proved frailer than his beloved pharmacist? He turned back to his beer.

All contemplations and conversations were cut short as the barroom door opened with a flourish.

'Boys!' cried William Williams, flinging his arms upwards and rolling his eyes. 'Boys! I come with news!'

'Come and sit down,' said the doctor. 'Take the weight off your dramatics.'

'Hey, listen,' growled the deacon, 'this is no dramatics, boy. Discoveries have been made. By damn, they have!'

'What sort of discoveries, William?' questioned Alexander, inspecting him over his steel-rimmed glasses.

'Listen to this: that bastard Nash-Thomas, pardon my French, has not only bought Hopkins' shop and put a bloody hairdresser in it, but he's gone an' bought Arthur James' three fields as well.'

'The fields behind the old pond?' inquired the doctor, interrupting a slurp.

'Them's the ones. And what is more, what is bloody more, the bugger has put in for planning permission for sixty-three eggsecative houses. Sixty-bloody-three!'

'How do you know about the planning permission, William?' inquired the doctor.

The deacon tapped the side of his nose meaningfully.

'So old Hopkins' place was the thin end of the wedge,' said Alexander Pritchard.

'Definite,' agreed the deacon. 'Apparently, he's got an office in the back room of the old newagent's ready for all the paperwork he'll be doing.' His face creased up in disgust.

'Would more houses really be so terrible?' asked John in a moment of rashness. 'I mean, there'll be more children for the school, and more people buying from local businesses. The library would have to be expanded, and there might be call for restaurants and shops. Even a small theatre, maybe.'

'A theatre?' boomed the deacon in disbelief. 'What planet are you on, boy? Houses this bugger is building. Breezeblock boxes with tiny rooms an' hundreds of toilets! *We* won't be able to afford 'em. For bloody eggsecatives, they are. They'll put pressure on the refuse services and the drains. An' as for local businesses doin' well out of it, you can bloody well forget that. The sort who'll buy 'em will have huge cars for driving miles to supermarkets, and they'll use that bloody Internet thing to order their clothes from France or somewhere. An' most of their little brats will be driven off every morning to bloody Bashford's.'

'The local public school,' whispered Alexander into John's ear. 'Not particularly good.'

John hid his face in his beer glass.

'Tell me, William,' inquired the doc, 'if Nash-Thomas has only just bought the fields, how come he's already submitted building plans?'

'How come? Cos he's bloody devious, that's how,' declared the deacon.

'But William,' added Alexander, 'just because he's put in for planning permission, it doesn't mean he'll *get* it.'

'He's gone to county level. He's gone to a level where *he* has influence and *I* don't.'

All were momentarily oppressed by the notion that there might be some plane of existence over which the deacon had no control. But one definite merit of alcohol is its capacity to make one forget, and so the baleful mood did not persist. By the time he'd finished his first pint, the

152

deacon had removed his black mackintosh, and re-gained his usual form.

'Well, boys, we must not let the bugger get away with it. We must act!'

Daniel Jones shot him a glance that the deacon chose to ignore.

'I will be convening a meeting about the situation after the service tomorrow morning. I expect everyone to be there.'

Mrs Lavinia Hughes made sure that John didn't miss the meeting at Moriah Chapel, even though – indeed, probably because – he had only just managed to return home before curfew time the previous night. He didn't mind too much. For a start, he'd had an extra hour's sleep as a result of Trecadno having been restored to Greenwich Mean Time. He was also interested to see how Trecadno's residents would respond to the news about the housing development. He was particularly keen to see Elisabeth-Mai's reaction. He was sure she wouldn't continue a relationship with Nash-Thomas in the circumstances.

Once again he had to sit through a chapel service while squashed between bulky ladies. The ordeal was worsened by the extreme length of mini-Hitler's rant and the unexpected absence of his beloved. At least the hymns were short, and he was soon in the vestry. Mrs Lavinia Hughes had control of the tea urn and smirked proudly as she handed out beakers of tea hot enough to cause blisters.

In due course, Mr William Williams appeared clutching a Bible. His spectacles glinted malevolently at the assemblage in an expectation of silence, and Mrs Hughes rushed away from her urn.

'I have called this meeting to discuss what to do about Roger Nash-Thomas,' said the deacon, clasping the Good Book to his bosom. 'Not long ago we were gathered here

153

to discuss the possible loss of our newsagent's shop. Brothers and sisters in the Lord, we were right to worry!' His audience brayed in agreement. 'Roger Nash-Thomas bought the place and turned it into a den of vanity!' He stared accusingly at Mrs Hughes' remarkably tight curls, causing her to squirm. 'Now we learn that he has purchased three fields from Arthur James. He told Arthur that he was going to put his horses in 'em, and Arthur, being a few sandwiches short of a picnic, believed him!' Giggles and murmurs of assent. 'Nash-Thomas has already put in planning permission for houses on those fields. Sixty-three so-called eggsecative houses.' The audience emitted sighs of despair. 'My friends, we cannot let this happen. We slipped up over the newsagents…' He glared at someone near the back of the room. '…But we cannot, must not, slip up over this.' He put the Bible down on the table behind him and clutched his shiny lapels. 'We are going to have a campaign.' Rumblings of approval. 'A Campaign to Undermine Nash-Thomas.' This caused such spluttering amongst the younger members of the congregation that Idwal Williams' illicit chewing gum landed on Phyllis Dunn's best hat.

John, trying to be helpful, cleared his throat and raised his hand. 'Mr Williams, may I suggest the "Campaign to Save Trecadno"? That might be more persuasive in council meetings.'

'If you say so, boy,' retorted the deacon, baffled. 'And seeing as you are so well-informed, Mr Simmonds, I'm appointing you as "seccatarry" for the campaign.'

John froze. Why on earth had he opened his mouth?

'You can write letters for us,' continued the deacon. 'You can write to the county council and the, er, RS and VP. You lot must all do your part as well. Find as many people as possible; go forth and euthanise.'

'Enthuse,' said a voice from the back.

'That as well. An' don' forget to write to the local MP. What's the bugger's name?' Someone shouted a name. Someone else disagreed. At least three names were bandied about. 'All right,' announced the deacon eventually, 'our new seccatarry will find out about the MP. And when he does, we *all* got to write to him.'

'Or her!' declared a female voice.

'But one thing we will *not* be doing – I repeat, *not* – is stepping inside Nash-Thomas' wicked hair-setting establishment!'

Several people approached John with words of support and commendation as the congregation departed. Despite dreading his new task, he felt a glow of appreciation. He was becoming accepted within the community; he was earning respect. How wonderful it would be if he could have the same effect on his pupils! Even better was the sight of Elisabeth-Mai, who had materialised behind a cluster of large ladies.

'It's going to be a very busy week for you,' she said, when he eventually reached her.

'Very busy. Lesson preparation, and now the campaign as well.'

'Perhaps I could help with some of the letters.'

'That would be wonderful!'

'You do agree with the campaign, don't you?' inquired Elisabeth-Mai. 'You do support our cause?'

'Certainly.'

'I know you've been here for less than two months, but hopefully you can see how Trecadno depends on rurality.'

'I think it would be dreadful to spoil the place. It's so very quaint.'

Elisabeth-Mai's expression became thunderous. '*Quaint*, did you say?'

'Er…'

'You think we're *quaint*, do you?'

'Well …'

'You think this town is a sleepy throwback to an age of English lords and Welsh yokels, I suppose? A discarded piece of history?'

'Er, no. I just…'

Her voice became quiet. 'You'll see how damn *quaint* we are when Halloween comes.'

She marched towards the vestry door. John hurriedly followed.

'Elisabeth-Mai!' he called after her as she proceeded down the chapel steps. 'Do you feel like a walk this afternoon?'

'No,' she hissed, and headed out of the square with her usual high velocity. John plodded back to Chapel View with his tail between his legs like an unloved Labrador.

Mrs Lavinia Hughes had prepared Sunday dinner well in advance. Perhaps too well in advance. The vegetables had been swimming in their saucepan since seven that morning, and Mrs Hughes' attempt to revive them in a hot oven after the service just added crusty edges to the otherwise pulpy mass. They were served up with two shrunken, over-cooked chops, and John pitied the poor lambs that had been sacrificed to produce such fare. The gravy accompanying these offerings had looked decent enough when made, but overnight a black skin had formed at the surface of the saucepan and a gelatinous mass coagulated at its base. Mrs Hughes' attempts to reconstitute this sludge resulted in a gravy with two distinct populations of lumps, neither of which improved her dinner. John forked all this into his mouth, helpless in the face of his landlady's relentless banter, and fully cognisant of the indigestion to come.

After dinner, John declined an invitation to watch Rock Hudson attempt to kiss Doris Day and slunk off upstairs.

He flopped down on the rose-covered bed, hoping to sink into sleep. It was not to be. Thoughts rushed into his forebrain: what classes did he have the following morning? Would he find all the necessary materials for his starch-breakdown practical with Year Nine? Where had he put the instruction sheet he'd written? Could he dodge Betty for another week? What about his new secretarial role?

But more pressing than all these questions were those about Elisabeth-Mai. Did she like him or didn't she, and what on earth had she meant by her reference to Halloween?

CHAPTER ELEVEN

The Campaign

Having had a whole week of getting up at lunchtime, it might have been expected that Trecadno's youth would be happy and compliant on the Monday after half-term. This assumption had prompted John to organise a practical class for form 9F immediately after assembly. He got into work early that morning, on account of Mrs Lavinia Hughes' 6am pacing, and an amazing lack of rain. After much searching in the dusty prep room, he found starch, iodine, and some powdered amylase that he hoped might retain a little enzymatic activity despite its advanced age. He had assembled dimpled tiles, pipettes and test-tubes, and even found four stop-clocks that worked. And all this before assembly, too. It would have been just wonderful if Mrs Perrig had decided to patrol her empire at this point. She would have found nothing to criticise. She might even have uttered some words of grudging praise for John's dedication and organisational skills.

In the event, the head of science appeared just as 9F's lesson was ending. She was thus able to observe the almighty rush from the lab as the break-time bell rang out. She also noted unwashed apparatus spread over bench-tops and several broken pipettes. There was no sign of John. Mrs Perrig had just decided he must be cowering in the prep room when she heard the sound of rubbing from the back of the lab. The new biology master was on his knees scrubbing iodine off grey linoleum with the aid of paper towels and an ancient can of Vim.

'It's like the Somme in here,' declared the head of science.

'Good morning, Mrs Perrig,' John mumbled, defeat writ large upon his weary face. 'I'm sorry about the mess.'

'It is inexcusable, Mr Simmonds.'

'I overestimated the ability of 9F to follow instructions,' he replied.

'Which shows that your judgement is sadly lacking.'

'Mrs Perrig,' he responded, slowly getting to his feet, 'I have taught in comprehensive schools in inner London. I have taught children who barely understand a word of English, children with learning deficiencies, and children from deprived and difficult backgrounds. I have never seen such a bunch of opportunistic criminals as the pupils who have just left this laboratory.'

Mrs Perrig snorted. 'You need to make more of an effort to understand your students. You have to be intuitive in small schools like this. You have to earn respect.'

John sighed and looked at his iodine-stained hands. 'I think I will have to stop giving practical classes.'

'Until you know what you're doing, I would agree.'

'Gosh,' muttered John under his breath.

'I'll let you know when we get a quote for the lino.'

'Sorry?'

'What it will cost you to replace the despoiled floor covering.'

'Now just hang on…' began John, but Mrs Perrig was already on her way out.

There was no time for a much-needed coffee, nor any sustaining banter with Alexander Pritchard. John had only just cleared away the dirty apparatus and removed the last bit of Vim from his nearly raw fingers when the Lower Sixth turned up. They were early for a change, as if tipped off about his unhappy state. Aimeé came in first. She dumped her floral bag on the front bench and leant back on a lab stool until her shoulders almost touched the bench behind. As usual, she was chewing gum and making no effort to hide the fact. Her long blonde hair was not remotely tied back as per school regulations, which were also contravened by her abundance of ear jewellery.

'Mr Simmonds,' drawled this Lolita, 'can I ask you something?'

'Yes, of course,' replied John as he seated himself in front of the blackboard, simultaneously striving, but failing, to throw a crumpled paper towel into the litter bin. 'My mother says you are wrong about "fitness",' Aimeé said, looking smarmy.

'Oh?' He was not really surprised. Since coming to Trecadno he'd been wrong about most things.

'According to my mother,' continued the little siren, '"fitness" is all about reproduction, and not about how physically fit something is, like you said.'

'And may I ask how your mother knows this?' asked John.

'She's got a PhD in biology. She's a lecturer at Swansea University.'

'Ah,' responded John, wondering how such expertise could lurk amongst the huddled terraces of Trecadno. 'Evolution depends on reproduction. So, when talking about 'survival of the fittest', it is quite correct to include reproduction, as your mother says, and not just things like running ability and so forth.'

'That's not what you said before half-term,' persisted Aimeé.

'No? Perhaps I was a bit rushed.'

Aimeé let her stool spring forward and flung a skein of golden hair over her shoulder in a gesture of vindication.

'Sir!' shouted Dan from the second bench, before John

had a chance to gather himself and begin the lesson. 'Sir, any chance of prac today? For a change, like?'

John looked at his pupil the way a weary cow might survey a buzzing bluebottle. 'No,' he sighed, and opened the textbook in front of him as calmly as he could. He was beginning to understand why his predecessor had spent so much time in the prep room in the company of fungi.

The next hour and a half somehow elapsed without mishap, aided by several tricky past paper questions and a video about Darwin, one of the resources procured from the deputy head by means of alcoholic bribery. It was a pleasant film, full of bracing sea voyages and Galapagos Islands creatures. John enjoyed watching the inflating red pouches of the frigate birds and the stretchy necks of the giant tortoises. He wondered, fleetingly, what Darwin would have made of his lesson. He would surely have been disappointed by the handful of dull-eyed pupils and their harassed teacher.

At twenty-five to one, John stumbled out of the biol lab and fought his way through throngs of kids to the canteen. One of the few advantages of being a teacher in Trecadno High School was the right to go to the front of the dinner queue. He asked for an especially large serving of cheese and potato pie, and vegetables, and likewise abundant rhubarb crumble. He took his loaded tray to an empty table in a distant corner, for he couldn't face recounting the morning's miseries to anyone. He put his head down and started shovelling. Haute cuisine it was not, but it was miles better than anything Mrs Hughes had produced.

Blessed isolation lasted for little more than five minutes before a pair of long, tanned legs came into view. Mrs Wontsmey advanced like a big cat, stopping when her glorious knees were level with John's left elbow, allowing him a close-up view of the region between her glossy thighs.

'May I join you?' she asked, in her most innocent voice.

161

'Er… yes. Of course.' John shifted in his chair, causing a sprout to fall onto his lap.

'It's been a while, hasn't it?' purred the lady, once seated.

'Yes. Absolutely.'

'You went away, I think?'

'I did. I went—'

'You went home to Surrey. Alexander told me. I had a holiday, too.'

'Did you have a good time?'

'We drank a lot. And skied a little.'

'Ah.' John imagined young male ski-instructors quaking in their snow-boots.

'It's good to have a break sometimes, isn't it?'

'Definitely.'

'And then get back to normal.'

'Right.'

John wondered what exactly would be classed as 'normal' in the Wontsmey household. He had a nasty feeling that it might involve him. 'Well, er, Betty. I'll have to go soon.' He eyed his uneaten crumble with longing. 'I hope you don't mind if I just finish my dessert.'

'Please continue.'

He spooned in some crumble plus cooling custard. It would have tasted better without an audience. He cleared his throat and attempted what he hoped was a diplomatic fob-off.

'Look, it's not exactly satisfactory in here, is it? Perhaps I can pay you a visit sometime soon.' He was thinking along the lines of a quick coffee in the cookery room.

'I'd really love to see you one evening, John.'

'Ah, well…'

'But I'm booked up at the moment.'

'You are?'

'Very much so. I'm even having to use my lunch-hours for marking.'

'Really?'

'I'm afraid so.'

'Oh, gosh. Well…'

'Of course, I'd do my best to fit you in.' She ran her tongue over her lips.

John coughed. 'That's, er, kind, but…'

'But it may not be possible.'

'Oh?'

'Not for some time.'

'Well, er …'

'Anyway, John, I really must go now.' She stood up. 'I'll see you around.'

He watched the waggle of her perfect posterior with mixed emotions. She had released him. He was a free man. Moreover, he could get stuck into his pudding in peace. On the downside, he'd lost a steady source of crumpet.

John had agreed to go to the Brush and Mask that night for the first campaign meeting. He was not happy about being press-ganged into helping, but he was on the side of anyone who had it in for Roger Nash-Thomas. It was also good to have an excuse to escape from Mrs Lavinia Hughes.

When he arrived at seven thirty, he was surprised to find the pub devoid of life. He could have sworn that this was the time agreed with Mr Williams. It was also strange that neither Dr Jones nor Mr Pritchard were in attendance. Still, Raymond the barman materialised before him.

'Where's everyone?' asked John, after he'd ordered a beer and whiskey chaser.

'Who knows?'

'Perhaps the doc has a surgery.'

'It's possible,' Raymond replied, looking unconvinced. 'Though there are other watering holes in Trecadno, you know. His ex-wife never saw much of him.'

'Is Alexander also a divorcee? He hasn't mentioned and

I didn't like to ask.'

'No, he never married.'

'I'm surprised. A personable fellow with a good job and a pleasant house.'

'Teachers often stay single.'

'I married.'

'Aye, but that was London, an' you was young. Once a teacher gets past a certain age, that's it.'

'That's not an encouraging thought,' said John.

'Beer's always good company,' said Raymond.

John ruminated on the prospect of eternal bachelorhood, and headed over to an inviting armchair. He thumbed through an old copy of the *Penymynydd & District Weekly News*, and sighed, repeatedly, as the unexpected wait got longer and longer.

Eventually, Mr William Williams sloped in, accompanied by a draught of damp air. He peered at the glasses on the table beside John's chair. 'You started early, did you? Slippery slope, boy. Slippery slope.'

'I've been waiting for you, Mr Williams. Didn't you say seven-thirty?'

'I certainly did, an' I'm a man of my word.'

'It's more like eight-thirty now.'

Mr William Williams looked at his watch, and then at the old clock above the bar. 'Does that say half past seven or doesn't it?'

John got up and peered at the clock which did indeed indicate seven thirty. 'I know what's happened!' he declared. 'You've both forgotten to put the clocks back.'

'Put the clocks back?' inquired the deacon.

'Yes, you know. End of British Summer Time. The clocks were meant to go back last Saturday night.'

Mr William Williams turned vexed eyes towards the bartender. 'Did you know about this, Raymond?'

'I have to admit…'

'See, the thing is,' continued the deacon, 'clocks are a domestic issue. Domestic issues is *Mrs* Williams' department.'

'But you arrived at Moriah Chapel at the right time yesterday.'

'Damn right I did. Never once been late. Anyway, boy, it's your round.'

The list of the necessary letters of supplication was exceedingly long. John imagined his London pals tackling such correspondence in minutes via emails generated on shiny new laptops. In Trecadno, he would have to resort to paper and typewriter. Not forgetting envelopes. He had none of these things, and his only chance of acquiring them was to appeal once again to the largesse of Mr Burrows-Morgan, deputy head. This required an alcoholic bribe, which was the only part of the whole plan that John approved of, given the obligatory visit to Elisabeth-Mai's pharmacy.

John left Trecadno High School at a quarter to four on Wednesday with a spring in his step. This was despite the unremitting rain and 10G's protracted gagging during a demonstration of rat dissection. The little dears over-did the revulsion, though there was no doubt that the rodent in question had been immersed in formaldehyde for a *very* long time.

As he squelched through the square in his wellies, John pictured the delicate arches of Elisabeth-Mai's eyebrows, her pink lips, and long-fingered hands. How had such a young woman managed to master chemicals, plants, and piano keys? And how could such a perfect creature cavort with a man whose chief aim was to despoil the countryside?

As this grim thought tormented him, John drew level with the façade of what had recently been Hopkins for News. All the grubby stickers advertising cola, crisps, and the *West Wales Argus* had been scraped away, and the windows were now adorned with frilly mauve curtains and pictures of coiffured female heads. A large mauve sign with the word 'Beverley's' had been placed above the window, and a pricelist attached to the inside of the glass door. All cuts, including those for gentlemen, were currently half-price. It was not clear whether the prices listed were pre- or post- discount, but either way, a Beverley's haircut was incredibly cheap compared to London. John ran a hand through his untidy locks and reflected on one of his mother's many criticisms:

'You should get your hair cut. You look like a spring poet.'

John had never met a spring poet. Nor, as far as he knew, had his mother. Back in Surrey he'd liked the idea of a literary persona. Moreover, he was determined to show his mother that he was his own man. But in Trecadno, neatness had the edge over individuality, and might make him more appealing to Elisabeth-Mai.

He reached the pharmacy, noting with relief that the light was on. But yet again, an aged lady had beaten him to the counter. She wore a black coat several sizes too big for her, and a hat resembling an inverted pink goldfish bowl.

'She's seeing to me,' declared the female, peering disdainfully at his dripping yellow oilskin.

'That's OK. I'll wait.'

'No you won't,' she said, puckering up her mouth and jutting out her bony chin.

'No?' John started to undo his mackintosh.

'No.'

He sighed. 'And why would that be?'

'Because I got five prescriptions, and three of 'em has to be made up special.'

'Oh?'

'See, I got neuralgia, an' shingles, an' arthritis, an'

osteoporosis.'

'Well!'

'An' there's my chilblains. Not forgetting the impetigo.'

John looked at her in despair. The woman was a walking pathology textbook, and indubitably an impediment to spending some quality time with Elisabeth-Mai.

'An' the pharmacy's closing in five minutes,' added the little woman. 'Special choir practise.'

'Really?'

'Damn nuisance, I say. People's got to be able to get their medicines. Mark my words, there's worse to come.'

'Sorry?'

'It was the same with Hopkins. Early closing for a few weeks, then caput!'

'Caput?'

'Place closed down, didn't it? This one could be next.'

'Really?'

There was no sign of Elisabeth-Mai, and clearly no point in hanging around. John started to button up his wet coat.

'Nice coat you got!' declared the medical phenomenon, as John advanced to the door. 'You'll never get lost.'

He made his soggy way back to Chapel View, contemplating how considerable ill-health could be compatible with great longevity, and also what Raymond would charge for his best whiskey. It was not until later, whilst halfway through an omelette the consistency and colour of leather, that he thought again about the little old lady's words. Could it be true that the pharmacy was under some sort of threat? Was Elisabeth-Mai's alliance with Nash-Thomas one of expediency? This was a comforting thought. It remained at the front of his mind as he dragged himself and his lurid oilskin through the darkness and driving rain to the Brush and Mask, once he'd finally managed to consume Mrs Hughes' dinner.

A small but fierce fire was burning, filling the lounge bar with dancing amber light and twisted shadows. Alexander Pritchard, Know-All, leant on the bar sipping a G & T.

'Hello, John. Strange to see you here mid-week.'

'Needs must.'

'That bad? Well, peel off your banana skin and take a seat.'

John did what he was told, settling on a barstool next to his colleague as Raymond poured him a beer.

'I'm surprised that Dr Jones isn't here.'

'So am I. He had to take a surgery for once.'

'To be honest, I'm amazed he's kept on. I don't mean to be unkind – I like Doc Jones very much – but it doesn't seem as if he sees many patients.'

'He has a part-time contract.'

'That's unusual, isn't it?'

'Daniel didn't want to be full-time. He doesn't really enjoy the job.'

'Oh dear.'

'He wanted to be a vet when we were in school. He and I were in the same class.'

'Oh?'

'His father was a doctor. Wouldn't let him be a vet. Said it was iniquitous to waste knowledge on mere creatures when there were people needing medical care.'

'I suppose he had a point.'

'I suppose he did. But Daniel never really took to humans. Especially after his wife left him. She was a nurse. They both worked at a hospital in Cardiff. Mrs Jones wanted Daniel to climb the greasy pole, the one with serpents entwined around it.'

'Sorry?'

'The Rod of Asclepius. Symbol of medical services.'

'Oh. Right. But the doc didn't want to climb the pole?

Or rod?'

'Correct. He didn't like the hospital or Cardiff and decided to retrain as a GP. Which upset wifey. She shifted her affections to a consultant anaesthetist, and Daniel shifted back here.'

'His home town?'

'That's right, with plenty of scope for walking and observing wildlife. He's very knowledgeable on small mammals. I'm sure the two of you could have a good conversation on water voles and what-not. Which might help you both to curb your alcohol intake.' Alexander grinned and nodded at John's beer glass.

'I'm not just here to imbibe,' he said defensively. 'Though goodness knows I'm glad of a drink. I need more whiskey for Burrows-Morgan. I'm hoping he'll get me a typewriter and some stationery for Mr Williams' campaign.'

'Ah. I'd heard you were roped in.'

John sighed and shook his head.

'It's a form of flattery, you know,' continued the Know-All. 'It shows that William values you.'

'It shows that he's good at delegating.'

'You'll need something decent,' Raymond said, when John explained his requirements. 'How about this?'

He produced a medium-sized bottle with a label depicting a cute group of young rabbits.

'Haven't seen that before,' said John.

'Scottish, I believe,' Raymond said, looking shifty.

Alexander peered at it through his intellectual half-moon glasses. 'The Bannock Bunny Whisky Company. Sounds like a soft toy manufacturer. I've never heard of it.'

'Good for a man called "Burrows" though, innit?' said Raymond with a chuckle, his blue eyes all a-twinkle. 'See, there are hundreds of little distilleries all around the British Isles.'

'No doubt. How much is it?' asked John.

'Twenty pounds,' came the prompt reply.

'Twenty pounds exactly?'

'Makes it easier, don' it?'

'I suppose it does.' John fished out a twenty-pound note, wondering how much change he should have been getting.

'I went to the pharmacy first to ask for whiskey,' John told Alexander, once Raymond had disappeared behind his curtain. 'But it was early closing today. Four fifteen. For choir practice, apparently.'

'Strange time to have choir practice.'

'That's what I thought.' John put down his beer glass with a furrowed brow. 'Alexander, do you know if the pharmacy is in financial difficulties? After all, it's pretty dim and ancient. Elisabeth-Mai hasn't invested much in the place.'

'Maybe people in Trecadno prefer it like that.'

'Maybe so. Or perhaps it doesn't take much money. That would explain why…' He stopped and stared into his beer.

'Why what?'

John gritted his teeth. 'It would explain why she hangs out with a land-grabbing slug like Nash-Thomas.'

Alexander arched his fine eyebrows. 'Your hypothesis being that she wants him to buy the place?'

'Yes.'

'Daniel would probably know. I have to say that I'd be surprised. The pharmacy has been in her family for years. I think she'd have to be desperate before she'd consider selling up.'

'Perhaps she is. Everyone has to eat.'

'There's no denying that, my boy.'

Burrows-Morgan must have been very fond of rabbits, for he surpassed himself in munificence. Instead of a mere typewriter, John was issued with a laptop plus modem, scanner and printer, and all of it arriving within two days! On Friday morning the gentlemen of the staffroom watched in bewildered silence as John struggled with two large boxes. No one had seen anything like it.

'This Nash-Thomas campaign must be serious,' said an old boy reputed to teach mathematics.

'Tell you what, though,' said another, 'there'll be a place if the ladies get to see all this.'

This sage remark was greeted with widespread agreement, and John was advised to disguise the computer's wrappings in carrier bags before disposal. But any lady worth her salt was bound to ask questions about a male biology teacher to-ing and fro-ing from the staffroom to the school wheelie-bin, and Mrs Perrig was worth a sizeable lump of sodium chloride. She stomped into the head's office, rousing him from a particularly pleasant nap. She didn't leave until she had extracted a promise from Mr Kane that the school would acquire laptops for any head of department who wished to order one. Old Ivor wasn't too bothered by this, for he knew that none of the male departmental heads had the faintest idea what a laptop was, never mind how to order one.

In due course, the laptop would transform John's rose-bower bedroom into a place of many possibilities. It certainly helped the production of teaching resources. But it turned out to be redundant as a tool for the Campaign to Save Trecadno. In the event, no letters were necessary, and no council or MP ever got to know of the peril that had threatened the town of the foxes.

CHAPTER TWELVE

Halloween

Not only was Friday the Day of the Laptop, but it was also the 31st of October: Halloween. John's pupils spent most of their lessons drawing skulls and talking about ghosts. John regarded them with amusement and wondered whether to go to quiz night. Alexander put him right.

'I think you'll find, my boy,' he said, as they gulped inferior coffee at the end of the afternoon, 'that the children have good reason to be excited.'

'Oh? Is trick or treat big around here, then?'

'Trick or treat? Good heavens, no! Trecadno has its own unique Halloween tradition: the Vigil. The townsfolk – children and adults – dress in dark capes, carry lanterns and form a great ring in the square.'

'Really?'

'Indeed. Then they troop up to the stone circle, where they assemble and say words of sorrow and respect for their dear departed.'

'Sounds a bit primeval. Are there druids?'

'Quite possibly. I've never been. Not my cup of tea.' He sniffed with disdain. 'It's supposed to be linked to the Christian festival of All Hallows and the earlier Celtic celebration of Samhain. Or Calan Gaeaf, as it is called in Wales.'

'Is that a sort of harvest festival?'

'That's right. A time when the souls of the departed can

come back to Earth. Apparently.'

'Right,' said John, looking uneasy. 'I'm beginning to see why you might prefer quiz night.'

'Oh, there'll be no quiz night tonight. Though the Wanderers' will be packed out by nine. Everyone goes there after the Vigil.'

John put down his cup, unable to take more of the foul brown liquid. 'The Vigil doesn't sound very appealing. But perhaps I should go. Impress the locals. Make me more accepted. What do you think?'

Alexander smiled benignly. 'I suggest consulting someone in authority. A deacon, perhaps. Or a pharmacist.'

What a day! 9F had been too obsessed with ghouls to think up any mischief. A wondrous laptop had appeared. The sun had even shone for a few minutes. Best of all, John found another excuse to contact his beloved. He decided on a more sophisticated approach this time, opting to phone her from the head's office. It was well-known that at four on a Friday, Mr Kane accelerated out of the school even faster than his students.

The head's office was a small and barren place. A couple of golf putters were propped up in one corner, and in another was a hatstand bearing a black tie and an old pair of ladies' tights. Any other intruder might have used the opportunity to investigate the papers old Ivor had left scattered on his desk, but John thought only of his phone call. He found the number of the pharmacy in a directory shoved under the phone. 'G' for 'Glyndwr'. With tingling fingers, he dialled the number.

'Trecadno Pharmacy,' said a female voice.

'Elisabeth-Mai? Is that you?' asked John.

'It is.'

'Oh good. It's John Simmonds here. I was talking to Alexander Pritchard earlier and he told me about the, er, traditions you follow for Halloween.'

'Yes?'

'And, well, I wondered if it would be all right for me to attend.'

'It's a community gathering, not an entertainment.'

'I understand.'

'Do you?'

'I understand that maybe you don't want all and sundry there. But I'd like to go. No problem if you think it's best that I keep away. But if it is OK to go, I'd like to accompany you. If you're going, that is.'

'I'm going.'

'Would you like an escort? Or do you already have one?'

'No one in particular.'

'So, could I call for you?'

'You could come here for tea first,' Elisabeth-Mai said after a pause. 'I'll be finished in the shop by five thirty. The Vigil begins at seven, so we'll have plenty of time. Would that be all right?'

'It would be wonderful.'

'Good. I'll see you at five thirty then.'

John put down the receiver in a state of ecstasy. The day was just getting better and better. There was the small matter of explaining to Mrs Lavinia Hughes that he wouldn't partake of her evening meal, but not even that thorny point could blight his sunny amble back to Chapel View. He broke the news in the kitchen, where his hostess was buttering a vast pile of bread.

'So,' she said in as supercilious a voice as she could manage, 'you're going to the Vigil, are you?'

'I'm really looking forward to it. Will you be there?'

'Definite. I'm making the sandwiches for after.'

'After?'

'In the Wanderers'.'

'Oh.'

174

'Mrs Bowen, Tŷ Newydd, is making queen cakes, Mrs Prosser is making apple turnovers, an' Mrs Evans, Bryn Mefus, is making walnut loaf, an'—'

'It'll be really good, then.'

'Oh, it's a good evening an' no mistake.'

'A bit unusual, though.'

'Eh?'

'I've never come across any Halloween rituals involving a whole town.'

'No? Well, I've told you before, we respect our dead here.'

'Yes.' It was a disquieting thought. 'You don't mind about me missing your meal, then?'

'I got it all ready. But it'll keep till tomorrow. Course, I'll be out shopping then.'

'Shopping again?'

'It's the run up to Christmas, see.' She put down the breadknife and puckered up her lips. 'You can sleep in tomorrow morning if you like.'

'Thanks, Mrs Hughes. I don't suppose...' His landlady's gimlet stare cut off the rest of his sentence. She knew he was going to ask about a key. He knew her answer.

'I'd better get myself sorted,' he muttered, and headed up to his room. Mrs Lavinia Hughes resumed her buttering with the sort of mocking expression often worn by Elisabeth-Mai. It suited Elisabeth Mai a great deal better.

At five thirty precisely John placed himself outside the pharmacy door. Elisabeth-Mai's bespectacled housekeeper once again slid the bolts and let him in.

'Through here,' she muttered, and led the way through a heavily curtained doorway into another dim room. She pointed at a chair then disappeared into the gloom. John sat and waited. Eventually Elisabeth-Mai appeared, looking lithe in black trousers and sweater, her red hair tumbling over her shoulders. She smiled at him and opened yet another curtain, to reveal a remarkably sunny conservatory full of potted plants. A table in the centre had been laid with white porcelain, a plate of sandwiches, and a cake-stand bearing a large Victoria sponge. Elisabeth-Mai led her dazed guest to the table.

'You have a very interesting house,' he said, seating himself in a rickety wooden chair next to a huge fern.

'Old and rambling are better adjectives.'

'Lovely, all the same.'

'You haven't seen much of it.'

'True.' He sat up a little to look outside. 'Though I can see a very charming garden. I didn't expect it to be quite so big.'

'All the gardens in Lôn y Gwenci are long. Ours is wider than most because this was originally two houses.' She picked up the teapot and poured. 'I don't tend to invite people here because of Mother. You've probably heard that my mother has multiple sclerosis. She's confined to a wheelchair.'

John nodded. 'I'm sorry.'

'We've learned to live with it. She has problems with her vision too. Hence the low light.'

'Ah.'

'She's staying at her sister's house this weekend.'

'Oh?'

'Do help yourself to sandwiches. We have cheese or ham.'

'Thanks. Mrs Hughes has been making sandwiches today as well. I think hers were egg and tomato.'

'The full menu includes egg, tomato, cheese, ham, and tuna. These are some of Mrs Hughes' sandwiches, actually.'

'Really?' John's opinion of them instantly diminished.

'I'm afraid there'll be nothing but sandwiches and cake after the Vigil also.'

'I don't mind. Especially when I'm with you.'

'That's a sweet thing to say.'

'You're a sweet girl.'

'Am I?' She gave a little snigger. 'I'll be even sweeter after some of this cake.' She cut them both large wedges that oozed cream and raspberry pips.

'I'm really looking forward to the Vigil. It sounds really, er...'

'Quaint, perhaps?'

'Definitely not. Different. Fascinating.'

'Do you feel like an anthropologist?'

'No! Gosh.' He cleared his throat. 'I don't just want to observe. I'm keen to take part.'

'And talk to the dead?'

Occult thoughts clouded John's mind. He stopped chewing.

'Because that's pretty much what happens,' Elisabeth-Mai said.

'Isn't it mainly just dressing up and candles? I mean, children go, don't they?'

'They do.' She took a delicate bite of her huge chunk of cake. 'But it's a serious matter for the older members of the community. And the hippies from Bryncadno. Deadly serious.'

John regarded his sponge cake. The dribbling raspberry jam looked a little like fresh blood.

'Well now,' Elisabeth-Mai announced, when she'd demolished her slice, 'we have just enough time to take a quick turn around the garden before donning our black capes.'

'Do I have to wear a cape?'

'Everyone else will be wearing one.'

'Ah.'

'And you'll have to carry a lantern.'

'Please say it's not a hollowed-out pumpkin!'

The lantern turned out to be a glass orb containing a

candle suspended from a long black staff. Not as naff as a pumpkin, but John still felt pretty self-conscious tramping along Lôn y Gwenci with it, his black cape tangling itself around his legs. With Elisabeth-Mai also sporting this daft rig-out, he reassured himself that it had to be all right.

As they approached the square, the last red remnants of sunset disappeared behind the church tower. The road circling the church and chapel was marked out by lanterns carried by black-garbed residents standing shoulder to shoulder. John and Elisabeth-Mai joined the circle of lights near the well. John's right-hand neighbour was a thin young man with dreadlocks and a black cardinal's hat, who stared at his lantern fixedly but without focus. Beyond Elisabeth-Mai to his left were two teenagers who looked vaguely familiar, though unusually neat hair and closed mouths precluded proper identification.

As the church clock struck seven o'clock, everyone became still and silent and bent their heads. The only moving things in the square were the flames from the lanterns and rustling capes. There were candles in the windows, too, forming a further ring of celestial lights above. It was all rather mystical and faintly disturbing, especially when a cold east wind wailed through the motionless throng. One or two candles flickered and died.

As the last chime rang out, a small figure walked out to the little road separating the church and chapel and began to sing in a clear soprano. John and Elisabeth-Mai couldn't see her but could just about hear her brief song. It opened with vigour and died away all too soon. John did not comprehend the words, but he sensed their meaning.

At length, a tall man raised his lantern aloft and advanced to the entrance to Heol y Carlwm. John assumed, correctly, that he was William Williams. This was the sign for the assembly to turn north-east and follow the deacon's lead towards the stone circle. John didn't dare speak to

Elisabeth-Mai as the procession moved forward. He had to be content to watch the swish of her cape and her tresses blowing in the wind. Every now and again he thought he saw glinting eyes behind the hedges, though with all the flickering of candles it was easy to be mistaken. It was a long walk, especially for the younger marchers, and John was surprised at their perfect conduct. It looked like the little blighters stored up all their naughtiness just for him.

It took around forty-five minutes for the silent procession to reach its destination. Gathering clouds had made the sky black and starless, so the lanterns were the only source of light. The townsfolk once again formed a ring, this time just inside the stones. Every now and again a gust of wind blew out a candle, creating a little black gap in the circle of light. No one tried to restore the lost lights. As the church bells rang out eight o'clock, heads were bent once again, and William Williams hoisted himself onto the altar stone. He stood rigidly, his right arm raised to Heaven like a grim Moses, and began to recite. John had no chance of understanding the words, but he listened intently to the stern tones. He found himself transported to a time gone by, a time when the land was wooded, when food was hunted and gathered, when a wattle-and-daub hut was a mansion. A time when remaining alive was an achievement. The deacon concluded with a tearful cry, taken up into a plaintive chant by the assembled throng. John joined in, crying out sounds he didn't understand. His heart broke just like theirs. Like them, he felt compelled to plead with powers unknown for the souls of those who had gone before. Like them, he yearned to feel the past.

After a few minutes, the dirge trailed off into diminuendo. John turned to look at Elisabeth-Mai but she was staring fixedly towards a dark area where a handful of lanterns had been extinguished. He was surprised to notice that this spot was not completely dark but contained several little lights at knee-level. John watched the greenish lights with a mixture of disbelief and apprehension. What on earth was going on? Had the spirits of the departed been summoned? Was he in the midst of a coven?

More little lights appeared, positioned between the megaliths. All at once, they dimmed, and there was an almighty scream. John grabbed Elisabeth-Mai's hand, but she just smiled and shook him off. Then the lights disappeared altogether. A silence descended, broken only by the whistling of the freezing wind. Capes blew open and candles blew out, including those held by John and Elisabeth-Mai. It was not long before the ring of townsfolk was plunged into impenetrable darkness.

To say that John was afraid was a gross understatement. What dark art would come next? Would spirits manifest? Was there to be some druidic ritual, even a human sacrifice?

No, only the re-lighting of the lanterns. Elisabeth-Mai used a disposable cigarette lighter. His disappointment at this banality was countered by the realisation that she had gently hooked her right arm through his left and was rubbing her face against his shoulder in a distinctly affectionate way. All thoughts of sorcery evaporated, and John shifted his arm so that it could curve itself around her waist. She did brush him off, but not immediately. There was the distinct hint of a cuddle in between.

The re-lighting of the lanterns marked the end of the Vigil, and people soon started to amble back to the town. Little knots of townsfolk ebbed and flowed, their chatter warming the night air. Small children flapped around people's legs like lost bats, and older ones pushed each other into the bracken. By nine fifteen the crowd was spilling into the Wanderers' Club. Capes were dumped on chairs and a small army of rotund females got weaving with tablecloths and sandwiches.

John went over to the bar to get Elisabeth-Mai a drink

– she'd asked for a port and lemon – and found Alexander Pritchard and Daniel Jones in their usual positions.

'Did you enjoy freezing to the point of rigidity?' Alexander asked.

'I didn't really notice the temperature,' John said. 'There were too many other things to take my attention.'

'Like your companion, perhaps?' inquired Mr Pritchard, inclining his head in the direction of Elisabeth-Mai.

'Certainly,' answered John, looking sheepish. 'Though the Vigil itself was pretty distracting.'

'Touch of hocus pocus?' asked the doctor.

'More than a touch. It was alarming at times, especially at the end when...' But he was interrupted by the arrival of William Williams.

'At the bar again, boy?'

'I've only just got here, Mr Williams,' protested John.

'Good night, eh?' said the deacon.

'Amazing. Tell me, what exactly happened at the end, when—'

'Have you seen my oldest boy?' the deacon asked of no one in particular. Getting no answer, he stomped off in the direction of the sandwiches.

By the time John had bought drinks, Elisabeth-Mai was nowhere to be seen. He would have searched for her, but he didn't want to lose their seats to the many people waiting to grab them. Many more minutes elapsed, and he thought of returning to the bar to join his friends. But he couldn't risk missing his beloved. He sat alone with his beer, feeling the chill of neglect.

After a while a couple of middle-aged ladies sidled up to his table. One was small with thick make-up, and the other well-built with pointed spectacles. John recognised her from Emanuel Parry's funeral, where she had been standing near the gladioli.

'Can we join you on this table?' asked the woman with

orange slap.

'You've got three empty chairs, see, Possum,' commented the other one.

There was still no sign of Elisabeth-Mai, so John had no pretext to turn away the two ladies. Nor could he refuse the orange lady's offer to take the undrunk port and lemon off his hands. He turned to his beer and tried not to listen to the ladies' conversation about socks. At least, that's what he thought they were talking about.

In their wisdom, The Wanderers' Club Bar Committee decided that, on this special evening, bar staff should wait at table between ten and eleven thirty. This proved very popular and led a considerable number of thoroughly sloshed townsfolk. Having little else to do, John soon joined their number. It was therefore a shock to feel a hand on his shoulder at around eleven, by which time the middle-aged ladies were discussing something that sounded like phoenix enlightenment. Joy of joys, the wondrous pharmacist had returned. More joy was to come.

'I'm sorry I had to go off for a while,' Elisabeth-Mai said. 'Look, let's leave this place. Let's get some coffee.'

In the sinful suburbs of London that John had once frequented, the concept of coffee at the end of an evening had little to do with beverages. Despite his sozzled condition, delicious notions of nookie percolated through his body. He reached over to take Elisabeth-Mai's hand but miscalculated and grasped the fingers of the orange-faced lady.

'What a boy, eh?' she chortled with a happy smirk.

'Uh… sorry,' mumbled John. He stood up, immediately tripping over his chair.

'Can you walk?' asked Elisabeth-Mai.

'Uh… yeah,' said the formless mass from the floor.

The petite and perfectly formed woman and the

crumpled, staggering man proceeded down Lôn y Bele back towards the town. It was a long trek for someone so well-pickled, as many townsfolk would later testify. John had so much trouble getting his feet working properly that he failed to notice that they did not stop at the pharmacy. Elisabeth-Mai steered him right up to the door of Chapel View.

'No!' cried John, when he saw Mrs Lavinia Hughes standing before him, arms outstretched.

'Come, come, John,' said that doughty lady. 'You need to go to bed.'

'Which one? What about coffee?'

Elisabeth-Mai chuckled and trotted off. In his drunken state, John thought that her distant form looked distinctly like a fox.

CHAPTER THIRTEEN

At Beverley's

If Mrs Lavinia Hughes had booted John out of the house at eight, which had been her inclination, he might have died of hypothermia. He would have been quite incapable of lifting himself off the pavement. In the event, he slept in his rosy boudoir until gone eleven, at which point he descended Mrs Hughes' precipitous staircase with great care and staggered into the kitchen. He was all set to apologise but found the room quiet and empty: his landlady was, of course, partaking of another shopping trip. He relaxed and made himself some toast and a strong cup of coffee. Ah, coffee! The recollection of his missed canoodle pierced his heart. But perhaps his darling would like to meet for lunch. Followed by a warming beverage.

Thoughts of postponed amour speeded him, and he hastened to the bathroom to make himself look lovely. He was taken aback by the wild man that stared back at him from the other side of the mirror. Dark rings circled his eyes, and the thick stubble on his chin made him look like a convict. His hair stuck out at a variety of angles, none of them improving. Not even Betty Wontsmey would give him coffee looking like that.

It was a quarter to twelve by this time, not too late to get a swift haircut and arrive at the pharmacy before it closed. He found his coat and rushed to Beverley's.

It wasn't until he was halfway down Heol y Carlwm

that he remembered he had no key and would be unable to get back in to Chapel View. If his mission failed, he'd be snookered. He was far too weary for a country ramble and had no facilities for planning lessons. Given the dark clouds gathering in the west, he was also at risk of a good soaking. But it was too late to ruminate on this oversight. He would go to Beverley's and hope that Elisabeth-Mai would be available to admire his new coiffeur.

Inside Beverley's, the air was buzzing with chatter and hairspray. Despite the shopping trip, there were enough females left in Trecadno to clog up the sinks and hairdryers, and they all beamed at him as he entered. He stood uncertainly in the doorway for a few moments, until a woman removed herself from under a dryer and pointed at a small window seat next to a pile of women's magazines. There were no other males in the establishment. Unbeknown to John, Trecadno's gentlemen always went to Glan the barber for their haircare. And other needs.

It didn't take long for Beverley herself to appear, all hips and peroxide, her tight black trousers not really suitable for someone of her age and ample proportions. Her red t-shirt, likewise, could barely contain its contents.

'Hello, love,' she said, waving a pair of scissors. 'What can I do for you?'

A cloud of perfume enveloped him as her black-rimmed eyes came up close. 'A cut, please. A trim,' said John nervously.

'I think I can fit you in,' Beverley replied, licking very red lips. 'You'll have to wait, but they say that the best things are worth waiting for, don't they?'

John gave an anxious laugh.

'We're busy here this morning, see,' Beverley continued. 'It's like the buses, in' it? They all come at once. We didn' 'ave anyone in yesterday. Not a single soul. Amazin'.'

'Oh dear.'

'D'you wan' a cup of tea while you wait?'

'That would be nice. Thanks.'

She straightened up, diminishing her chemical haze. 'Ju-lie!' she yelled. 'Get the gentleman some tea!'

'OK,' muttered a weary girl, busy brushing hair clippings along a stretch of lino.

'Here you are,' said Beverley a few minutes later, proffering a mug. 'I'll do you soon as I can.' She fluttered her excessive eyelashes.

'Oh, fine. Thanks.'

'We don't often get young men in here, do we, ladies?'

Titters circulated amidst the driers and sinks.

'The owner must come here for his haircuts,' John remarked.

Beverley picked up her scissors and resumed snipping a nearby head. 'Yeah, he comes in. If he can be bothered.'

'All men are trouble,' commented the female being trimmed.

'Too bloody right,' said Beverley.

'Wass' up then?' asked another female from under her drier, clearly determined to root out any gossip.

Beverley sniffed. 'The bugger didn't come home last night.'

'No!' exclaimed the lady in the drier.

'Where'd he go, then?' asked the one being trimmed.

'Search me,' responded Beverley. 'I still 'aven't seen the swine.'

'Has your husband got a big black car,' asked the woman under the drier.

John's curiosity was roused. 'Is Roger Nash-Thomas your husband?' he asked, staring at Beverley.

'Yeah, for my sins,' she said. 'Why then, love? Was you hoping I was single?'

Another set of giggles permeated the hairspray haze.

'I, er, just wondered.' Elisabeth-Mai could not possibly

186

know that the rogue was married. Yet she knew all about his building plans and business acquisitions. Was it possible that she cared for him so very much?

Beverley looked back at the reddening drier-woman. 'What d'you say about a car, Nerys?'

'I was asking about a big black car,' replied the head wobbling within its apparatus.

'Yeah, Rog has got one. Mercedes.'

'It's just that there was a big black car in the Wanderers' car-park last night. There all night, it was.'

Beverley stopped trimming and turned to Nerys under the hairdryer. 'Was that sod in the Wanderers' all night?'

'No idea. I didn't see him myself.'

'Neither did I,' declared the trimmed female, 'an' I was there until gone twelve.' There were murmurs of agreement throughout the establishment. Mr Nash-Thomas had not been spotted within the WC.

'What the hell was his car doing there, then?' asked Beverley.

Nerys shrugged her ample shoulders.

Beverley looked around the salon, but no-one seemed to know. Plenty of possibilities were offered, and the volume of banter increased accordingly. Beverley's face tightened in agitation, and she began to tap her scissors on the back of a chair in a distinctly threatening way.

Then one woman sat up from a sink, wet hair dripping all over the floor, and yelled at her neighbour, 'That Wontsmey woman is shameless! They shouldn't let sex-mad Yanks into the country!'

This was too much for boiling Beverley. 'If that woman had my husband at 'er place last night, I'll kill 'er,' she declared. 'I swear to God I'll kill 'er. An' I'll castrate 'im!' With that dramatic riposte, she flung her scissors to the floor, grabbed her handbag, and stomped off.

John looked around in a dazed state. But the ladies

weren't for dazing. They flung curlers, grabbed towels, and yelled at Julie about incomplete hairdos. It was inevitable that the poor girl would end up in tears. It was a wonder that she maintained just enough calm to turn off the driers and move all the scissors to safe ground. John got out of there smartish. His first and only thought was to get to the pharmacy and tell Elisabeth-Mai that she'd been the victim of a heartless predatory adulterer.

It took him little more than a minute to hare to her door, which he hammered as if his life depended on it. No one came to open it. John looked at his watch. It was only ten minutes after closing time. Surely Elisabeth-Mai must still be inside? He took a couple of steps back and surveyed the upper windows. Gentle rain dampened his hair and trickled into his eyes. He shook his head and crossed the road to survey all the house's windows. He could see no light or movement in any of them. As his forehead furrowed in perplexity, the faint sound of piano music reached his ears. Chopin again, he thought; quite a jaunty tune. It ended with a flourish and a peal of merry laughter. What on earth was he to make of Elisabeth-Mai?

The rain became heavier, and John knew that an indoor refuge would have to be located. The chip shop was open, but there was nowhere to sit. That left the Brush and Mask, where Raymond furnished him with a toasted sandwich and some warm beer. John gratefully took his lunch to an armchair next to the fire. Within minutes of consuming the last piece of sandwich, he was, predictably, fast asleep. When his eyes finally opened, he stared at the clock in confusion.

'Have you put the clock forward instead of back, Raymond?' he called over to the bar.

'Eh? I haven't got round to doing anything with it to tell the truth.'

John consulted his wristwatch. 'Is it really half-past

five?' he asked.

'Probably.'

John shook his head in disbelief.

'The last twenty-four hours have been truly surreal,' he said.

'Oh?'

'Last night's vigil was weird, and this morning I had an unsettling time at the hairdresser's.'

'Oh dear.'

'Look, Raymond,' began John, all conspiratorial, 'did you know that Roger Nash-Thomas was seeing ladies other than his wife?'

'There have been rumours,' replied the barman, his bushy red eyebrows a-twitch.

'Apparently his car was outside the Wanderers' Club all night. But he himself wasn't there. That's strange, isn't it?'

'I wouldn't know about what happens at the Wanderers',' said Raymond with a pompous sniff.

'Of course. Sorry. I think it's odd, anyway. Not as odd as the Vigil, though. That was disturbing. I think I'd better have another pint.'

'Drinking helps to minimise life's mysteries.'

'You are a wise man, Raymond.'

'Thank you, young sir.' He glanced towards the door. 'I believe you are about to have company.'

Doc Jones entered, followed soon after by William Williams swirling his black mackintosh in the manner of a nineteenth century cad. A posse of males followed in his wake, ones with the youth and vigour of rugby players.

'Mr Simmonds, yr athro!' declared William Williams. 'You're never out of this place, are you?' He and the doctor squeezed themselves onto barstools, while the rugby boys formed a haphazard queue behind. 'Major news, boys,' the deacon announced, with a wink directed towards the first lad in the queue, who happened to be his son.

'What have you got for us then, William,' asked Daniel Jones wearily.

The deacon got himself comfortable on his barstool, took a frothy sip from his beer, and grinned. 'Are you ready for this?' he asked.

'Please put us out of our misery.'

Mr Williams took another leisurely sip, then declared, 'He's dead.'

'Who?'

'Nash-Thomas.'

John sprayed beer all over his pullover.

The doctor removed the pipe from his mouth and stared at the deacon. 'You like your little joke, William.'

'Honest to God. He's just been found.'

'How do you know that?'

'I am a deacon, a borough councillor, and a magistrate. I get to hear a lot of things.'

'His wife said he hadn't been home last night,' interjected John, pleased to be able to make a contribution. 'And according to another woman in the hairdresser's—'

'Hairdresser's?' intoned Mr Williams, daggers glinting in his eyes.

'I had to get out of the rain,' responded John shamefacedly. 'Anyway, according to a lady I heard talking in there, his car was outside the Wanderers' Club all last night.'

'Thas' right,' said Idwal Williams, son of deacon. 'The boys noticed it before rugby. He came for a bar-meal around midday, but we didn't see him after that.'

'Where was he found?' asked Daniel Jones.

'You'll never guess,' answered the deacon playfully.

'No, I won't. Hurry up and tell us.'

'In the middle of the stone circle.'

Both John and Daniel froze.

'But,' began John, 'but...'

'He was found there a couple of hours ago by our local constabulary,' said William Williams. 'They reckon he'd been dead for about twenty-four hours.'

'But,' began John again, 'that means he would have been dead last night. When we were up there. When the whole town was up there.'

'Indeed.'

'We would have seen him.'

'You think so? It was very dark, boy.'

John turned white. 'Are you saying that people just walked past him?'

'He was underneath the altar stone.'

'That slab is only two or three feet above the ground,' said Daniel Jones. He was so shocked that he hadn't yet managed to restore his pipe to his mouth.

'That's where he was, whatever,' said William Williams.

'Is there any indication of the cause of death?' asked the medical man.

'Looks like suicide.'

'Suicide?' gasped John. 'How on earth could that be?'

'They found a half-drunk bottle of whiskey and some tablets of, er, *parazone*.'

'*Prozac*, more like,' said Daniel.

'Could be.' Mr Williams took a slurp of his beer, thus managing to suppress a chortle of delight.

'He might have been alive when we arrived there last night,' John said, his distress overcoming him. 'We might have been able to save him!'

'Now listen here, boy,' said the deacon, putting his glass down firmly on the bar. 'There's human life, which is worth bemoaning, and then there's rept—'

'That's enough, William,' interrupted Daniel. 'It's a tragedy. Awful.'

'There was a note,' announced the deacon with glee. 'I

haven't seen it, mind, but the constable let slip that there was reference to a woman.'

'But, but...' wailed John, not quite knowing where to begin.

'I'm sure we'll hear all the details in due course,' said Doc Jones, plonking down his glass. 'Come along, John. I think the ladies will be back from their shopping trip by now. I'll walk back to Chapel View with you.'

It was not until Monday that a journalist's version of events appeared. By lunchtime, three copies of the *West Wales Argus* had found their way into the gentlemen's staffroom, and John managed to read the frontpage over the shoulder of an elderly Geography master.

DEAD BODY AT HALLOWEEN SHOCK

By Argus reporter Ed Lyne

L ast Saturday, local policemen made the chilling discovery of a dead body within the stone circle to the south-east of Trecadno. The body is believed to be that of Roger Nash-Thomas, a property developer from Penymynydd. The discovery is all the more disturbing because it was made on the day after Halloween, and it is thought that his body may have been present in the vicinity of the annual Trecadno Vigil ceremony whilst it was underway. Mr William Williams, Deacon of Moriah Chapel, commented: 'This awful finding has shaken the community. To think that we were saying prayers to the dearly departed with Mr Nash-Thomas in our midst.'

Roger Nash-Thomas, 49, was reported missing by his wife, hairdresser Beverley Nash-Thomas, 47, on Saturday afternoon. He had apparently lunched at the Wanderers' Club in Trecadno the previous day, and his car remained at the club carpark overnight. No-one has yet come forward with a later sighting of him, nor does anyone know how he reached the stone circle. A member of the Wanderers' Club told the Argus that the only means of access is a steep path.

The area around the stones is currently cordoned off. Police have not yet commented on events, though it is understood that foul play is not suspected. The results of the post-mortem are expected next Friday.

CHAPTER FOURTEEN

The Part-time Police Station

Penymynydd, with a population nudging five thousand, merited a reasonable-sized police station, contained within a small house. The force had a manning level of sixty man-hours, comprising one policeman's presence for forty hours, and another two for ten each, though staffing permutations were known to fluctuate during the rugby season.

Trecadno, by contrast, deserved only a converted garage and ten man-hours. These were usually provided by PC Samuels, Trecadno resident, member of Moriah Chapel, and man seeking quiet life.

PC Samuels had been making up his hours at Trecadno Station on the Saturday when Beverley Nash-Thomas phoned to notify the constabulary of her husband's absence. PC Samuels was used to missing sheep and cats, not people. Those reported to him were usually young, feckless, and came home once they got hungry. Nash-Thomas was a different kettle of fish, for sure, but PC Samuels expected that he'd turn up once he'd tired of his current floozy.

Mrs Nash-Thomas was less easy to ignore. She phoned the police station repeatedly that Saturday, 1st November, her voice moving up an octave with each new call. PC Samuels decided to enlist the help of WPC Pope. Hysterical wives were known to cool in her presence. Despite her middle years, she had maintained a blank, doll-like appearance. She had never been known to smile, possibly due to a hatred of humanity, possibly as a consequence of cosmetic intervention.

Around four, a mobile phone was handed in, which turned out to belong to Nash-Thomas. A man who liked to trumpet his importance and connections as much as Nash-Thomas would not be caught dead without his mobile. PC Samuels called Penymynydd for assistance. PC Vaughan, who was young and keen, was sent down to Trecadno to ask around, and after some fruitless wanderings ended up picking around the stone circle with a flashlight and a walkie-talkie. When he came back down again, he had to be revived with hot toddies. PC Samuels shoved his portable TV in a cupboard and called in the heavies.

Detective Inspector Lionel Smith (known to all as 'Agent Smith') arrived with a scene-of-crime team at half-past five. He was a small but solid man with nicotine-stained fingertips and fair, receding hair swept back over a high forehead. He fancied himself as Philip Marlowe and didn't think it fitting for one so suave to have to tramp uphill on a damp and darkening evening.

There were no signs of violence at the stone circle. In fact, the corpse looked quite cosy curled up under the altar slab with his bottle and packet of pills. As William Williams had stated, a note was indeed found inside a jacket pocket, and the handwriting was soon verified as that of the deceased. But it wasn't a typical suicide note. It started 'My darling One,' and went on to say: 'I didn't want us to part. It has come at a bad time. I don't feel a complete man. I wish…'

It looked like Nash-Thomas had been dumped, possibly because of poor performance. But Agent Smith didn't believe that a bit of flaccidity would cause a successful entrepreneur to down a load of *Prozac* whilst huddling at a relic in the dead of night. Questions needed to be asked.

Mrs Nash-Thomas was first in the queue for quizzing the following morning. As a token of sympathy for her grief – of which there was little – the lady was interviewed at her home in Penymynydd with WPC Pope in attendance. Decked out as she was in in pencil skirt and heels, Beverley Nash-Thomas didn't look capable of getting anywhere near the stone circle. He bumped her down his list of suspects.

All the same, it was clear that there had been marital discord. Her husband asked too much of her when it came to business, she said. She was expected to run a hairdresser's shop as well as dealing with his correspondence and convoluted accounts. She was getting headaches with all the arithmetic involved, she maintained. But when it came to the bedroom, he didn't ask for enough. At least, he hadn't for the past couple of months. Which was unusual. Normally, it was a case of Roger by name, Roger by nature. He'd been embarrassed by this failure and had had tried various remedies.

When asked if another woman might have been involved, Beverley admitted that she had suspicions. A name soon emerged: Betty Wontsmey.

Mrs Wontsmey was duly contacted, and a car sent to bring her to Trecadno's part-time police station on Sunday afternoon. DI Smith decided that some privacy should be afforded to lady interviewees, which left PC Samuels wrestling to close Venetian blinds whose angle and position had not been altered for at least ten years.

WPC Pope noted, with annoyance, that DI Smith was immediately smitten by Mrs Wontsmey. Maybe it was the soft Canadian accent, or possibly the long legs. By the end of the interview the lady was almost on his lap, and there were certainly whisperings into his left ear of which no formal record was made. In between cooing, giggling, and lingering touches to various parts of DI Smith's person, it was established that Betty had an alibi: she and her husband had set off for London immediately after school had ended on Friday, and had only returned that morning. DI Smith learned that there had indeed been a dalliance between Mrs Wontsmey and the deceased, though she insisted that they had not seen each other for a couple of months. They had parted on account of 'difficulties' on his part. She believed that Roger had subsequently embarked on a new relationship with the local pharmacist.

A car was duly sent to Trecadno Pharmacy, and in due course Agent Smith was delighted to be faced with yet another glamorous female; this investigation was turning out to be one of his favourites. Elisabeth-Mai arrived at half-past five, bearing Friday's leftover sandwiches and cake for the boys and girls in blue. She admitted seeing Nash-Thomas, though emphasised that he had been the one doing all the chasing. Which was easy enough to believe. She had been flattered by his approaches, she said, but was uncomfortable about some of his business activities and the fact that he was a married man. In fact, when they had met the previous Thursday evening, she had kindly but firmly terminated their relationship.

In the face of such pristine beauty, Agent Smith somehow forgot to ask about the exact nature of their relationship, or whether there had been limitations in the bedroom department. Neither did he ask about an alibi. He simply couldn't believe that such a wondrous creature could kill. It was left to WPC Pope to extract the key information that Elisabeth-Mai had been at work all day Friday and had subsequently had a guest to tea.

DI Smith was quite content about this until the name of the friend was provided.

'It was a man?' he exclaimed.

'That's right,' replied Elisabeth-Mai. 'The new biology teacher.'

The DI scowled.

'Is he your new boyfriend?' asked WPC Pope, diving in.

'Just a friend,' she replied with a sweet smile. The detective couldn't help smiling back. Philip Marlowe wouldn't have been so fickle. Philip Marlowe would have asked about the *Prozac.* This was another point left to WPC Pope. Miss Glyndwr stated that Roger Nash-Thomas often called at the pharmacy for cold remedies and toiletries but rarely for prescription medicines. A diligent search of her prescription records the following morning confirmed that she had never dispensed *Prozac,* or anything else, to the Nash-Thomases over the previous two years. It looked like she was in the clear.

Since the new biology teacher had been mentioned, and looked like being in competition with Roger Nash-Thomas for Miss Glyndwr's affections, he was next in line for questioning once all statements had been typed up.

It came as a shock to John to find a uniformed constable standing at the door of Chapel View Guest House at 5pm on a Monday afternoon. Mrs Lavinia Hughes was incandescent.

'The police are here!' she shouted. 'They're outside my house! What have you done, you wicked man?'

John was alarmed and bewildered. But at least he had an excuse to abandon Mrs Hughes' food. As he climbed into the police car, John assured her that he had done nothing whatsoever. He didn't know why he needed to be questioned.

'It'll be about that dead man,' said Mrs Hughes in a loud whisper. 'That Nash-Thomas.'

'But why do *I* need to be questioned?'

'All will be explained at the station,' responded PC Vaughan, in an attempt to sound mysterious.

John expected a building with some gravitas, but the

'station' had crumbling brick walls and a corrugated tin roof. It was hard for anyone to be nonchalant in such a place, but DI Smith tried.

'Thank you for coming, Mr Simmonds. Sit down.'

John lowered himself into the same sort of metal-framed canvas chair commonplace in Trecadno High School. Agent Smith sat opposite him.

'I believe that this is about Roger Nash-Thomas,' said John. 'But I don't understand why you need to speak to me.'

'I've been told that you are a friend of Miss Elisabeth Glyndwr.'

'Elisabeth-Mai. Yes. We have gone walking together occasionally.'

'Nothing more?'

'Not really, no. Last Friday she was kind enough to invite me to tea, and we then went together to the Vigil.'

'You make her sound like a maiden aunt.'

'She is very far from that, Inspector. Though I think "maidenly" would be appropriate.'

A flicker of satisfaction passed over the DI's face. 'Would it be correct to say that you admire her?'

'Certainly.'

'And that you might be jealous of other admirers?'

'I'm only human.'

'Indeed. And it is a very human reaction to get rid of the competition. Such as Mr Nash-Thomas.'

This was ridiculous, and John said so. 'I didn't like the idea that she was seeing him. I very much hoped that she'd eventually prefer me to him. But I had no intention of interfering.'

'No?'

'It was none of my business. I never actually met the man.'

'You must have seen him around, surely?'

'I saw them together once, at a distance,' John said.

'Where was that?'

'At the pharmacy. I had intended going in. To buy paracetamol.'

'Not *Prozac*, by any chance?'

'Certainly not.'

'You saw them and didn't go in?'

'That's right. It would have been embarrassing.'

'He's out of the way, now, isn't he? You must feel pleased.'

'Not at all. I didn't wish the man ill. Though I believe there were a few who did.'

'Really?'

'I understand that he was a ruthless businessman. Some thought he was a threat to the town.'

'Do you know anyone that he might have upset?'

'No one in particular,' replied John, though Mr William Williams' dour visage loomed large in his mind's eye. 'I just picked up general rumours.'

'There must be some happy people around here then,' remarked the detective.

'I don't think "happy" is the right word at all,' said John. 'I think the town is horrified by what happened.'

'Pretty grim, eh?'

'Very. I wish I hadn't gone to that Vigil.'

'No?'

'The whole thing was quite bad enough before I knew about poor Roger Nash-Thomas. When I heard… well, it's all very disturbing.'

'Damn weird thing, that Vigil.'

'Definitely.'

'But at least it's given you an alibi.'

'An alibi? Oh. I See.'

The constabulary interviewed several other people over the next few days. Even Hopkins the ex-newsagent was located and transported to Trecadno's part-time police station. PC

Samuels thought that William Williams, not to mention various other Williamses, would be worth bringing in, but he chose not to air this view. Agent Smith failed to come to the conclusion himself; indeed he failed to think of anyone with the motivation, means or opportunity for committing the evil deed. All the people who might have nurtured murderous thoughts towards the deceased businessman had a perfect alibi. Most had been at the Vigil and could produce at least twenty witnesses to the fact.

The pathologist Dr Mackintosh, Mack the Knife, had finished his proddings by the following Friday lunchtime. It soon became common knowledge that Nash-Thomas' last meal had been chicken and chips washed down with copious whiskey and several tablets of Prozac. The more well-informed in the town knew that *this* was an anti-depressant so concluded that Nash-Thomas must have been depressed. Which was baffling. A man of such means, about to complete his biggest deal yet… Then the rumours of female rejection started to circulate. There were no signs of injury on the body, and the cause of death was a heart attack. The consensus of local opinion was that Nash-Thomas went for a long walk out of dejection, got tired on account of the drink and pills, and found a dry spot for a nap. Beneath the altar stone, high above the town, his heart finally broke.

DI Smith's investigations came up with no better story. There was no evidence of malpractice and several reasons why Roger Nash-Thomas might have been suicidal. The inquest would eventually turn up nothing different. Agent Smith would soon head back to Penymynydd Police Station, never to return. In years to pass, he would occasionally remember the case of the tragic businessman, and leer at the thought of the dissatisfied hareem. But deep down he remained convinced that there was something fishy about Nash-Thomas' demise. He wasn't wrong.

CHAPTER FIFTEEN

Fireworks and Shandies

For once, the students of Trecadno High School had a reasonable excuse for their complete lack of attention. It was Wednesday 5th November, and they were eagerly anticipating fireworks.

'Are you coming, sir?' Gwydion Bevan of 9F asked John.

'I'm too busy.'

'No one's too busy for fireworks, sir.'

'I'll be busy preparing lessons for you lot.'

'Oh, sir!' came an amazed cry, echoed around the room.

'We don't care if you don't prepare our lessons,' someone said.

Out of the mouths of babes and nuisances, thought John.

Alexander Pritchard was similarly surprised by John's lack of enthusiasm. 'Why not go?' he asked between sips of break-time coffee. 'Little enough happens in this town, and the display is usually very good. I'd go myself were it not for a meeting of the *Dyfed History Society*.'

'Don't you think it's inappropriate, Alexander?'

'Inappropriate? Why?'

'Because of the Nash-Thomas business. It seems in poor taste to have a celebration when the poor man only died a few days ago. Especially a celebration of a failed plot followed by executions.'

'Come now, a bit of jollity is surely no bad thing in the circumstances. I'm sure Mr Nash-Thomas would not have wanted the town to grind to a halt on account of his bereavement. We mustn't let death have dominion, must we?'

John sniffed. 'I don't much feel like joining any more of Trecadno's mass gatherings.'

'It must have been unnerving to discover that poor old Nash-Thomas was amongst you at the Vigil.'

'Very. The event itself was scary enough. All that chanting over Neolithic stones.'

'Neolithic? Not those stones, my boy. Those were put up in 1954 for the National Eisteddfod.'

'What?'

'You didn't know?'

'I thought they were ancient, just like in Stonehenge. I'm sure Elisabeth-Mai....'

'I daresay you got the wrong end of the stick. They were just for show, I'm afraid. Part of a ritual dreamt up in the eighteenth century by a chap calling himself Iolo Morgannwg. Now used in a ritual dreamt up by our own William Williams. Funnily enough, Iolo Morgannwg *was* actually a Williams.'

'So, the Vigil isn't an old local custom?'

'Not at all. But it's very popular. There aren't any Eisteddfodau in the winter months, so it gives would-be druids like William something to do. And the Crusties love all that nonsense.'

'They're fond of certain mushrooms, too, I understand.'

'Indeed. So was your predecessor, Tom Pugh.'

'Really?'

'That is to say, he was a mycologist. Anyway, must fly, my boy. The Upper Sixth need my guidance for the uncomfortable matter of the Anschluss.'

'Ah.'

That night, Mrs Lavinia Hughes dished up bangers and

mash, adorned with a countable number of peas.

'Food for Fireworks Night,' she announced as she plonked the plate down in front of John.

'Great,' he replied without enthusiasm.

His landlady surveyed his distinctly un-jolly face. 'You are going, aren't you?'

'I'm too busy, Mrs Hughes.'

'Come on now. It's only once a year, and it doesn't last long.'

'Honestly, I have far too much marking. And I'm rather tired.'

Mrs Lavinia Hughes tut-tutted and turned her attention to a saucepan of custard bubbling on the stove. John wouldn't have been surprised if it also contained eye of newt and toe of frog.

'You do realise that *I* want to go,' she said some moments later.

'That's not a problem, Mrs Hughes. I'll stay and hold the fort.'

She screwed up her mouth into a tiny pink circle. 'I don't like to leave people in the house.'

'What about Saturdays? You don't mind me staying then.'

She gave him the evil eye and seemed about to embark on a new course of vituperation when she was interrupted by a loud whizzing sound. 'It's started!' she exclaimed, beaming.

'It's only half-past six,' John said.

'Small boys get excited.'

John nodded, looking decidedly unexcited himself. Mrs Hughes huffed and dished out an unusually small bowlful of rhubarb and custard. John thanked her, sighed, and dug into the small yellow mound, grateful to find the intense heat of the custard counteracted by the coldness of the rhubarb (stewed two days earlier). He was also glad of Mrs

Hughes' uncharacteristic silence, which persisted through the pouring of tea. She seemed to have accepted that he would not accompany her to the fireworks.

But rule number one at Chapel View was 'never underestimate your landlady'. Just as John spooned in the last of the custard, Mrs Hughes produced a plateful of large, individually wrapped chocolate biscuits, which she placed very carefully at a spot on the table just out of John's reach.

'Biscuit?' she inquired, staring at him with intent.

'Ah,' said John, transfixed by the gloriously shiny orange foil wrappings.

'Have one,' said Mrs Hughes, just as the Wicked Queen tempted Snow White with apples. She edged the plate forward.

'Thank you!' said John. He grabbed one and wolfed it down swiftly. It was the most edible thing he'd come across at Chapel View.

'I'd offer you another,' Mrs Hughes said sweetly, 'but I'll be taking them to the fireworks.'

'Ah.'

'If you come with me, I could pass you one. Or two.'

'Oh?'

'And after all, we wouldn't be there for long. We'll be back here by eight for a nice cup of cocoa and some Viennese whirls.'

Viennese whirls? Where did she hide such wondrous things? The thought of all this saccharine indulgence was too much for John. He didn't really have much marking anyway for few of his students had thought it proper to hand in homework that day.

'It's stopped raining, you know,' remarked Mrs Hughes in a final thrust.

John sensed defeat pulsing through him. 'All right, Mrs Hughes. I'll come. But for no more than an hour.'

'Right-o,' she said perkily. 'You'll need a scarf and

gloves.'

She wasn't wrong. The wind whistled with merry iciness through the square and along Lôn y Bele as Trecadno's residents trouped towards the Wanderers' Club. Their final destination was a patch of scrubby land next to the rugby pitch. The pitch itself was sacrosanct; only ignorant infants ever dared to toddle onto it, and they were rapidly removed. John and Mrs Hughes arrived just as the huge bonfire was being lit. At its base, bits of twig crackled with promising orange flames.

Somewhere on the other side of the pitch a group of people were attaching fireworks to supports. At seven thirty precisely, a rocket whizzed up above the crowd and broke up into a shower of yellow sparkles. The crowd 'ooohed' and 'aaahed' and little faces glowed delightedly in the firelight. John recognised a handful from 8W and 11B. On the far side of the bonfire, the gaunt figure of Mr William Williams was momentarily illuminated. To John's great shock the deacon was laughing, his face a grotesque mask of leery happiness reminiscent of a *Hammer House of Horror* villain.

Another firework exploded with a whoosh of mauve stars.

'It's marvellous, in' it?' declared Mrs Hughes.

'Lovely,' replied John.

He looked around to see if there was anyone else he recognised. A little way off on his left was a lady who taught English. He waved at her, but she looked away. Standing behind her was Raymond from the Brush and Mask, which meant that the pub must be closed. A strange and alarming thought. The golden figure of Betty Wontsmey appeared fleetingly from the mass of figures to his right. She looked very beautiful in the orange glow of the fire, and John could not help recalling her tanned shoulders and inviting bosom. Ah, what might have been! He could certainly forget about an invite that evening, for someone already had his arm around her waist. John couldn't quite make out the features of the lucky man, but he was taller than her husband.

Three multi-coloured fountains of fire simultaneously exploded, and the townsfolk clapped and cheered.

'How do they do it?' cooed Mrs Hughes. '*So* pretty!'

John continued his scan of faces, hoping that he might just spot...

'Hello, sir!' said a jolly boy from 7B wearing a hat worthy of a *Hero of Telemark*.

'Hello, Medwyn.'

'Good, in' it, sir?'

'Very good.'

'Sir?'

'Yes?'

'We've got you first lesson tomorrow.'

'Is that so?' John's heart sank.

'Sir?'

'Yes?'

'Cos it's a late night tonight, can we have first lesson off?'

'No.'

'Please, sir!'

'You know I'm not going to say yes.'

'Can we do something easy, then?'

'I don't think I've come across anything that you've found easy, Medwyn.'

'How about sleeping, sir? I'm good at that.'

John rolled his eyes, and Mrs Lavinia Hughes chuckled.

'Run away now, there's a good boy,' she clucked. 'Don't bother Mr Simmonds on his night off.'

John watched the boy waddle off accompanied by the whizz of a couple of rockets. Fireworks weren't so bad, he mused. Football was better, though. And the cinema. He couldn't do those things in Trecadno. He did what everyone else did. He was standing in a cold dark field watching exploding fireworks because that is what one did in Trecadno on the 5th of November. John wondered if he had completely lost control of his life.

The bonfire was burning well now and producing a much better light. Beyond the bits of stick and wavering flames, John at last saw the face he'd been looking for. Though only for a second or two. It must have been the distortions of the heat, but somehow the face of Elisabeth-Mai looked as if it was *in* the fire, as if his darling's amber locks had mingled with the flames. But then the face vanished. A gust of wind suddenly caught hold of a bright yellow flame and expanded it upwards, forming a flare of oil-rig proportions. All eyes were drawn upwards by this enormous flame, including John's, and he found himself looking up at the guy stuck high on a pole at the apex of the bonfire. A face had been painted onto the roughly fashioned head. It looked very much like the face of the late Roger Nash-Thomas.

The fireworks display and the Halloween Vigil remained in John's thoughts for the rest of the week, as he explained, marked and shouted. An unsettling mix of questions kept circling around his head. Why had Nash-Thomas breathed his last beneath an altar stone on Halloween? Why had his effigy been used for a guy? Why had Elisabeth-Mai bothered with him, and crucially, what had she meant when she said that John would learn just how quaint Trecadno was at Halloween? Was it possible that she'd known what would happen? These were not happy thoughts. John began to wonder if his new home was governed by a malign sect, and if the woman he desired was some sort of witch.

By Friday teatime, John felt a powerful urge to get out – of everything. When he'd finally got rid of 10G, he made straight for the secretary's office.

'It's too early,' said Miss Morse, putting her lipstick away quickly. 'I'm not leaving until four and I might still need to use the phone. And for once, Mr Kane is still in his office, so you can't use his, either.'

'I don't need to use a phone today, Miss Morse. I just wanted the *Times Educational Supplement.*'

'Really? Oh dear. It normally takes two terms before new staff start reaching for that.'

'I just wanted a quick glance.'

'I believe it was taken down to the ladies' staffroom at lunch-time.'

'Hell!'

'But most of the ladies will have left by now.'

Armed with that comforting thought, John hastened along the corridor and knocked on the dreaded door. Hardly daring to breath, he listened for any signs of life. None came. After a further minute or two he pushed open the door. He had expected the sofas to be neat with magazines and fragrant tea-towels tidily arranged on pristine work-surfaces. He was faced with disarray worse than anything the men could have managed. Dust and spilt coffee contaminated the tables. Chairs had been abandoned at a variety of angles. Exercise books, newspapers and back-issues of *Cosmopolitan* were strewn all over the floor. John tip-toed over to the centre of the room and scanned the floor for the *TES*. He was bending down to inspect a promising piece of newsprint when a terrifying sound arose behind him.

'What do you think you are doing?' it growled.

John froze. 'Er... er...'

'This room is for ladies only.'

The speaker was that human equivalent of a rottweiler, Mrs Evadne Perrig.

'I was looking for, er...'

'What?'

'The *Times*.'

'The *Times*? We don't take that. It's either the *Guardian* or the *Telegraph* in here. We ladies are not as pathetically lukewarm as you men.'

'Oh? Well, I just wanted—'

'The *Times* is always in the men's staffroom.'

'Ah. Well, you see—'

'What?'

'I was, er, misinformed.'

'By whom?'

'It must have been Miss Morse.'

'Balderdash! She is never wrong. It is *you*, Mr Simmonds, who are at fault. Either you have ventured in here for your own mysterious motives, or you wanted some other newspaper. The *Times Educational Supplement*, perhaps?'

'Oh, er…'

'Why you should want to look at that I don't know.'

'Well, er…'

'Because people only read that for the job advertisements. Presumably because they wish to leave their current posts.'

'Oh?'

'And you have only just got yours.'

'Quite. I mean—'

'I think, Mr Simmonds, that you had better leave.'

Meekly, John did as he was told, rushing out, only squeaking a little rebellious 'Bye!' once well out of slapping distance.

Having collected his laptop and wellies he sloped dejectedly out of the school. His walk back to Chapel View was slow and ponderous. His day had been swallowed up by inattentive pupils and vicious females, and all he had to look forward to that Friday night was an incinerated piece

210

of meat drowning in cold gravy. He ended up watching *Who Wants to be a Millionaire?* with his landlady and silently interrogating every one of his life decisions.

'See?' remarked Mrs Hughes, 'you don' need to go to that blessed Wanderers' Club. You can get your quiz night right here in my middle room!'

Mrs Hughes departed on yet another shopping trip that Saturday. John lay in bed until tantalising fragments of sunshine began to flicker through the rosebud curtains. He pulled back the nearest one to watch little wisps of cloud gliding calmly across the windowpane, gulls swooping alongside them. He was reminded of the seaside.

He closed his eyes and pictured seagulls from long ago flying through air rich with the smells of seaweed and fried onions. Beneath them, foamy waves broke on shingle banks and bodies draped themselves in towels. His parents struggled with deckchairs, he struggled with a dripping ice cream, and Grandma's tights kept falling down.

Alas, it was not August 1978, and he was not on Brighton beach. It was ten thirty on Saturday 8th November 2003, and he was stuck in a room guaranteed to bring on claustrophobia. He didn't just feel disappointed. He felt strangely fearful. He was afraid of being stuck, alone, in an alien place forever.

But hunger always conquers wild imaginings, and by eleven John was up and making toast. Since sunshine had managed to reach Trecadno for once, he decided that he would have an *al fresco* breakfast in Mrs Lavinia Hughes' back garden. He sat on the blue garden bench and tried to find something to admire within her little strip of land. He hadn't been seated for five minutes when an emaciated woman popped her head over the privet hedge.

'Are you sunbathing?' she asked.

'I'm trying to enjoy a bit of sun,' John said.

'Nice, in' it? Good for drying.'

'Of course.'

'You can wait for weeks 'round here to get a good drying day.'

'I can imagine.'

The woman headed back to her clothesline and another appeared in the garden to his right. This one was more Mrs Hughes-sized.

'Nice day for it,' she said to him.

'Yes,' he replied, wondering what on earth she had in mind. He did not have an opportunity to find out, for which he was most relieved, for the two ladies soon embarked on an animated over-hedge conversation, all in Welsh. Within minutes several more ladies had appeared in their respective gardens, all bearing laundry and broadcasting loudly to each other over John's head. This was too much for a displaced man. With a weary sigh he picked up his empty mug and plate and plodded back into the house.

He couldn't face marking or even thinking about next week's lessons. And there was no point embarking on an amble because he wouldn't be able to get back into the house. He wandered forlornly back to his room and lay once again on his rose-bud bed, remonstrating with himself for not taking charge of his life. Things would have to change, and fast. He resolved to buy a car. That would allow him to escape whenever and wherever he wanted without fear of getting soaked. It would be an easy matter to reach decent shops and bars, and he could even take trips to watch the odd football match or film. Estate agents would be readily accessible, and he would find himself a lovely new home. These thoughts caused such contentment that John fell sweetly back to sleep.

His slumbers were interrupted by a knock on the door. He didn't rush, assuming it was the milkman or bread-man calling. He shuffled down the stairs with a yawn, a hangdog look, crumpled hair, and his shirt hanging out of his trousers, to find Elisabeth-Mai standing before him.

'Hello, John,' she said with a broad grin. 'I hope I haven't disturbed you.'

'Oh no,' he replied, wondering if he would ever get out of disaster mode. 'I mean...'

'I just thought I'd pay you a visit.'

'Right. Gosh.' He pushed his shirttails under his waistband.

'Can I come in?'

'Of course. Yes. I think it's OK if you come into the parlour.'

Elisabeth-Mai smiled at the honour implied by an invite into Mrs Hughes' sacred inner sanctum, and seated herself in an armchair facing the window.

'Would you like a cup of tea or something?' John asked, realising that he had no idea where Mrs Hughes kept tea, coffee, or cups.

'No, thanks.'

'Oh.'

'I just wanted a little chat.'

'Right. Great.' He sat down opposite her, feeling pleased, embarrassed, and strangely apprehensive.

'It's a lovely day outside, you know,' remarked Elisabeth-Mai. Her hair gleamed copper and her emerald eyes twinkled.

'Yes indeed.'

'I'm surprised you haven't ventured out for a walk.'

'I did think of it, but...'

'Spirit willing, but flesh weak?'

'Something like that.'

'Perhaps I can spur you on. I feel like a hike, and I don't particularly want to walk alone.'

John inwardly glowed. 'Well, er. Thanks. I still haven't got a key, though.'

'Perhaps we can time things so that you arrive back

213

around the time Mrs Hughes returns.'

'What if it rains?'

'I'll think of a route that passes a couple of pubs.'

John nodded in an uncommitted sort of way. Despite being flattered by her presence, he was a little unsettled by her unexpected arrival, and he was not oblivious of the way she was trying to direct his activities. Thoughts of Nash-Thomas and the Vigil had not left his mind.

'You know, I thought that maybe you'd be feeling a little down at the moment,' he said after a pause. 'I didn't think you'd feel like country rambles.'

'Because of Roger's death?'

'Exactly.'

'Moping won't help him now, will it?'

'Aren't you upset?'

'No more than anyone else.'

'But I thought, you know, that you and he—'

'You thought wrong.'

'I saw you kissing him. It wasn't just a peck on the cheek.'

'Look, John, Trecadno is a very small place. Opportunities for romance do not come along often.'

'But—'

'Please, let me finish. I am not proud of a flirtation with a married man. It was nothing. A mistake. I soon ended things. He was pretty cut up when I told him. That was the day before he died.'

'My goodness!'

'We never really had a relationship. I'm not overly distressed. But I do feel guilty. Horrified, frankly.'

Horrified she might have been, but John's initial reaction was joy. His darling had never been in love with Nash-Thomas! Then he remembered what she'd said before he died.

'Elisabeth-Mai, do you remember telling me that I'd find out quite how quaint Trecadno was at Halloween?

What did you mean?'

Her alabaster brow puckered. 'I was referring to the Vigil, of course. It's quite impressive, don't you think? Daunting, even.'

'Definitely. But I wondered whether you might also have been referring to Nash-Thomas' fate.'

'Certainly not,' she said, looking irate. 'How could I have had him in mind? I had no knowledge of what he would do.'

'You just said yourself that he was cut up over you. That you ended things between you the previous day. That he was upset.'

'He never mentioned suicide. Not that it's any of your business.'

'No. Sorry.'

She stood up huffily. 'Look, I've got the car outside. Do you want to join me on a walk or don't you?'

Obviously he did. Thoughts of ritual sacrifice were rapidly put aside, and John was soon back in faithful hound mode, occupying the passenger seat of Elisabeth-Mai's car. Her little green MG had a noisy engine which made conversation difficult. This was handy, as underneath it all, a prickling sense of unease still soured John's hopes. Elisabeth-Mai's explanation had made him feel a little better, but he knew that she hadn't told him everything. He also sensed that he was being used. As they passed Bryncadno he had a whiff of the strange smell that he'd noticed on the day of his headache. It didn't help.

Elisabeth-Mai drove them up hill and down dale until they reached a flat stretch of road running parallel to a river, the Afanc. Trees and cow-pasture gave way to sheep-nibbled tummocks and mudflats, and eventually they entered the town of Aberafanc. Elisabeth-Mai parked the car next to the sea wall.

Once out of the car, John gazed at the houses behind

them, and the square church tower with rocky promontory behind it. The village was delightful, but its true merit was the view out to sea, with sailing boats moored at angles along the shoreline and mountains dominating the skyline to the north-east. The tide was going out, leaving sandbanks interspersed with sparkling pools. High above them, the wind pushed clouds as slow and white as cruise liners up the estuary.

'This is the jewel in the crown of our local beauty spots,' said Elisabeth-Mai.

'Magnificent!' John replied, enraptured by the way the breeze blew wisps of hair across her face.

'The view from the other side of the Afanc estuary is even better,' she said. 'At night, the sweep of Aberafanc's town lights resembles a Van Gogh painting.'

'Lovely….' John rhapsodised.

Trying to recover his faculties, he squinted towards the mountains, 'Is that a castle?'

She nodded, though didn't seem too keen.

'I thought that you'd like castles,' John said.

'I like Welsh castles.'

'Isn't that one Welsh?'

'Norman.'

'As in William the Conqueror?'

'That's right. Twelfth-century, I believe.'

'Looks imposing.'

'In contrast to Trecadno's quaintness, perhaps?'

The sun disappeared behind a bank of cloud. 'I just think it looks grand and picturesque,' he said.

'A lot of people around here would say it is a symbol of English subjugation.'

'French, surely?'

'Back then, they were pretty much the same thing to the Welsh,' Elisabeth-Mai said.

'And what about me? Am I a reminder of all things

English? Am I fatally flawed?'

Elisabeth-Mai leaned over and placed a small and delicate kiss on his stubbly chin. He stared at her with disbelief as a large drop of rain plopped onto his forehead.

'Come on!' she cried, taking his hand. 'This shower will be heavy.'

They ran towards the village, stopping at the first pub. It was called the Fish and Bucket, and unlike most of the public houses in the area, it was large, busy and possessed a sound system, through which Abba perpetually belted forth. High-backed wooden benches were arranged in cubicles around the edge of the room, and John and Elisabeth-Mai headed to the only empty one. After peeling off his wet coat, John went to the bar to order couple of shandies and pick up the bar menu. Elisabeth-Mai chose a jacket potato with cheese and mushroom filling. John, unable to think, ordered the same.

'I'm sorry about the rain, and this place,' she said. 'I'd planned a walk on the beach and then lunch at the Eagle's Nest, a pub on the headland.'

'It doesn't matter. I'm with you, and that's all I care about.'

'Flatterer.'

Elisabeth-Mai was spared more devotional gazing by the prompt arrival of food (the baked potatoes had been sitting on a hotplate for several hours). As John chewed experimentally, his attention was taken by the conversation in the cubicle behind them. He suddenly recognised the voice of the female.

'What's the matter?' asked Elisabeth-Mai, noting his fork poised in mid-air and the look of horror on his face.

'Behind me.' John whispered. 'It's Beverley Nash-Thomas.'

'I did notice.'

'You're not bothered?'

217

'Why should I be?'

'You know… Roger.'

'I don't think she knows about me. Not yet. She will do if I'm called to give evidence at the inquest, of course. Though I'm not sure she'd care. She knew that Roger liked to play away. I don't think she was too bothered who he played with. I think she suspected Mrs Wontsmey.'

'That's no surprise.'

They were quiet for a moment, listening to Mrs Nash-Thomas' chatter.

'You know, Arthur, you're a man a girl can trust,' said the widow, loudly. John could imagine the coquettish simper on the made-up face, could picture the gaping cleavage. 'You're a beer and chips man. You don't go in for all the fancy stuff that my husband liked.'

A distinctly male response vibrated through the wooden corral, but John couldn't discern the actual words. They must have amused Mrs Nash-Thomas, for she laughed and took a noisy slurp of her drink.

'You're right there!' she said. 'Big car, small you-know-what, eh?'

More bassy vibration.

'It's quite true what they been saying, you know,' continued Beverley in a high-volume whisper. 'He'd become completely impotent. He couldn't understand it. I couldn't understand it. And he was so fussy about his health these last few months. Went to the gym, an' took them steroid things. He'd even been using herbs to help with his painful knees. Liquorice for indigestion, too.' John noticed a smirk on Elisabeth-Mai's face. 'He never failed at anything. Especially not in the bedroom. Hurt him, it did. Made him miserable. Went to the doctor about it, an' that's how he got the *Prozac*. He didn't want me to find out, but I saw the tablets in his drawer. He had money trouble too. There were loans. God knows what will happen about them. I hope I won't be hard up.' Arthur mumbled something which caused giggling, and their bench started to rock. 'Shall we go back to my place?' Beverley asked, loudly enough to be heard over the Abba.

Clearly no further words were needed for her interlocutor, who stood without warning. Arthur was a big man with an unwashed look and biceps that severely tested the fabric of his shirtsleeves. John had the perfect vantage to observe all this, as the other man turned and caught him mid-gawp.

'What you lookin' at?' asked the piece of rough.

'Er…um…'

'Oh, it's you!' chortled Mrs Nash-Thomas, standing herself. 'It's all right, Arthur, he's a customer of mine. Nice to see you. You must come and have another haircut soon. Right, love?'

'Oh. Yes.' John didn't bother to point out that his hair had yet to come into contact with a pair of scissors.

'Special rate, love,' she added with a wink. 'Professional man.' Arthur mumbled something unpleasant under his breath and dragged Beverley towards the door. 'By-eee!' she shouted as they left, red fingernails held aloft in a wave.

'I'm just off to powder my nose,' Elisabeth-Mai said, and started to shuffle to the end of her bench.

'Hang on a moment,' John said. 'Tell me about the herbs.'

'Sorry?'

'Did you give Nash-Thomas herbs and liquorice?'

'He asked me about herbal remedies,' she replied.

'Like what?'

'I recommended liquorice and a plant called *arnica*.'

'But you didn't sell him any?'

'I didn't have any to sell. He asked me where he could get some.'

'What did you say?'

'I told him that there's a healthy clump of *arnica* on the

outskirts of Trecadno. I pointed it out to you.'

John's eyes widened.

'I remember. It grows by the stone circle!'

CHAPTER SIXTEEN

Influenza

John was quiet as they drove back to Trecadno. Thoughts of coffee and canoodling had been replaced by meditations on a plant. Elisabeth-Mai dropped him back at Chapel View Guest House just as the bus delivered Mrs Lavinia Hughes and her many friends back to the square.

After the fuss of arrival had subsided, Mrs Hughes presented John with her attempt at a quiche. The circular object on the plate placed in front of him consisted of nothing but pale egg and pastry.

'A nice change for you,' announced his hostess. 'Got it ready last night. See, it's difficult getting a dinner sorted when you've got to go out.'

'Indeed.'

'Don't worry, I'll make you some gravy to go over it.'

'Gravy? For a quiche?'

'What's wrong with that?'

'Er, nothing. Nothing at all.'

'Funnily enough, my sister Evadne doesn't like gravy on it either. Don't know why not.'

'Evadne? There's an Evadne at Trecadno High School. She's the—'

'Look, do you want gravy or don't you?'

'I wouldn't want you to go to any trouble, Mrs Hughes.'

'It's no trouble. I'm tired, it's true. But I don't mind doing things if they're appreciated.' She flashed him a grin that would have incapacitated a Panzer tank.

John decided that digestion would only be possible with the aid of alcohol. By seven thirty he was once again treading Trecadno's glistening pavements on the way to the Brush and Mask. Predictably, Doc Jones was already leaning on the bar with pipe and whiskey.

'Evening, John,' he said amicably.

Raymond appeared and poured them both beers.

'How are things?' asked Daniel Jones. 'Making progress at the school?'

'Slow progress.'

'Pleased to hear it.' The doc took a swig of his beer.

'Doc, would you happen to know if my landlady and my line manager are sisters?'

'Didn't you know? An indomitable pair.'

John remained silent for a while as he contemplated the magnitude of the sisterhood arrayed against him. But he had another, more pressing query. 'Was Roger Nash-Thomas your patient?' asked John.

'No. He went to the surgery in Penymynydd, I believe.'

'Would you have prescribed him *Prozac*?'

Doc Jones sniffed and fiddled with his pipe. 'It's best to avoid such things as a rule,' he replied. 'But if he was seriously depressed, then yes. Sometimes people need a bit of help.'

'Can *Prozac* have adverse reactions if mixed with other things?'

'Like alcohol, you mean? The mix would have made him sleepy, for sure.'

'What about herbal remedies?'

Doc Jones' eyes narrowed, though he kept them on his glass. He began to rotate the receptacle, causing his beer to swirl and froth. 'Most of them are pretty harmless,' he said.

'What about *arnica*?'

Doc Jones puffed on his pipe. He looked as if he was trying to recollect the word. Or thinking up a noncommittal response. Either way, John didn't get an answer, for that moment William Williams lurched in, closely followed by his son and his brother.

'You in here again, John? You're getting as bad as the doctor.'

'I've only been here since—'

'You two will get reputations as drunkards.'

'Mine is well-established,' said the doc with a grin.

The deacon chuckled and instructed Raymond to get a round in.

'We can't stay long, mind,' added Emyr Williams, cobbler and brother of deacon. His morose face looked especially ugly in the dim light. 'We got work to do.'

'But first we had to come and see you, doc,' declared the elder Mr Williams.

'Not that colon of yours again?'

'You leave my colon out of it.'

'What do you want, then?'

'There's someone who's poorly.'

'There usually is.'

'Truth to tell, more than one.'

'It's the rugby team,' interjected Williams Junior, peering down at the doctor from his great height.

'Oh bugger,' muttered the doctor. 'Have I got time to finish my drink?'

'It's not especially urgent,' said the deacon. 'It's not as if they've been knifing each other or anything.'

'Do they often knife each other?' asked John with a wide grin.

'Well, a couple of weeks ago—' Idwal Williams began, but his father nudged him hard in the ribs.

Perfect with his timing, as he was with everything else, Mr Alexander Pritchard let himself into the hallowed chamber. 'Well, well! It's Father, Son, and Holy Ghost!'

'Do you dare to mock our Lord's name? Er, names?' demanded William Williams with flared nostrils.

'Come, now, William,' said Alexander. 'Are you ready for a drink?'

'All right, seeing as the doc is taking ages to finish his.'

Alexander brought out his ornate leather wallet and waved a ten pound note at Raymond.

'Mind, we'll be going soon,' said Emyr Williams once again.

'Indeed?' inquired Mr Pritchard after a quick sip of his gin and lemon. 'Am I unworthy of your company, oh flock of Williamses?'

'People are ill,' said the deacon. 'We've come to get the doc here.'

'Would it be influenza by any chance?'

'You're such a bloody know-all, Pritchard. How come you know that?'

'See?' said the doctor to John. 'I am not needed in this town. Mr Pritchard has the knowledge to deal with all problems.'

'I would love to agree with you, Daniel,' said the Know-All, 'but I do not have a licence to treat. I know about the 'flu because Mrs Robbins, my home help, has come down with it. Likewise, Mr Tapscott-Davies of the Historical Society, and Edgar Evans, Quizmaster.'

'This is worrying news,' commented the doctor. 'Surprising, too. I've only seen one person recently who might have 'flu, and that's old Mrs Leyshon. And she has every ailment known to science already, so I didn't pay much attention.'

John remembered the little old lady lurking in the pharmacy. 'Could it be an epidemic?' he asked.

'Not impossible,' replied Daniel Jones. He was beginning to look worried.

William Williams drained his second whiskey and deposited his glass on the bar with a thud. 'Enough of this small talk. Come on, doc. Let's see if you remember what to do with your steth... stethy... er...'

'All right, William, I get the gist. Goodbye, all.'

The three Williamses and the doctor trouped out, leaving the dim room strangely quiet.

'Interesting times,' said Alexander. 'Monday will be easy, at least.'

'What makes you say that?' asked John.

'Our dear pupils will have got word about the contagion and will take full advantage. Your classes will be small next week, mark my words.'

'How on earth will they know already?'

'Gossip moves around this place in real time these days. People used to have to make do with notes in their daily papers.'

'Notes?'

'The paper boys slipped them into the middle pages.'

'What sort of notes? Where from?'

'From Mr Williams, most likely.'

'Was that why he was so bothered when Hopkins sold the newsagent's?'

'Exactly. That was a major blow to the deacon's communications strategy. But at least it brought Trecadno into the twenty-first century. People can text each other these days.'

'I couldn't get a signal of any sort on my mobile phone.'

'I think you'll find that there's good coverage since they put up the mast.'

'The mast?'

'Haven't you noticed it? It's right on top of the chapel.'

'You mean the new cross?'

'That's right.'

'Good grief!'

John spent another hour with the Know-All receiving instruction on the merits of the Historical Society and past itineraries of the Choral Society. When a couple of members of the latter organisation happened to enter the pub, John gladly took his leave. He was tired and slightly drunk, and still troubled by thoughts of herbal remedies and Elisabeth-Mai.

Despite his uncertainties about his beloved, he dawdled as he passed the pharmacy. The place was in darkness, but from an upstairs window, piano playing could be heard. Notes accelerated into a crescendo that made John's spine tingle with pleasure. He would never forget that moment of sensory perfection, when his ears vibrated with the joys of a polonaise and his nostrils filled with chip fumes.

Shortly, the recital came to an end and a lithe shadow hovered behind one of the curtained windows. The curtains parted, and Elisabeth-Mai appeared. Not only did she appear unsurprised to see him, she seemed almost as if she'd been expecting him. She waved at him. He waved back. As quickly as she had appeared, she was gone again, disappearing behind the curtain without a word. The street became silent and still but for the odd twitch of a curtain and a large moth flying towards a streetlight. Further down the road, just within focusing distance, a particularly pretty fox trotted away into the darkness.

'Our Minister wasn't well this morning,' announced Mrs Hughes as she spooned out Sunday dinner next day. 'He kept coughing.'

'Oh dear.'

'Terrible, it was. He couldn't read the lesson. In the end, Mr Williams had to take over.'

'Flu, perhaps?' suggested John. 'The rugby team has also been affected.'

'I know. Young boys. Makes you think, don' it?'

'It does.'

'These parsnips are a bit hard, but they'll be fine when they're covered with some gravy.'

Barely half the school assembled in the hall on Monday morning. Just three pupils from 9F turned up for John's first lesson, and all had handkerchiefs clamped to their snivelling noses. He gave them homework questions and directed them to the library.

Pleased at this unexpected respite, John treated himself to an early coffee in the gentlemen's staff room. The place was packed out and smoke-filled. Mr Philips, Geography, was running a book on the likelihood of school closure and was touting for business. Frank Erskine, the balding physics master, was hitting golf balls into a chipped mug at the end of the room. Not far from him, Mr Erasmus-Jones, Classics, was assembling his favourite jigsaw, depicting Pliny the Elder's lewder observations of the last days of Pompeii. As usual, Mr Burrows-Morgan, the deputy head, was asleep next to his collection of bottles. Mr Alexander Pritchard was holding forth on the subject of epidemics, indeed pandemics, making special reference to the 1919 influenza outbreak.

'Almost killed as many as the First World War,' he declared. 'Let that be a warning to us, brethren. This virus is no nancy.'

'What action should we take?' asked a gent concealed behind a leaflet on thermal underwear.

'Go home and prepare to vegetate!' announced Mr Pritchard, finishing off his tea. 'Ah! Young Mr Simmonds!'

'Hello, Alexander. It's very festive in here.'

'Certainly, my boy. As befits the absence of pupils.'

'I'm amazed that so many of them are affected.'

'That's influenza for you, as I was explaining to my esteemed colleagues. Though I think most of our absentees

227

are anticipating illness more than experiencing it.'

'In short,' muttered the thermal gent, 'they're skiving.'

'Surely we should do something about that?' inquired John.

'Get them back in, you mean?' asked Alexander with a look of amazement. 'Are you mad?'

John had no further opportunity to bunk off himself, for a reasonable number of pupils turned up to his other classes, either too honest or too lacking in initiative to ham up some symptoms. At half-past three, when the last of the little snivellers had finally departed, he grasped his mac and wellies and hastened through heavy rain towards the pharmacy. He was still unsure about Elisabeth-Mai and the nature of her dealings with Roger Nash-Thomas, but you couldn't just turn your back on a woman like her. After all, she had waved at him on Saturday night!

To his great distress, when he arrived, the *Ar Gau* sign was displayed on the door, indicating the shop was closed. He gazed forlornly at all the medicine bottles and pillboxes shut up in darkness. But the light was on in the cobbler's shop, and Emyr Williams had somehow spotted his approach.

'She's not in,' he shouted down the road, a large boot dangling from his left hand.

'No,' replied John with a sigh.

'Leave her alone,' continued the cobbler. 'She hasn' got time for you. Find someone else to pester. You'll get into big trouble if you carry on annoying 'er.'

'Why?' asked John, but Emyr Williams had retreated into his den.

An unusual sight met John's eyes when he went down to the kitchen the following morning. Instead of the tight curls and neat cardigan that were such key parts of her normal daytime attire, his landlady was sporting a hairnet and pink

Bri-nylon dressing-gown. Moreover, she was slumped over the table sipping a beverage with a distinctly alcoholic smell.

'Mrs Hughes! Are you unwell?'

'I am. I feel terrible. Terrible!'

'I'm very sorry. Why don't you go back to bed? I can get my own breakfast.'

'No, you can't. You'll get egg all over my stove.'

'Perhaps I could have cereal this morning for a change.'

'Cereal? That's not proper food for a working man. Anyway, I haven't got any.'

'How about toast, then? I can just about make that.'

Mrs Lavinia Hughes turned bleary eyes upon him. 'I suppose.'

'Good. Now you go back to bed.'

'All right.' She got up and staggered slowly towards the hallway.

'Would you like me to help you up the stairs?' asked John with concern.

Mrs Hughes grimaced at him. 'Certainly not! You stay out of my bedroom!'

The school hall was practically empty that Tuesday morning. The headmaster scanned the few bodies before him in a state of annoyance and indecision. Staff numbers were also unusually low, though Mrs Wontsmey was present and correct, flashing her golden legs and smiling at anything with testicles.

It was clear that the head needed to say something about the situation. But quite what escaped him. Should he close the school? How long for? Should there be special sessions on the merits of fresh air and the pitfalls of close human contact? Even with so few pupils, there just weren't enough teachers to go around. He glanced at Mrs Wontsmey and sighed.

His inadequate compromise was to declare that

registration would run longer than usual, taking in first three lessons. In effect, this left John with four of his usual thirty tutees, all boys, for over two hours. During this time, he was compelled to learn their favourite football teams, which of them had sisters, and the names of all their dogs.

Lack of dinner ladies precluded a hot lunch, but a delivery of sandwiches had been organised from the council offices at Penymynydd. As John inspected the sorry selection, a hand took firm hold of his left elbow.

'It has been too long since we spoke,' purred Mrs Wontsmey.

Oh bugger, thought John. *She's been ditched and is on the prowl again.* 'Betty! Lovely to see you.'

'Don't choose the tuna mayonnaise. Trust me on that, John.'

'Right.'

'May I join you?' she asked, as they turned towards the refectory tables.

'Of course.'

'I just wanted a little chat.' She sat down, smirking. 'You know, these days I only see Andy on Friday evenings.'

'Really?' replied John with mounting trepidation.

'He has other diversions.' Her eyelashes were starting to flutter, and his gut was starting to knot.

'Ah.'

'I've been very busy myself.'

'Have you?' He very much hoped she would remain so.

'And you, I understand, have been busy pursuing a certain lady.'

John couldn't prevent a blush spreading over his shaving regions. 'Well, I suppose…'

'She must be very busy, too,' Betty said. 'All those 'flu remedies to dispense.' She discarded her sandwich with a look of disgust. 'This is worse than cardboard,' she declared, setting her elbows on the table. 'Look, John, it's none of my business what you do with Elisabeth-Mai. But I feel I need to warn you. You are not doing yourself any favours by seeing her.'

'Why do you say that?' he asked, grimacing as he bit into his own dismal pieces of bread.

'Let's just say that I've heard things.'

'Like what?'

'There are a lot of stressed people in this town. You might find that some of them turn against you.'

'Turn against me? Why? I don't see what you're getting at.'

Betty smiled slowly and stood up. 'Look what happened to Roger,' she said, and wiggled out of the canteen.

CHAPTER SEVENTEEN

Revelations

All that afternoon John mulled over Betty's words. Emyr Williams' caution also came back to him. Why would he be in big trouble if he pursued Elisabeth-Mai? Why would people in Trecadno turn against him? Did they think he wasn't good enough for their pharmacist? Was it because he was English? Could he possibly be in danger? He needed to find out what Elisabeth-Mai herself thought.

Weak, apologetic rays of sunshine struggled through gaps in the cloud as John stomped into Lôn y Gwenci that evening after school. The 'closed' sign had been put on the pharmacy door yet again, but that didn't put him off. He knocked and waited, scanning the shop window for movement. He heard a collared dove cooing softly from somewhere nearby, and then the approach of a vehicle. A car resembling William William's aged brown Rover advanced with dangerous speed and pulled up with a screech right alongside him. Three large men in dark coats and balaclavas jumped out, gangster-like, and headed straight for him.

'Hello,' John said uncertainly. 'What, er…?'

'Get in,' ordered one of the men.

John found himself unable to process the command. He couldn't believe what he was seeing, let alone hearing. 'You've… you've used the wrong balaclavas. What's this all about, Idwal?'

The knitting pattern for the balaclavas had indeed been intended for recreation rather than thuggery, leaving John able to see the face of Idwal Williams, son of deacon.

'Don't argue. Just get in.'

John stood his ground, but that didn't prove too useful against three burly rugby boys. He was soon wedged in the back seat between Idwal and an accomplice equally lacking in fragrance. The car was definitely the deacon's, which presumably meant that he'd sanctioned this outrage. Betty's warning flashed through his mind. Had he visited the pharmacy one time too many? But what if he'd just wanted some cough mixture? He glanced at Idwal. He didn't look as if he'd be persuaded by minor pharmaceutical needs.

The car headed down Lôn y Bele, out of town. The cold uncertainty of the fate of Roger Nash-Thomas was now forefront in John's mind. Was he to become the next victim of some hellish plan? Would he also end up an apparent suicide case, found at a scenic spot on the outskirts of Trecadno?

'Where are we going?' he asked Idwal nervously.

'Somewhere,' came the bored reply.

Within minutes the car halted, and Idwal draped an old scarf round John's eyes to act as a blindfold. The scarf smelt strongly of camphor; it had probably languished in one of Mrs Williams' cupboards for years.

'Why are you doing that?' cried John.

'You're not supposed to see where we're taking you.'

'This is beyond a joke. Take this thing off.'

'Can't be done, mate. I'm goin' to have to tie your hands, un' all.'

'It's stupid. Not to mention criminal. Whatever it is you think you're playing at, you'll be punished for this.'

'No, I won't.'

'Is this what you and your rugby team do in your spare time?' John asked as he was pushed out of the car. 'Is this what you did to Roger Nash-Thomas?'

Idwal and his companions laughed. 'Look, don' worry, all right? It won't be long now.'

'It won't be long before what?'

'Start walking,' Idwal instructed.

The four of them proceeded in single file through damp foliage onto uneven grassland. John could smell sheep droppings, and something sweetish, like the air around Bryncadno. The sickly aroma got stronger as they progressed, especially when their path started to incline upwards, and John began to feel dizzy. Before long they stopped, and John heard a creaking noise like the hinges of an ancient trapdoor.

'Mind the steps,' said Idwal, prodding him forward.

The air became suddenly cooler, damper. It felt like they were descending into the earth. John shivered. Were they heading to a dungeon, maybe? The route seemed to level after a while, before John was yanked onto a large wooden chair.

'Oh God! For pity's sake...' But he stopped speaking when the blindfold was removed.

He was in a cave. The dim light from several little camping lamps showed that it was filled with boxes and crates. After a few moments, John noticed a pair of fiery eyes watching him from a corner. The devilish creature began to move through the gloom, heading towards him.

'Mmmm...' began John, terror reducing him to incoherence. It was not a balrog or a cave troll. It was worse.

'You didn't expect to see *me here*, did you?' It was Mrs Perrig.

'Aaaa…'

'Get this ninny a glass of water, Idwal,' commanded the head of science, as she pulled up a seat next to John. She adjusted her horn-rimmed glasses. 'I want you to know,

John, that if it were up to me you wouldn't be here.'

'Oh, good... please...'

'Mr William Williams assured me that you would be suitable.'

'He's wrong. I'm not wicked like Nash-Thomas. I... well... I'm nothing. I'd be a completely useless sacrifice to the moon god, or whatever it is.'

'What are you talking about? Idwal, your father told me he was a Baptist.'

'Aye. Funny bugger, whatever,' commented Idwal.

'I'm not a—' began John.

'I don't wish to know anything about the perversities that fill your addled mind. You are here now, and I hope you will make a significant contribution in our time of need.'

John stared at her, baffled. Was it the stress of capture that was interfering with his brain, or the developing headache?

'My giddy aunt! I've never seen anything quite so gormless in all my life,' declared Mrs Perrig. 'Idwal, I fear I must question your father's judgement. His dose of influenza has inactivated his brain.'

'He's very poorly, right enough,' said Idwal, as he handed John a glass of water.

'Ridiculous situation,' commented the lady. 'It won't happen again, I can tell you. That Daniel Jones will be vaccinating from September next year, or he'll be out on his ear.' Mrs Perrig stood up. 'Well,' she announced, 'I haven't got time to sit here and chat. It's time for your vow.'

John's sweaty brow creased in agitation. 'My *what?*' he inquired.

'Vow. Promise. That what you see and do in this place will remain secret. You will not mention a word about it to anyone whom you do not meet down here.'

'Down where? I don't—'

'You have no alternative. You must promise.'

'But, er…'

'Do as the lady asks,' growled Idwal from behind the captive's back.

'Quite. And don't forget that young Idwal and his associates will take the necessary action should you consider breaking your sacred vow.'

'Right. Well. I promise. But I wish I knew—'

'Good. Now, I have to go. The fox mistress will tell you everything you need to know.'

John let the words form slowly on his lips. *Fox mistress…* In the distance of his mind footsteps receded and approached, and a silence of dancing fumes crept around him. He surely had to be dreaming. Nothing as outlandish as this could possibly…

A crash and splintering of glass broke the calm, and liquid dribbled around his feet.

It was her.

When he eventually opened his eyes, he was surprised to find a distinct lack of rosebuds in his environs. This did not worry him. It was quite normal first thing in the morning for his lenses to lack the ability to focus. Mrs Hughes' questionable design choices would reassert themselves soon enough. He shut his eyes again and tried to remember which class would be inflicted upon him first that morning. But no pupils materialised from his mental filing cabinet. Instead, John found himself recalling the head of science's sadistic spectacles.

He sat up with a start. He was in a small room lit by the same sort of battery-operated lamps that he'd seen in the cavern. It was furnished in Spartan fashion, just a small table and his modest bed. A bucket had been thoughtfully placed in the corner. The room was dry and warm, though the green paint on the walls – or was it mould? – was flaking badly. There was no window, just a door with a ventilation grill. John groaned with the realisation that either he was deep inside a nightmare or he'd been imprisoned. He looked at his wristwatch. It said seven o'clock, though close inspection revealed this to be wildly inaccurate, as he'd forgotten to wind the mechanism.

He reached out to touch the walls. Alas, the damp flakes of plaster felt distressingly real. He could hardly dream such a thing, he thought, as he swung his feet to the floor and reached over to the glass of water on the table. It felt rigid and cold, like a glass normally did. He could feel water trickling down his throat. Surely, he couldn't conjure up such sensations during sleep?

The door opened, and the third man from the abduction team towered over him, a gormless grin making his round head resemble the man in the moon.

'Welcome to the desert of the real,' he said with a chuckle.

'Smart arse,' commented another male voice from somewhere behind the door.

'You feelin' better, now?' asked the third man.

'Er, yes. Look, where am I? Why I am being kept a prisoner?'

'I'm supposed to ask you if you're hungry.'

'Yes. I suppose I am.'

'We got sandwiches.'

'Oh. OK.'

The third man trouped out, closing the door behind him. Within five minutes he was back with a mug of tea, and two packs of sandwiches that closely resembled those sent to the school canteen by Penymynydd Council offices.

'Don't go,' entreated John as the third man turned to depart.

'Eh?'

'I need to ask. About the, er, fox mistress.'

'You'll see her soon enough. She went off when you fainted.'

'I fainted?'

"Fraid so, mate. But don' worry. I'll send word that you've come round. I 'spect they'll send me to get you before long.'

'Right. Thanks.'

Half an hour passed. John scanned the walls and the ceiling, and then the walls again. He studied the pattern of the metal mesh in the ventilation grill. He drank a little more water.

An hour passed. John could now relate to any interested party the locations of each bit of flaking paint and could describe with great precision every intricacy of the grill. He had also learnt that imprisonment could turn a person completely bonkers very quickly.

An hour and a half later the door finally opened. The third man smiled benignly at his charge.

'OK, mate?'

'Can I leave now?'

'Yep.'

'Thank God. Look, is there a bathroom here?'

'What's wrong with the bucket?'

'I'm not used to using buckets, and anyway, I'd like a wash and brush up.'

'Eh?' The concept was clearly a new one to the third man.

'If I'm to see a lady.'

'Oh. Fair enough. OK, follow me.'

During the short walk to the gents' conveniences, John peered around the gloomy corridor, trying to take in every detail. But there was little to see. Once he'd completed his ablutions, they retraced their steps back up the corridor, past the 'cell' door, then proceeded a little further to a larger room. There was less peeling paint in evidence here, and a large wooden table and chairs had been provided. Furthermore, the room contained a machine dispensing hot drinks, and a large tin bearing a country cottage scene which turned out to contain at least three different types of biscuit. Such niceties would be unlikely privileges for the average prisoner, he reflected, and happily took a seat as directed.

Before long, a gentle whiff of lily of the valley reached his nostrils, and he sat up rigidly in anticipation.

'Hello, John,' said Elisabeth-Mai. 'I'm really sorry about all of this. I was going to explain everything earlier, but you had some problems.'

'I was told that I passed out.'

'That's not unusual.'

'Really?'

'All will become clear. But first I want to apologise for the way you were brought here. Idwal Williams has been watching too many Al Capone movies.'

'Ah.'

'I'm sure you would have come of your own accord if you'd just been asked nicely.'

'Quite possibly,' he said, though he thought it unlikely.

'The thing is, we have an emergency. So many people have the 'flu that we barely have anyone left, and we have to make two big deliveries, one on Saturday and the other on Tuesday.'

'Deliveries? What are you talking about?'

'It's easiest if I just show you. Follow me.'

She left the room, closely followed by John, and led the way to the cave where he had encountered the creature of doom. 'As you can see, this room is used for storage.'

She moved swiftly on to a corridor. The sweet aroma so reminiscent of Bryncadno was strong here. They stopped at a door.

'This is the centre of the operation. Are you ready?'

For what? thought John.

She opened the door to reveal an even larger cavern

than the boxroom. It contained glassware that shone beautifully in the dim light, and many glass orbs filled with a clear, brownish liquid. The corridor's heady perfume clearly emanated from this room, and John was beginning to realise why it had so affected him.

'This is distillation apparatus,' he said quietly, his gaze held by the glistening glassware.

'That's right. We have five stills here, and as you can see, just two people to look after them at present.'

He looked around. Phyllis from the chip shop waved at him from a corner of the cave, and Dai Pinter, the diminutive school caretaker, nodded from another.

'I'm inside a distillery,' John said.

'That's right.'

'An underground distillery.'

'It spans a couple of the naturally occurring caves beneath Bryncadno, plus some old mine workings.'

'Coal mines, you mean?'

'Indeed. We've put these old tunnels to good use, don't you think?'

'But...' began John.

'Bryncadno is an old slagheap. It was still mostly black when I was a child.'

'So it's not an Iron Age burial mound?'

'Certainly not.'

'Nothing in Trecadno is what it seems.'

Elisabeth-Mai shrugged. 'Unfortunately, the outbreak of influenza is very real,' she said. 'We have very few people who are well enough to do any work down here. Apart from Phyllis and Dai the only other people who can run the stills are myself and Mrs Perrig.'

'Mrs Perrig?'

'She's the still mistress.'

'The *what*?'

'She's in charge of distillation, all the operations in this room.'

'But she's head of science at Trecadno High School.'

'You just observed that nothing in Trecadno is what it seems. Haven't you also worked out that everyone here leads a double life? Isn't it obvious that our townsfolk are very good at multi-tasking?'

'Well…'

'Most people have to work here at night for obvious reasons, but if we should find some unexpected availability we put a candle in an upstairs window.'

'Really? So they have nothing to do with venerating the—'

'Getting back to the point: we have major problems at present. We can normally tolerate a shut down here for a week or two because of our liquor stores, but they are now beginning to run low.'

'Whiskey?'

'Of course.'

'With a special Trecadno label?'

Elisabeth-Mai raised her eyebrows. 'Why do you think all of this is underground?'

'I don't—'

'It's a secret operation producing illicit hooch. Americans might call it "Moonshine". It's a very apt term.'

'How do you sell it?'

'We have a team of highly skilled sales personnel who make contact with suitable establishments, mostly in Wales. Sometimes they venture as far as Bristol, even London. Always on Saturdays.'

'Saturdays?'

'Can't you work it out?'

'The only thing I've noticed on Saturdays is that Mrs Hughes and her friends… oh!'

'You've got it. The famous shopping trips are not for shopping at all. Although the ladies do like to participate in a little diversional spending along their way.'

'So, Mrs Hughes and all those ladies…'

'Indeed. They are very effective. On one trip, Mrs Hughes got us seven major orders armed only with a pack of chocolate biscuits'

John inhaled deeply. 'Let me get this straight. You make whiskey, and sell it to – what? –pubs?'

'Pubs, clubs, off-licenses. That sort of thing.'

'But why would they buy *your* whiskey? Is it really cheap? And why all this secrecy?'

'We undercut most suppliers. We label up our bottles to look like popular commercial brands. We ensure that the whiskey they contain tastes much like the usual versions.'

'How on earth do you manage that?'

'Different batches are modified so that they taste just right. That takes great skill. Come with me.'

She led him out of the distillation room, through a short corridor, and into another large room filled with bottles and jars, materials of various consistencies and hues therein. Sitting on an armchair in the middle of it all was Mr Burrows-Morgan, deputy head of Trecadno High School, a glass of amber liquid in his hand.

'Good grief!' cried John.

'Hello,' slurred the deputy head with a sheepish grin. 'Glad to hear you can help.'

'Mr Burrows-Morgan is the taste master,' said Elisabeth-Mai, heading back into the corridor. 'He decides which flavourings are added to which batches. His decisions make or break us.'

'Is that why he's always asleep in school?'

Elisabeth-Mai sniggered. 'No one is as good as he is for matching flavours, though many have tried. The poor man has to be here at least three nights a week. He's only just started his shift.'

'Isn't it morning?'

'It's about half past eight in the evening. You've missed a day.'

'Blimey.'

She led the way to a small room with barrels positioned on stands, and crates of empty bottles stacked high. 'Raymond from the Brush and Mask is the bottle master. Unfortunately, he has also been laid low by 'flu.'

'Ah.'

'So we need someone reliable to take his place, and to transfer ten barrels of liquor into bottles.'

John looked at the barrels. They were huge. 'How does anyone go about that? It looks like an enormous amount of work.'

'It is. And it's urgent. If we don't get at least three barrels bottled up by tomorrow night, we stand to lose a lot of money.'

'Oh.' He started to feel even weaker than he already had.

'You'll have help. The rugby team can lend you some manpower, but they're quite busy, too.'

'Busy intimidating people?'

Elisabeth-Mai giggled. 'Don't be silly. They move barrels, drive lorries, attend to security matters.'

'What sort of security matters?'

'The nature of our operation means that we cannot invoice. All sales are cash on delivery. Four rugby boys travel with every delivery to make sure that customers always produce the required cash.'

'Ah.' John shook himself to check once again that he wasn't dreaming. 'Am I allowed to ask what happens to the cash?'

'Emyr Williams keeps the accounts. He's the cash master.'

'Really?'

'Well, he has a till.'

'Ah.'

'The money doesn't go towards Rolls Royces or Italian villas, you know. Some goes on salaries for the rugby boys. Most goes on community projects. Things like Mrs Hughes' central heating, for example. Half of Trecadno High School was paid for using whiskey money.'

'Really? So the distillery is not really about profit?'

'No, though it has to cover overheads and generate enough income for the town's needs, of course. You could say that we're a charity. We certainly will if we're ever found out.'

'It's amazing that you haven't already been discovered,' John said, stroking a barrel.

'People in Trecadno are good at keeping secrets, and Mr Williams is good at ensuring that they do. He's the stealth master.'

'Stealth master?' John repeated. This was getting more and more surreal.

'And now I need to show you your room,' Elisabeth-Mai said. 'It's just over here, next to the bottling area. Very convenient.'

'*My* room?'

'A better room than the one you were in earlier. We have several rooms down here, for weary workers or emergencies or what have you. Idwal Williams will be staying down here full-time for the next week or so, as well as Mr Burrows-Morgan.'

'And what about you?' John asked hopefully.

'I have to go home to see to mother.'

'Ah. I suppose your car is parked at the bottom of the hill.'

'Oh no. These are mine-workings, don't forget. A narrow-gauge railway runs from here into town.'

John stared at her, disbelieving. 'But there's no railway station at Trecadno. You told me that the nearest one was somewhere down in the valley. And it hasn't been used for years.'

'That's quite correct. But there's an underground line following the coal seam. Which happens to pass beneath the town. The line terminates right under Moriah Chapel. Prayer meetings and choir practises are held at the start and end of shifts to disguise our comings and goings.'

'Unbelievable!'

She opened a door to indicate John's new room. It wasn't exactly leagues above the one he'd started off in. 'I must go now,' she said, taking John's right hand in both of hers. 'This won't be for long. Just until we've got these two big consignments out of the way.'

'What about the small matter of my teaching job?'

'The school will be closed down for the next week or so.'

'Ah.'

'You may recognise some sixth-formers down here. Desperate times. It's a tight operation at the best of times, and the 'flu has knocked us for six. I'm trusting you to help. I persuaded William Williams to take you on.'

'So it was you who got me bundled into a car and led blindfolded into an underground prison?'

'I've apologised for Idwal.'

He gently removed his hand from hers. He needed one more explanation. 'You have to tell me what actually happened to Nash-Thomas,' he said. 'You have to explain about the pills and the herbs. I need to know the part you played.'

Elisabeth-Mai sighed and sat down on the single bed, patting a patch next to her to indicate that John should sit alongside. 'I gave him information about medicinal herbs,' she said, 'but I didn't tell him everything.'

'What do you mean?'

'I didn't mention side effects. He could have asked. He could have looked things up. He could, *should*, have sought advice from his own doctor.'

'What sort of side effects?'

'Both *arnica* and liquorice can cause a rise in blood pressure. Which can cause impotence. Which can make some men anxious, even turn them to anti-depressants. Unfortunately, some anti-depressants can also raise blood pressure. Some hearts can't cope.'

'There was no coercion at any point?' John asked.

'Not at all. We wanted him embarrassed, weakened in spirit. We wanted him gone. But not the way it turned out. We just wanted him to go back to Penymynydd and stop meddling with Trecadno.'

You led him towards more than embarrassment, John thought. *You pointed out the path to death.*

'He fell for you, didn't he?' he said, very quietly. *Who wouldn't,* he reflected, gazing at her lustrous eyes.

She nodded. John felt wounded. And angry. He had been dragged into an illicit scheme linked to a man's death. He ought to refuse to have anything to do with their damned distillery. He should insist on being released. He should leave the town, pronto.

As if sensing the tensions in this cornered animal, Elisabeth-Mai leant up close to him and placed a soft and tender kiss on his left cheek. 'Please help us,' she said.

He looked deep into the foxy green eyes. 'You are the fox mistress,' he said, with a hint of accusation.

'Yes.'

'What does that mean?'

'It means that I take care of the foxes.'

He sighed. More excessive weirdness. 'What do you *mean*, take care of the foxes. Why?'

'Because Trecadno is the town of foxes.'

'Oh, right, of course,' John said in exasperation.

Elisabeth-Mai leant back a little. 'The wort that we put into the stills – the mix of grains, water and yeast – is filtered before distillation, giving a residue. A further residue remains in the stills after distillation. When distillation started up in the seventies...'

'The seventies?'

'This is a well-established operation. It started shortly after the coal mines closed. There were no other jobs, no other sources of income. But as I was saying, when distillation started up, the wort residues were treated as waste. They were dumped on Bryncadno at the end of every shift. After a few weeks, people noticed that foxes had started to congregate at the dumping points just after shifts changed, early morning and early evening. Coincidentally, the times when foxes are most likely to be out and about.'

'So...'

'So, a mutually beneficial relationship was struck up. The foxes got a nutritious dietary supplement, and we got an ecologically sound waste-disposal system. With a little training, the foxes soon provided an excellent early warning system as well. Which became especially important when the Crusties arrived. The foxes have been trained to gather and watch any visitors to Bryncadno, and to howl hideously if anyone unknown to them approaches the mine entrance. The job of the fox mistress is to supervise the training of foxes and oversee their welfare. Dr Jones is the fox doctor. He treats any injuries or diseases in the foxes. And any in the distillery workers, of course.'

'Doc Jones is in on it, too?'

Elisabeth-Mai nodded.

'The foxes follow you, don't they?'

'Like Pavlov's dogs, they are trained to respond to particular stimuli. Our foxes respond to the smells of wort and lily of the valley. Though I like to think that they follow me out of affection as much as anything else.'

'I half imagined that *you* were a fox,' John said with adoring eyes. 'That you could change form from fox to woman and back again.'

'Like the *kitsune*? I'm not a spirit, John.'

'No?'

'This flesh is very real.'

Perhaps she could read from his eager face that he would quite like to verify that last point, for she blushed delicately and stood up.

'Now I really do have to go.'

And she did. She drifted from the room and disappeared into the low, laughing light beyond.

John went back to the distillation room and walked around slowly. He touched bottles and examined machines whose purpose he knew not. He opened cupboard doors to find boxes of corks, and labels bearing the words '*Teachers Whiskey*' and '*Glenfiddich*'. He thought of Mr Burrows-Morgan and chuckled.

'Hey,' said a voice, 'you're not having fun, are you? By damn, my father will hear about this.'

'Hello, Idwal. Have you come to interrogate me?'

Idwal grimaced at him. 'Why? What 'ave you done?'

'Nothing. That didn't stop you from kidnapping me.'

'You can't be half-baked about security, mate. D'you want a cup of coffee?'

'Wouldn't mind.'

'OK. Tell you what, I'll run through what you've got to do tomorrow morning, and then I'll bring a mug of coffee and some cake to your room. Food's a bit iffy at the moment, to be honest. Only, see, the food mistress is ill.'

'Oh?'

'Don't you know who that is? It's your landlady!' John had never seen such glee in a Williams.

'That can't possibly be right,' said John, picturing congealed custard and shrivelled chops.

'It sure is. She's coughing her lungs out at the moment,

poor dab. Doc's had to go round a few times.'

'Does everyone in Trecadno have a role here?'

'Most of 'em. Not newcomers.'

'I'm privileged, then?'

'We were desperate, weren't we? The biol teacher before you was in on things, too.'

'Did he grow magic mushrooms?'

'You knew about that, then? There were a few growing around Bryncadno anyway, but old Pugh made sure there were plenty more. To help keep the Crusties quiet. Trouble was, old Pugh got a liking for them himself. In the end, all his lessons were about dinosaurs 'cos he kept seeing 'em everywhere. Taught me for a while. Nice guy, but off his head. Stayed in the prep room most of the time hiding from *T-rexes*.' Idwal grinned at the happy memory.

'What about Alexander Pritchard?' asked John. 'What job does he do down here?'

'He's one of the ones who don' know. Ha! Some bloody Know-All, eh?'

'He knows everything except what's going on right underneath his feet?'

'Spot on, mate. He's ill at the moment, an' all. Tell you what, there'll be plenty of funerals after all of this. An' we 'aven't even got to January yet. Joss Edwards, the undertaker, will be rubbing his hands.'

'Oh dear,' said John, deciding that he'd never understand Trecadno's obsession with death.

'Anyway, we got to get down to business. Time for the bottling room. Just need to pick up a couple of crates from the boxroom first.'

John followed him. He was starting to get a feel for the geography of the place. The boxroom turned out to be the large cavern where John had first become acquainted with Trecadno's underground world.

'You know, this would be a perfect place for a disco,'

John remarked, as Idwal groped around between the little camping lights. The big man looked up at John, his face seeming to snarl. Had he been too flippant? Was he going to get a clip on the ear, or worse?

'Thas' not a new idea, mate. My *Best of the Bee Gees* cassette has had plenty of use, as it happens. But don' tell my dad, for God's sake.'

They trouped to the bottling room, John trying to imagine how 'Night Fever' might manifest itself in Trecadno.

'I don't know as much as Raymond about bottling,' Idwal said, as they entered the room, 'but I'll have to do. What you've got to do is turn this tap 'ere,' he indicated the tap at the base of the barrel nearest the door, 'an' run the stuff into a bottle. When it's full, turn the tap off, put the bottle on the table, an' get another one to fill. When you've collected a tableful of bottles, you start corking with this gizmo.' Idwal took a cork from a nearby box and demonstrated with an empty bottle. 'Nothing to it. Pull down the lever and check that the cork is right down. Then you put a seal on top of the cork with this other gadget.' He pointed to a device at the far end of the table. 'You stick the labels on after that and put all the finished bottles in an empty crate. Take care you got the right labels, mind. Check with old Burrows-Morgan before you start. Watch out for some odd labels, 'cos Raymond gets bored sometimes an' makes up names.'

John remembered the Bannock Bunny Whisky Company.

'When you get to the bottom of one barrel,' continued Idwal, 'you just start again with the next one.' He indicated the barrel alongside, which also bore a tap. 'If you finish all the barrels, you press this buzzer 'ere.' He pointed at a button on the wall that resembled a front doorbell. 'Someone will come to help you change barrels. If we can spare anyone, there might be help with the corking, an' all. We got two corking machines, see.'

'Ah.'

'It's easy, even for someone like you. Careful with the sealing machine, though. The plastic gets really hot. You can get some beautiful burns if you're not careful.'

'Then I'll try to be careful.'

'There you are, then. That's your lesson for today. 'Fraid you'll 'ave to go to your room now.'

John felt like a naughty dog. But at least he had some new, clean, white walls to study, not to mention an alarm clock and radio, as well as some back copies of *Chemistry Today*. What more could anyone want?

'What about, er, washing and so forth?' he asked Idwal, picturing the bucket.

'Oh aye. Look, I tell you what: I won't lock your door, so that you can get out to the gents. But the doors both ends of the corridor will be locked. Security, see.'

'Right.'

'I'll be round with cake in a minute. It's one that Mrs Hughes baked last week.'

'Coconut,' muttered John, with a forlorn expression.

A combination of alcoholic fumes, pages on the oxides of aluminium, and possibly doctored coffee ensured that John had a sound night's sleep. He'd needed one. He certainly couldn't have roused himself at the right time the following morning without the aid of the alarm clock.

His sleeping brain decided that the clock's strident ring was a fire alarm. At the tail end of his dream, he ran out of Trecadno High School fearing for his life and pelted down Heol y Dyfrgi. When the alarm stopped ringing, he came to a sudden halt. The world became silent and still save for a movement behind him, delicate, like a fox's nose touching a leaf.

251

He awoke and looked up at the clockface. He sensed, still, that something alive was near him. He sat up with a start, but he was completely alone. The creature watching him was a thought-fox only, a fox with large green eyes and a beautiful auburn pelt.

The third man arrived with a tray of tea and cornflakes within minutes of the alarm going off, and at 8am John was led to the bottling room to start his day's work.

At eleven, Idwal came round with coffee and biscuits. 'You can 'ave ten minutes break now,' he said. 'How's it goin'?'

'Not too bad. Though I've already burnt myself on the sealing machine a couple of times.'

'It's a bugger, that one.'

'I'll get a break for lunch, will I?'

'Half-hour. Then ten minutes at four, and a half-hour for something to eat at six. That'll be in the boardroom, the room where you met Elisabeth-Mai yesterday. Clock off at eight.'

'Long shift.'

'S'pose. It's what we've always done. Days or nights.'

'You're not really unemployed at all, are you?'

'I'm busy as hell. Though I 'aven't got what people like to call a "proper" job.'

'What would happen if the social security find you one?'

'I wouldn' take it, would I? I'd find some excuse. 'Aven' got the right skills. Or too unwell.'

'You wouldn't feel guilty about that?'

'Eh?'

'Some people would say that you're defrauding the state.'

'Not to my face they wouldn't.'

John took the point and changed the subject. 'Where will today's bottles end up?'

'That's confidential.'

'Oh.'

'Though I reckon they'll make a lot of travellers to Ireland very happy.'

'Ah. And where exactly do you load the lorries? It can't be down here, can it?'

'At the Wanderers' Club.'

'Don't tell me there's a shaft under there as well?'

'Aye, there is.'

'Is that why the club is so big? For storage?'

'Yeah, though most crates are kept in the cellar. We got a conveyor belt up to a hatch for filling up the lorries.' Idwal beamed with pride.

'Really? Gosh.'

'The rugby team has a thousand an' one tasks to see to,' said Idwal, strutting a little. 'Thousand an' one.'

'Including security.'

'Quite right,' replied Idwal, puffing out his chest even further.

John took a swig of his coffee to give himself courage for his next question. 'Were you involved in the Nash-Thomas business, Idwal?'

'Nah.'

'After all, the last place he was seen alive was in the Wanderers' Club.'

'Listen, that smarmy git did for himself, all right? All I did was supply him a few tablets. For bodybuilding. An' one of the boys who's got green fingers made sure that plant he wanted was growing good up by the stones.'

'You mean *arnica*?'

'Yeah, I suppose. We know it as "wolf's bane".'

'*Wolf's* bane?' John went a little pale.

'Drink up, mate. Time to get back to work.'

The following day – Friday – passed in much the same way, though a bulky chap called Dorian came in to help for an hour during the morning. He didn't say a word the whole time despite John's attempts to be friendly. Still, by six in the evening all the empty bottles in the bottling room were full of amber liquid.

'Good job done,' announced Idwal, as he and the third man came to pick up the crates. 'Raymond would be pleased with you.'

'Shall I help carry them out?'

'No, you get along to the boardroom for an early dinner. There's rumours of fish an' chips tonight.'

'Great. But before you go, could you possibly arrange for me to have something else to read?'

'Don't you like Mrs Perrig's chemistry magazines? I thought you was a learned man.'

'There are limits to what any man wants to learn. Especially after a day of bottling.'

'OK. I think Dad's got some *Amateur Gardener* somewhere.'

John rolled his eyes. 'Great.'

Things carried on thus for another three days. Idwal said that there would normally be at least one day off at the weekend, but that this had to be waived on account of the emergency. He apologised for the extra work by bringing in four cans of lager and a Kit-Kat on Saturday night. If all went well, he maintained, John would be out after all the crates had been loaded on Tuesday morning. 'Out' was starting to seem like an alien concept. John was beginning to feel like a prisoner who'd become institutionalised, or a public schoolboy who'd forgotten his parents. All the same, he relished thoughts of green fields and sunlit estuaries.

When Tuesday finally arrived, John found that he was more anxious than excited. What if another big order materialised? Worse: what if Trecadno's residents decided that their tame biology teacher now knew too much? As he placed the last bottle in the last crate, he looked around with apprehension. His worst fears seemed confirmed when the bottling room door opened to reveal William Williams, deacon and stealth master, looming in the doorway.

'Mr Williams!' exclaimed John nervously.

The deacon took out a handkerchief and mopped his brow.

'Sit down,' he instructed.

'I've bottled everything,' said John, desperate to show himself in a good light. 'Despite being brought here under duress, I have done everything that was asked of me. Now I'm ready to leave.'

'Ah.'

'You can't keep me here any longer. I mean—'

'We're not going to.' Mr Williams sat down himself, clutching his raincoat's lapels to his throat as if cold and ailing.

'Oh.'

'I have struggled out of my sick bed simply to thank you, boy.'

'Oh?'

'You helped us in our hour of need. We got all the loads ready for delivery. A good job has been done.'

'Well...'

'It 'asn' gone unnoticed, an' won't go unrewarded.'

'Really?'

'When you get back to Trecadno, you'll find that a very nice apartment has been found for you. Got a lovely view over the Afon Dyfrgi, it has.'

'Gosh. But what about—'

'Mrs Lavinia Hughes will be heartbroken, of course. Until we find her another young man to swoon over, you'll have to promise to visit every Sunday for dinner.'

'Oh well...'

'Your laboratory has been refurbished, an' the prep-room is full of agents.'

'Do you mean "reagents"?'

'How should I know? Mind, that's not all. There's new textbooks on the shelves, an' there's a fancy white board an' projector. Though what's wrong with chalk I don't know.'

'My goodness!' John's lower jaw was wobbling.

'See, we look after people who help us.'

'Thank you, Mr Williams. Thank you very much indeed.'

The deacon coughed, causing a female voice in the corridor to tut.

'You shouldn't have come down here,' the voice pronounced, in distinctly American tones. Its owner put her head around the door and looped an arm through one of the deacon's. His glasses started to steam up.

'What on earth…?' began John.

'Hello,' said Mrs Wontsmey. 'Are you surprised to see me?'

He certainly was. He nearly fell over when she proceeded to kiss Mr Williams on the cheek.

'All right, all right,' said the latter, looking shamefaced. 'I suppose I should explain.' He gently removed the lady's arm. 'In case you are wonderin', this is not adultery you are looking at. See, I was abandoned.'

'Abandoned?'

'About three weeks ago, it was. I had just come home from a long day in chapel, and I sat down in the kitchen expecting a bit of food to appear. Ten minutes I waited, hungry and thirsty after all the praising of the Lord. There was no sign of Daphne, so I went upstairs to look for her. There she was, on the landing in her best coat, a suitcase in each hand. "Don't try to stop me!" she said. "I've had enough. I'm off to my sister's in Shrewsbury, an' I'm not coming back." An' she hasn', either.'

'Oh dear!'

'Aye, there you are. Frailty, thy name…'

'Is woman.'

'Definite.' He looked towards Betty and gave a little embarrassed cough. 'As it happens, Mrs Wontsmey here was also abandoned by her spouse.'

'Circumstances threw us together,' said Betty with a sultry simper.

'Oh well. Wonderful!' commented John, deciding that her desperation must have reached new depths.

'It is wonderful, an' all,' muttered the deacon, with a lascivious wink in Betty's direction. 'But I got to get going,' he continued, getting to his feet. 'If I stay here any longer, I might catch another chill.'

'I'll accompany you, shall I?' John ventured.

'Eh?'

'I'll leave with you. After all, as you said, I've done my bit. I've finished my shift.'

'You're not coming with *us*, boy,' replied the deacon, escorting his companion through the doorway. 'Three's a crowd, see.'

'Right. So will Idwal show me the way to Trecadno after you've gone?'

Mr Williams paused and reflected. 'I doubt it,' he said, before stomping off arm-in-arm with the glorious Canadian cookery teacher.

John flopped, exasperated, back onto his stool. Was he to be released or wasn't he? He didn't have long to mull over the situation because Idwal soon arrived with instructions.

'You're supposed to have a shower,' he said with bonhomie.

'You don't like knifing sweaty folk, then?' John quipped.

'Eh?'

'Joke.' He hoped it was.

'Right,' replied an uncertain Idwal.

'Am I allowed to ask *why* I need a shower?'

'You're not clean enough.'

'Am I going anywhere special?'

'I think you're going for a meal.'

'The Last Supper, perhaps? In the boardroom?'

'I'm not allowed to say. 'Ave your shower, go to your room, an' wait.'

Despite feeling thoroughly fed up, John did as he was told. His tameness wore thin when Idwal came into his room after his ablutions and put a blindfold on him that smelt like an old vest.

'What is the point of this again?' he demanded to know, pulling it away from his nose.

'If you're goin' to take it off, I'll have to tie your hands.'

'It's dark down here. I'll have no idea where I'm going. Though presumably I'll be heading up the tunnel that ends with Moriah Chapel. So where's the mystery?'

'Maybe you're not going there.'

'Where am I going, then?'

'It's a surprise.'

'Nice or nasty?'

'That depends on whether you're a good boy.'

'Look, I've been working very hard. Don't you think I deserve to be treated with a bit more consideration?'

'This is as considerate as it gets, mate.'

John sighed and pulled the blindfold back up. 'OK. Let's get on with it.'

He was guided out of the room and down the corridor. At one point he was fairly sure that they were passing through the storage cavern, for he could hear his footsteps echoing. But it wasn't long before he felt completely disorientated. He couldn't have re-traced his steps even with the aid of his eyes.

After a while they came to a stop.

'Be careful here,' commanded Idwal. 'Take one step up and turn to sit on your right.'

John did as he was bid, managing to bash his leg against some sort of large box.

'It's a bit tight, in' it?' observed Idwal. 'I'll be right behind you.'

'Oh good.'

There were some sounds of doors shutting, and then the sensation of movement. He recalled his eleven-year-old self riding on the ghost train at a visiting fair in the local park. He had the same dread now as he'd had then, and the same lurching of guts.

The little train came to a halt twenty minutes' later and John was led up some steep steps into a warm place that smelt of woodsmoke.

'Can I take this thing off now?' he asked, as the Idwal let go of his arm.

'Leave it on for a minute. But you can sit down.'

John was led to a cushioned bench.

'Where are you going?' he asked, when he heard his companion's footsteps receding.

'Just a minute, right?'

John sighed. But, he reasoned, it had only been a week. Some people were held captive for decades, after all. He could be stoical for another few minutes, though it irked him terribly. He turned his head and felt a slight draught. He took a deep breath of air that smelt of mountains and sea. And lily of the valley.

He pulled off the blindfold.

His vision was impaired by light that seemed painfully bright, but he knew who was in front of him.

'I'm sorry,' Elisabeth-Mai said. 'I'm afraid that mean trick was my idea. I wanted to surprise you.'

'You succeeded,' John said, his eyes starting to adapt to their new environment.

'Look out of the window,' instructed Elisabeth-Mai. John saw a gorse-edged field that dipped towards the sea.

Sunlight spreading from a gap in the cloud lit up the waves and the hovering gulls. 'We're at the Eagles' Nest, the pub I mentioned when we were at Aberafanc. I hope you like it.'

'I certainly do,' he replied. 'So the tunnels reach this far?'

'That's right. The tunnel beneath us pre-dates the mines by many decades, in fact. This place has dealt in liquor for a very long time.'

'Smuggling?'

'Good guess. The loot from wrecks was brought to the Eagle's Nest before being divided up.'

'Gosh.'

'Time to eat.' She indicated the single large table in the centre of the room. 'We'll soon be served what I hope is a very fine meal.'

'I hope I get my favourites,' replied John whimsically, pulling out a chair. 'After all the prison fare I think I deserve melon to start, then beef Stroganoff, and sherry trifle. Washed down with a pint of Guinness and a bottle of Cabernet Sauvignon.'

Elisabeth-Mai sniggered and sat down. Within moments, a whiskery old man hobbled up bearing a large glass of Guinness in one hand, and a bottle of red in the other.

'Remarkable,' murmured John as he peered at the bottle. It was a Cabernet Sauvignon.

A middle-aged woman in an overall arrived bearing two glass bowls of melon balls.

'Thanks,' muttered John, raising nervous eyes towards Elisabeth-Mai. 'How could you possibly know? You've got magical powers, haven't you?'

'You can think that if you like. Or you can accept that you talk in your sleep.'

'Ah.'

'Either way, you've got what you want.'

'True.'

'A good meal in a delightful place.'

'And the best company.'

'Thank you.'

'I must also thank you,' John said. 'Or at least, the townsfolk of Trecadno. I believe that various perks may come my way as a result of my stint at the distillery. Including my very own apartment.'

'I hope you approve of it.'

The melon ball on the way to his mouth paused in mid-air. 'You've seen it?' he asked.

Her laugh was like a gentle trill from a piano. 'I chose it. I even selected the colour of the décor.' He stared at her. 'I could hardly leave it to William Williams. He'd have picked somewhere close to the chapel. And everything would have been magnolia. Or black.'

'Fair point,' replied John with a grin. 'Though normally I like to be the one deciding where I live and what it looks like.'

Elisabeth-Mai popped a melon ball into her mouth with delicacy and shrugged her shoulders. 'If you don't like it, you can find somewhere else. It'll be rent-free for the first six months so you might as well give it a try.'

'All right, I will. Look, I don't want to sound ungrateful. I just want to make my own decisions.' He gazed out of the window, down towards the sea, as he chewed on a piece of melon. 'I'd like to live somewhere with that view.'

'Mmm.'

'I think you would, too, wouldn't you?' he asked, as he picked up his wine glass.

'Certainly.'

'Perhaps you could open a pharmacy in Aberafanc one day.'

She put down her melon fork. 'I won't be doing that. There is something else I have to tell you.'

John stopped chewing too. What further revelation might there still be?

'You see,' she continued, 'I'm not a pharmacist at all.'

'What? But… but what about the plaque on the wall for a start?'

'The qualified pharmacist is Emily Margaret Glyndwr. My mother.'

'Your mother?'

'Both my parents were pharmacists. I ended up following in their footsteps, but it wasn't my plan. My father died suddenly when I was seventeen. By that time my mother was already affected by her MS. There was no one else to run the pharmacy except me. There was no time for university and qualifications. But I didn't really need them. I'd worked alongside my parents for years and my mother gave me directions. Still does.'

'But that's…'

'Illegal?'

'No. Well, yes.' John noticed a tinge of sadness darkening her expression. 'It must have been very difficult for you. A big responsibility.'

'I just got on with it. I liked learning the names of all the medicines and what they did. I became quite expert at plant names and properties.' She flashed a little smile at John which made him quiver with delight. And apprehension. He hadn't forgotten about Roger Nash-Thomas. But delight won out, and he reached forward to take her hand.

'I wish I'd known,' he said tenderly.

She raised her eyebrows. 'What difference would it have made?'

'I understand now why you've had to be so strong, and a little aloof.'

'I'm not aloof now, am I?'

'Definitely not. I'm very glad. You know, Elisabeth-Mai,

I have dreamt of times like this. I dream of you constantly.'

'Occasionally, I dream of you.'

'You do?'

'Mmm.' Her eyes took on a dreamy quality that was thoroughly bewitching.

'Just like the foxes, I have to be where you are,' John said. 'I can't help myself.'

'I like your company, too, you know.'

'Elisabeth Mai!' he cried, overwhelmed. 'I want to be with you always, every second of the day.'

'Isn't that just a bit over-dramatic?'

'I mean it. Truly. Don't you think it would be wonderful to buy a little house overlooking the estuary, and set up a home together? I could carry on working at Trecadno High School, and you could get yourself properly qualified. You're still young, after all.'

'You're very endearing.'

'Don't you think it sounds good?'

'I do. Though I wouldn't do the pharmacy training. I've always wanted to be a concert pianist.'

John rose from his chair and leant over to kiss her on the nose. 'You would make an exquisite concert pianist!' Tiny tears of joy started to form in the corners of his eyes.

'I only ever learnt to play Chopin. Mother doesn't like anything else.'

'That's good enough for me.'

'Funnily enough,' she said, removing a key from her pocket, 'there is a fine piano in one of the upstairs rooms.'

They took the wine and the glasses, but the melon balls were abandoned.

Those few within the Eagle's Nest that afternoon stopped what they were doing as Elisabeth-Mai started to play. Notes rose and fell in exquisite showers as Polonaise melted into Sonata, Sonata into Nocturne.

Dusk was falling by the time John and Elisabeth-Mai returned to the dining room to resume their meal. The hills had grown dim and were spangled with frost, and the foxes danced all the way back to Trecadno.

The End

About the Author

C P Davies is a retired academic and teacher living in South West Wales.

Originally a science specialist, she now focuses on writing and local history, and also enjoys hiking and open water swimming.

Listen to the *Trecadno* Spotify playlist…